"*EXTREME MEASURES* IS A DAZZLING AND DELICIOUS DEBUT FROM A BRIGHT NEW TALENT!"
—TERESA MEDEIROS, AUTHOR OF *A KISS TO REMEMBER*

BREAKING THE RULES

DuBois's voice lunged into the stiff tension between them. "Do you remember the rules of our deal?"

"No drinking. No drugs. No whoring." Faith was surprised at how clear and strong her words came out.

"And yet you're here, tonight, after what happened this afternoon."

"Ask me, André." It was the first time she'd ever used his given name, and she recognized the intimacy it drew them toward. "Ask me what I was doing at Mattie's." Her heartache raised her voice to a higher tone. "Then ask me how I'm acquainted with her."

His eyes roamed over her face. The longing and the pain and the depth of raging emotions in his gaze silenced her. "I don't want to know why you were there. God help us both, I don't want to know." He moved quickly and wrapped his fingers around her shoulders. With one great tug, he pulled her in his arms. "Don't you understand? I *can't* know."

"But it's not—"

His mouth swallowed the rest of her words. Unlike any they'd shared before, this kiss was filled with pure, hot, furious need. His lips moved across hers, demanding her full participation and filling her with his uncontrolled passion.

EXTREME MEASURES

RENEE HALVERSON

LEISURE BOOKS  NEW YORK CITY

A LEISURE BOOK®

July 2002

Published by

Dorchester Publishing Co., Inc.
276 Fifth Avenue
New York, NY 10001

ISBN 0-8439-5062-5

Printed in the United States of America.

With love to my husband, Mark.
Through the years you have taught me the true meaning of unconditional love. You are my heart.

And to my daughter, Hillary, and son, Daniel.
Your laughter, joy of living and daily enthusiasm inspire me beyond words. When I grow up, I want to be just like you.

EXTREME MEASURES

Chapter One

Denver, Colorado, August 1879

Faith O'Malley knew from years of poverty just when desperation took over a situation. And once it did, an otherwise reasonable woman could become quite reckless. Perhaps that explained why she now found herself in a losing poker game, boldly eyeing the stern-looking gambler sitting directly across from her.

She tried to ignore the thumping of her heart, but couldn't rid herself of the notion that trouble stared back at her. Determined to maintain some semblance of control, she aimed a frown at him.

His lips curled around a fixed smile. "It's the lady's deal," he announced.

Silence rounded the table, trapping Faith in its cloaked menace. She took a hidden, calming breath, but continued to hold the gambler's stare.

He angled his head. "Or perhaps you're finished for the

evening?" The challenge crackled in the air between them.

Pretending that the hint of alarm tripping along her spine was caused by nothing more than nervousness, Faith produced a sweet, innocent smile. "I'm still in the game."

He dropped a glance to the paltry winnings in front of her. "Are you certain? It appears you're . . . busted."

She lowered her gaze and drew her lower lip between her teeth. He was right, of course. Down to her last fifty dollars, and the only woman surrounded by four men, she had few choices left. She just hoped he didn't realize that was part of her plan. "I'm certain."

He lifted a single brow. "You realize there is no shame in removing yourself from a losing game."

The silky warning weakened her resolve. But she couldn't give up before she'd even begun the second half of her plan. Seeking an ally, Faith flashed her brightest smile at the player sitting on her left. "Oh, my, must I accept the deal? Can't I simply join in the fun as before?"

The gray-haired gentleman tugged a long drag from his cigar, then blew the smoke into the already congested air. Patting her hand with a benevolent, fatherly touch, he said, "Unfortunately, my dear, those were the rules you agreed to follow when you took cards."

Knowing full well the unusual rules of play had been the sole reason she'd joined this particular game, Faith shook her head in pretend shock. "Oh, of course. How could I have forgotten? Dealer must deal a minimum of five rounds before passing the duty on." Batting her eyelashes for good measure, she added, "Well, honestly, I've never heard of such a thing but I suppose I have no other choice." She joined in the responding laughter, adding a careless toss of her head and an empty smile.

Enunciating each word with slow precision, the forbidding gambler gained her attention once more. "Gather the cards or walk away clean. Before it's too late."

Her breathing hitched at the open accusation in his eyes. She hadn't planned on drawing suspicion while she lost. What would this man do once she began to win?

The children, she told herself. *Think of the orphans*. The silent reminder helped her recover the necessary courage to finish what she'd come here to do. She had, after all, tasted hopelessness too many times in the last ten hours to allow a stranger's skepticism to send her into a panic now.

Stalling for a moment, she whipped open her fan and peered at her nemesis through the slats. At first glance he looked perfectly harmless. Rather than taking away from his severe good looks, the crisp white shirt, red silk vest, and matching tie added a refined dignity. A girl could go all wobbly inside if she liked the hard, brooding type. Good thing the arrogant, brutish sort didn't appeal to *her*.

In an effort to calm her racing pulse, she resorted to playing the role she'd adopted for the evening. Over her fan she threw out a silly question. "Is the choice of play mine as well?"

The air grew heavier with his impatience. "Call your game and deal." He placed his palms flat against the table and leaned forward. "Now."

Faith swallowed hard. This man was different from any she'd ever known, a dangerous combination of hunter and prey. The unruly, dark curls dipping across his forehead added to the image of a fallen angel. On deeper inspection she detected a familiar savagery in his eyes, the kind garnered from an unfortunate past like her own. She suddenly wanted to thread her fingers through those locks, perhaps in the hopes of taming the hair or even the man himself.

By heavens.

With a snap, Faith closed her fan and cleared her throat. "Five card draw?"

Three heads bobbed in agreement. The fourth kept his gaze unreadable and steady. Faith ignored the look, along with the man himself. "Here we go then."

With a long-suffering sigh, she scanned the cards from the last hand lying face-up. With fingers intentionally shaking, she made a marvelous show of picking up cards in what appeared to be no certain order. A deuce first, an eight, a ten, a three, and a king. She repeated this method four more times, ensuring that a king always landed in the pile every fifth card.

In an attempt to draw attention away from her active hands, she said, "I don't think I've ever seen a more opulent saloon. Don't you agree, Mr. Greene?"

"Most definitely."

While the conversation steered to the wonders of the newly renovated saloon, Faith checked her surroundings again. When selecting her seat, she'd ensured that the flawless mirror behind the bar gave her a clear view of the entire room. Elegant lanterns provided dim lighting throughout. A swift, circling glance revealed five other poker games, two billiard matches, three active faro tables, and a piano in the far right corner.

Her eyes rested briefly on the exit, insuring she still had a direct path to the swinging doors. She only hoped she wouldn't have to depart in haste.

The gambler's clipped, rigid command brought her attention back to the table. "Let us get down to business, shall we?"

Calling upon the recklessness born from her childhood alone on the streets, she allowed herself a slight smile. "Of course."

Unable to resist, she glanced one final time at the player across the table. A violent quiver captured her heart.

Powerless to move her eyes from his, she squared the deck. As she went to deal the first card, his hand shot across the table and wrapped around her wrist. "You forgot a step."

Her pulse jerked, but she quickly schooled her features to hide her reaction to the simple joining of his flesh with hers.

This was supposed to happen, she reminded herself. One of the four men at the table needed to prompt her to shuffle. She just hadn't expected the warning to come from . . . *him*.

She slowly lowered her gaze to his hand and back again. She told herself that frail nerves, and nothing more, caused the tremble kicking her pulse into an erratic rhythm. A niggling doubt of conscience screamed at her to leave the saloon at once.

She disregarded it.

Furrowing her brow in practiced confusion, she widened her eyes for additional effect. "Oh, silly me. I'm supposed to shuffle the cards before I deal." She let out a tinkling, senseless laugh.

He gradually released her wrist and leaned back into his chair. "Indeed." His lips curved slightly upward, but the hard look in his eyes remained.

Spurred on by his smugness, Faith brightened her expression before returning her gaze to the cards. Her shuffling hinted at nervousness and incompetence. With practiced flummery and illusion, every card appeared to find a new spot in the deck. But only the bottom cards landed in different positions, while the top half stayed in the order she'd intentionally placed them in at the start. Her fingers worked quickly. Unless the gambler was some sort of medium, even he wouldn't detect her method.

Would he?

As doubt reared, she ruthlessly forced it down. She could do this. She *had* to do this, for the abandoned children who needed the safety of a home she alone provided for them.

Swallowing the last of her indecision, she tossed ten dollars into the middle of the table. "Ante up."

With a theatrical flourish, Faith placed the first card in front of the player on her left, then continued clockwise around the table. As she drew upon the image of the children sleeping soundly in their beds, the thought of cheating at cards filled her with only mild apprehension.

Now that he had permanent ownership of The Dancing Belles saloon, André Du Bois thought his days of play were over. But the bright laughter and phenomenal losses of the beautiful young woman had called to him from across the room. She'd played with appallingly poor judgment, considering neither the odds nor the risks. Yet something in her manner alerted him that she was far smarter than she pretended. It was his duty to find out whether his gut instinct was right.

While she dealt, he watched. And waited. She giggled again, causing him to shift his attention back to her face. Her ridiculous expression told him nothing.

After three turns around the table, she pivoted toward Joshua Greene. "Am I doing this correctly?" she asked in a childlike voice.

The old fool responded with a smitten smile. "Perfectly, my dear."

André swallowed his distaste behind a grunt. He'd known enough actresses to recognize that he sat in the company of one of the greats. The woman was no more a dim-witted innocent than Pearl LaRue had been.

And thanks to Pearl's heartless betrayal, André had learned an important lesson. An actress was merely an accomplished liar. And a liar was the same as a cheat.

He hadn't been wise enough to stop Pearl before she'd walked away with his pride, and all his money. But tonight, he would stop this particular fraud. He'd worked too hard to regain his wealth to allow a woman, any woman, to swindle so much as a dollar from him or his saloon. She'd frivolously chosen to ignore his warnings. Now she would pay the consequences.

He just had to catch her in the act.

"Place your bets, gentlemen," she said.

André picked up his cards. A pair of threes, two jacks, and a ten stared back at him. He stole another glimpse at the woman's face. As before, her expression held a remarkably unreadable pout, but then her right eyebrow began twitching. The tiny gesture confirmed his earlier suspicion. Not only was she cunning, she'd just dealt herself an unbeatable hand.

"I'm in," Greene declared.

The other two men at the table agreed simultaneously. André said nothing as he dropped twenty dollars into the center of the table. As the next round of betting started around the table, he took the opportunity to study the woman.

She'd swept her rich, mahogany hair atop her head, leaving several loose strands cascading into a careless image of idle sensuality. The effect enticed, but it was her eyes that had held his fascination all evening. He'd been both stunned and strangely enraptured by their odd beauty, the color matching the finest Kentucky bourbon he'd ever come across.

Her red dress complimented those extraordinary eyes to perfection. The tight-fitting bodice was cut low enough to show a considerable amount of cleavage. He'd noticed right from the start how every man at the table watched her exposed skin more than their own cards.

Stupid fools.

André, on the other hand, knew better than to let a beautiful set of eyes and creamy white flesh send his logic disappearing into his pants. If his experience with Pearl had taught him anything, it was that a man could trust no woman.

And this woman, dressed in the height of fashion, had the audacity of a whore with the look of a practiced innocent.

"Cards, gentlemen?" Her velvety purr circled the table, reminding André of a sleek mountain lion ready to pounce.

With more savagery than necessary, he discarded the ten and took a new card. She dealt him a jack, completing his full house. Several rounds of betting ensued. One by one each player folded, leaving only André and the woman in the game.

André called. "Show your cards, ma'am."

Her four kings easily beat his full house.

"Oh, my. It appears my luck has finally changed." She gave a high-pitched laugh as she swept her gaze across the table, avoiding direct eye contact with any of the players. André could only marvel at her daring.

"Do I get to deal again?" she asked.

He leaned forward, commanding her attention. For a dramatic moment, they stared at one another. "I insist," he said.

She drew in a deep breath, blinked, then began picking up the cards. André focused on her right brow. The moment the twitching began, he lowered his gaze to her hands and watched the shuffle. Though outwardly clumsy, her fingers worked too quickly for him to detect any fancy dealing.

Three hands later, too much of André's money, along with a considerable amount from the others, sat in front of the woman. Damn, she was good. A grudging respect enveloped him while loathing twisted in his gut at her brazen conduct.

"One more hand?" she suggested, her manner concealing all signs of excitement, except the slight quivering of her brow.

Two of the gentlemen declined her offer and left the table, grumbling about their unconscionable bad luck. Joshua Greene agreed, leaving André the last to accept. He inclined his head, then examined her movements as she picked up the cards from the table. For the first time he noticed the neat pattern she used.

A deuce, a ten, a three . . . *I'll be damned.* He hadn't realized, hadn't thought to look. All night, she'd used the simplest method of them all, stacking the deck *before* she shuffled.

Annoyed by his own lack of insight, André played the last hand with one thought in mind—he had her. As she began sweeping the pile of winnings toward her, he said, "I would like a word with you in private."

Her gaze shot to his, measuring. "Excuse me? I don't think I quite heard what you said." Pasting that sublimely foolish smile on her face, she fanned a hand in front of her and looked to the entrance of the saloon. "Oh, my, it's suddenly quite warm in here. I think I am need of a bit of fresh air."

She turned to the only other player at the table. "Mr. Greene, would you care to take some air with me?"

The old fool sputtered at the outrageous comment. "Of course, young lady. What a wonderful suggestion."

With lightning speed André rose from his chair and walked around the table, stopping directly behind the brash woman. "I'd like to speak with you first."

Her back ramrod straight, the little cheat remained motionless, never once acknowledging his presence. André bent over her, resting his lips against her earlobe. "I said, come with me." He lowered his voice to a hushed whisper, guaranteeing his words fell only on her ears. "Or would you prefer I make my accusation in public?"

He felt her betraying tremble, just as he felt her physically capture her rigid control afterward. The gesture proved his earlier assessment of her character. Only a professional could stifle fear so completely.

A sneer tugged at his lips. "I see you understand me perfectly."

"Sir, who do you think you are?" she demanded, an impeccable mixture of outrage and shock sounding in her voice.

He straightened, and with hard-earned authority said, "André Du Bois." She opened her mouth to speak, but he beat her to it. "The owner of this saloon."

She shot him a disbelieving gaze before she arranged her features into a presumed air of senselessness.

"I assure you it is the truth," he said.

"Then I must compliment you on such a fine establishment."

"And *I* must, once more, ask you to come with me."

As though finally realizing that something was amiss, Joshua Greene chose that moment to interfere. "Now see here, my good man. What do you wish with this sweet, young lady?"

André was not intimidated by the elder gentleman. "That's between the . . . *lady* and myself."

"I'm certain whatever you have to say could be said here."

André held the man's stare. "Indeed."

Greene's confidence slipped under the relentless scrutiny. "If she doesn't wish to go with you—"

"Oh, she does. Isn't that correct, miss?"

The woman cut André a cold, hard glare, then cleared her expression as she turned her head toward the older man. "Thank you for your concern, Mr. Greene, but I can handle myself perfectly." She blessed André with another unwavering look.

Greene looked unconvinced. "Well, my dear, if you're certain."

André blew out a hiss. God save him from well-meaning gentlemen. "On my honor, I guarantee this woman is in no more danger than the circumstances warrant. Perhaps you would care to wait for her at one of my faro tables?"

Greene, a well-known mark for faro, nodded, suddenly distracted as his gaze connected with the tables on his left. "Splendid idea."

The moment the other man rose, André motioned to his security man, Hank, watching from across the room. Hank sauntered over in a casual manner that gained little notice from the other patrons in the saloon.

"Hank, please escort Miss—" André leveled a look on the woman. "I'm afraid I haven't had the pleasure of learning your name."

She silently stared at the exit with an unblinking expression.

André leaned into her line of vision. "I wouldn't do anything rash if I were you."

She sniffed, tilted forward, and angled her head so she could fix her eyes once more on the swinging doors.

"Now, now. That wouldn't be wise, Miss . . ."

She snapped her gaze to his and lifted her chin, outrage masked any signs of fear. "Oh, this is absurd. My name is Faith. Faith O'Malley."

André lifted a single brow, then turned to Hank. "Please escort Miss O'Malley to my office." André bent forward and grabbed the sides of her chair, pinning her from behind. He lowered his lips once more to her ear. "If you would be so kind as to cooperate without a fight."

Faith refused to panic. She'd been in worse scrapes than this and had managed to get herself out of each one. She wasn't about to give up now, nor would she allow the two men to usher her out of the saloon without her money. "What of my winnings?"

André smiled unpleasantly at her. "Not to worry. The

money will be safe." He widened his grin. Superiority radiated from his facial features. "Then again, there's just no telling what sort of unscrupulous dealings are underfoot."

Before she allowed her tongue to get away from her, Faith closed her eyes against the brute's arrogance. She reminded herself that she still held some of the control. André Du Bois might think he'd caught her, but he had no material evidence. She would simply deny any wrongdoing.

Simple, really.

With her defenses fortified, Faith stood and turned to face her accuser. He took a step toward her, closing the distance to mere inches between them. Her breath caught on a gasp as the unfamiliar racing of her heart began again. Towering a full head taller than her, he was much more solidly built than she'd imagined. She drew in another ragged whiff of air, and the hint of limes, covered over with cigar smoke, filled her senses.

The impression of danger overwhelmed her for a brief moment. She coaxed her fear into compliance and graciously allowed André to take her hand. But instead of escorting her himself, he pulled her forward and hooked her fingers into the crook of Hank's arm. As the hulking man led her toward the back of the saloon, Du Bois fell in step closely behind.

Hank's hold remained remarkably light. Faith considered making a hasty retreat, but decided against it. She sensed if she tried to draw away, the hired ruffian would tighten his grip to painful proportions. Of course, there was also the matter of André Du Bois. She could feel both his heat and suppressed anger as he walked directly behind her. She doubted she'd make it any farther than a step or two.

As though guessing her thoughts, the beast let out a deep rumble of amusement. "I wouldn't try to run if I were you." His warning sizzled in the air. "You're no match for Hank or myself."

Faith seethed at the man's easy self-assurance, but cleared her expression of all emotion. She walked with dignity, chin held high, and let Hank usher her inside a small room in the back corner of the saloon. Du Bois entered behind them and shut the door with a resounding click.

She spun around and faced the gambler-owner-brute. Prepared to express her outrage, she was shocked to discover words eluded her. As she fidgeted from foot to foot, the noisy din from the saloon pervaded the cold silence seeping into her resolve.

Concerned her agitation might be wrongly misinterpreted, Faith paused. She stared at her captor with unconcealed scrutiny, evaluating her next move. She ignored the thundering of her pulse, putting it down to simple desperation over potential disaster. And yet, the look in the man's eyes awakened in her a feeling of restlessness she didn't quite understand. What was wrong with her? This wasn't the first time she'd stumbled into an unpleasant mishap.

Du Bois turned to Hank. "Please retrieve the money Miss O'Malley"—he paused and lowered a look of censure—"*won* at my poker table."

Faith stifled the urge to lash out at his sarcastic tone. No matter what happened in the next few minutes, she would *never* confess what she'd done. Or why.

Resorting to the role she'd played all evening, she flashed a sweet smile at both men, then spoke to the least deadly of the two. "That would be very kind of you, Hank."

Hank presented her with a bemused grin. He opened his mouth to speak, but Du Bois's gruff command cut off the response. "Leave us now."

Faith continued to smile as Hank nodded, then turned

to go. Using the silly, nonchalant tone that she'd adopted for the evening, she said, "My, what a fine office you have, Mr. Du Bois."

She spun in a slow circle, taking in the room from the perspective of a captive—searching for a route of escape. An odd squeaking sound came from the back of the room, but when she looked for its origin she found nothing. Shrugging, she continued her hunt for a way out. It took no time to detect the lack of a back door. There was only a small window high up in the far right-hand corner of the room. She'd have to get closer to judge if she might fit through it.

She sidled toward a sturdy-looking desk, gazing up at the window.

The size was right, but she'd never make it in her borrowed dress. Having eyed an armoire, she walked toward it and boldly threw open the large cabinet's doors. She pressed the smile curving on her lips into a tight line, hiding her excitement in mundane speech. "You keep several sets of clothes in your office? You must spend an awful lot of time here."

He lifted a shoulder, leaned against a nearby wall, then crossed his arms over his chest. "Through with your assessment yet? As I'm sure you've already concluded, there is no escape."

She giggled softly. "I don't have any idea what you mean."

An insulting smirk slid onto his lips. "Naturally."

How she hated that self-righteous tone. It reminded her of the banker who'd only this morning refused to give her more time on the remaining portion of her loan. Driven by both men's sanctimonious attitudes, she closed the cabinet's doors and twirled in a circle again. Another part of the room captured her attention. "Oh, look. You even have a fireplace. I say, this room is truly abundance at its finest."

"Some of us work hard for what we have."

"I couldn't agree with you more."

Oh, she knew all about hard work. And regardless of the hidden message in his words, she doubted André Du Bois had any idea what it meant to be penniless and scared, never knowing when the next meal would come. But Faith did. And she'd pledged long ago that the abandoned children she now housed would know the comfort of a bed and the security of three meals a day. No selfish, sinfully wealthy saloon owner would stand in her way tonight.

Drawing confidence from the thought of her honorable mission, she walked toward the mantel that held tin photographs arranged haphazardly on the top. How odd, she thought. The man leaning against the wall, watching her with two small slits in the place of eyes, didn't seem like a man with a history. And yet photographs meant friends and loved ones. Drawn to one in particular, she touched the frame of a beautiful young woman.

The curious squeaking sounded again, but this time Faith ignored it. She concentrated on the photograph, looking from the picture to Du Bois, then back again. The girl had the same incredible eyes as the man. A sister? No, he seemed too hard to have a sister. And yet the resemblance was uncanny. Just as she started to question the identity of the woman, the office door swung open.

Out of sheer reflex, Faith pivoted on her heel and dug the tip of her right shoe into a crack between two of the hardwood slats. At the same moment, Du Bois reached out and slammed the door shut. "Not a chance, honey."

Undaunted, she shifted her weight, then reached toward Hank to receive the heap of money laden in his arms. "Oh, how kind of you—"

André moved with remarkable speed as he filled the space between her and Hank. "Put the money in the safe and leave us."

"Sure, Boss."

Refusing to panic, Faith forced her voice into a sultry hush. "The safe? Come now, Mr. Du Bois. I assure you that won't be necessary. I find the hour has grown quite late." She placed three fingers over a feigned yawn, then leaning to her right, cast her brightest smile onto the other man. "Isn't that right, Hank?"

Hank flashed a grin. "Yes, ma'am. It is getting late."

"Well, then, considering the hour, perhaps you might wish to give me my money now and I'll just be on my way."

Hank took a step forward, but stopped abruptly at the sound of André's growl. "Ignore her, Hank. She's not to be trusted."

Hank cocked his head and stared at her for a long moment. She thought she detected sympathy in his eyes, but the look turned slowly into suspicion.

"You may continue as before," André ordered harshly.

Grimacing, Hank nodded and turned toward a small, metal safe flushed against the back wall beside the desk. Faith inched into a position so that she could watch Hank's every move. The melodic tick of the spinning lock filled the silence, diminishing her chances of an easy escape with each turn.

All pretense of the innocent victim disappeared as she fought for her right to the winnings. "You can't do this."

Neither man acknowledged her statement.

"Wait," she yelled as the safe's lock clicked and Hank swung the small door open. "I won that money fair and . . ."

André turned and raised his eyebrows. "Fair and . . ." he prompted.

Shamefully, Faith found she couldn't finish the statement now that he'd called her bluff. "You were there . . . you saw what happened."

"Yes, I did."

Faith glanced to the heavens and prayed for quick guidance. What had started as her last chance to save her orphanage was quickly turning into her greatest failure yet. She softly cursed André Du Bois and his wicked cunning.

"I didn't quite get that," he declared. "What did you say?"

Faith stifled a groan. "Nothing."

He chuckled. "That's what I thought."

Dear God, she needed that money to pay off the loan before the three-day deadline arrived. Frantic now, she pushed past the arrogant gambler, intent on taking her money by force if it came to that.

But as she approached his side, Du Bois reached out and tugged her to him. She landed hard against his big, solid body. He wrapped his arms around her, pinning her back into his chest with his firm hold. "Stay still." His breath hissed against the nape of her neck. "I don't want to hurt you. So I expect your full cooperation from this moment forward."

The menace in his threat sent a shiver licking across her spine, making her rethink her plan. Swallowing an oath, she fidgeted in his clutches. Du Bois tightened his grip. Each time she squirmed, he increased the pressure a bit more, until her breath came in shallow gasps.

Struggling for air, she watched helplessly as Hank dropped her two thousand dollars in the safe. "You can't do this," she sputtered.

As though used to this sort of episode, Hank studiously ignored the tension in the room as he shoved the money deeper inside the tiny compartment, then closed the door with a snap. A single flick of the wrist cleared the lock, as if spinning Faith's chances of success away.

"That's my money." Her words came out in a whisper as the futility of fighting the inevitable settled in her brain.

"That'll be all, Hank. I'll call if I need you."

The moment the other man left the room, André turned Faith in his arms. They stood face-to-face, neither speaking—both breathing hard. Instead of releasing her right away, André continued to stare at her for a long, breathless moment. His gut wrenched the moment his gaze collided with her large, expressive eyes. No woman should have been given that much mesmerizing beauty. God must have a cruel sense of humor, he thought, putting a conniving, cheating heart inside such a sweet package.

With insolence, he slid a frank glance along her face, stopping at her lips. What would they taste like? He hated the intense craving to find out.

He lowered his gaze further until it rested on her creamy cleavage. Her shiver washed through him, joining with the one building inside him. She parted her lips and whispered something unintelligible. Oddly compelled, he leaned his head closer . . . closer . . .

Her trembling voice broke the spell. "Please. I must have that money."

André pulled back. He closed his eyes against the sound of desperation in her voice. Her ill-concealed alarm made him rethink his initial judgment of her character. When he reopened his eyes, something unimaginable tugged at the back of his conscious.

Dammit. The woman's hopelessness and fear looked real. But he hardened his heart as her expression slowly filled with resolve. In that moment he knew Faith O'Malley would do anything to get the money Hank had just locked in the safe. *Anything.*

He tightened the embrace as the truth ripped through him. She was just like every other woman he'd ever known. The momentary slice of doubt had merely been a trick of his imagination, a weak hope that he might have found a woman different from the rest.

He'd been wrong.

Revolted, he pushed her out of his arms. "You're an accomplished liar and cheat, Miss O'Malley."

Her frantic plea ripped through him like a jagged piece of glass. "Won't you at least let me explain?"

He refused to be drawn in by her false innocence. He dropped a cold glare on the woman with the extraordinary eyes and lying heart. "The money will remain in the safe, and you will stay in this office until I decide what to do next."

She raised panicked eyes to him. "Please, I beg you. Don't—"

"You should have thought about the consequences before you sat at a table in my saloon. No one cheats André Du Bois."

A shudder passed through her. "I . . . I had no other choice."

André should have been pleased by her subtle admission to the crime, but instead felt as if he'd suddenly become a dastardly villain in a dime novel. "There's always a choice."

"Not always."

"*Always*. But I wouldn't expect a woman, especially a woman like you, to understand."

He ignored the defeat wavering in her eyes just before he slammed out of the office. The sound of her soft plea only added to the deep feeling of loss growing inside him.

Dammit. Why did he have to meet a woman like Faith O'Malley tonight of all nights? Almighty God certainly had a unique way of punishing a man for his past mistakes.

Chapter Two

At the sound of the lock striking into place, Faith's useless cry for mercy died an immediate death. She blew all the air out of her lungs, cleared her mind, and waited for the tension to seep out of her body. Unfortunately, the calm she sought never came. Instead, the roaring of her pulse grew louder and her breathing quickened into short, painful intakes of air.

Unwilling to accept defeat, she rushed to the door and twisted the knob. The gesture turned out to be as fruitless as her efforts to calm herself. She pounded on the door. "Let me out, Du Bois."

The only response was the sound of raucous laughter accompanied by the most wretched piano playing she'd ever heard.

She slammed her palm against the door. "Let me out this instant."

If it were possible, the noise grew louder, as though it

had a life of its own and was determined to drown out her demands.

Banging on the door was an obvious waste of her time. With her plans exhausted and her ego severely wounded, she didn't have many options left. She placed one hand on her hip and with the other, tapped a long tapered finger on her chin.

Think, think.

Well, she could meekly wait for Du Bois to return. Then again, she could exit through the door he'd just left—with the help of a hairpin, of course—thereby facing the brute sooner rather than later. Or she could simply escape through the window above the desk.

Given her three options, there seemed no alternative. André Du Bois was too formidable a foe to face a second time in one evening. The memory of his turbulent expression as he'd held her tightly in his embrace sent her heart hammering in her chest. His sharp, stinging gaze had called to a hidden point deep within her, unearthing feelings she'd rather not name.

The burning image of his face lowering toward hers darted along her nerves with delicious vengeance. She'd been right to think him dangerous. And for one brief moment, she'd hungered for the arrogant saloon owner to close the distance between them and join his lips to hers.

Dear God, out of desperation she'd gleefully defied one of her strictest rules of decency and in the process had nearly compromised every value she'd ever held dear. Was she like her mother after all? A wanton, willing to do anything for the feel of a man's warm body against her own?

Faith pressed her lips together to keep her cry of dismay silent. An unfamiliar panic prickled at the back of her neck. She rested her head against the door, swallowing her despair as the cold silence in the room grew to deafening proportions.

She couldn't give into hysteria now. The children needed her. "Get control, girl," she muttered.

A shrieking, high-pitched echo reverberated through the tiny room. "Get control, girl. Get control, girl."

Gasping, Faith pivoted in the direction of the voice.

Her own words came at her again. "Get control, girl."

She flattened herself against the door. With her heart pounding and her knees trembling, she furiously looked around for the owner of the peculiar voice.

"Who's there?" she demanded, her words shaking through the air in time with her knees.

Her question rumbled back toward her. "Who's there? Who's there? Get control, girl."

The odd, raspy voice came from the vicinity of the desk, but she couldn't see anyone else in the tiny space. Faith took several determined breaths, then lunged toward the back of the room. Her knees buckled, forcing her to grasp the edge of the desk for support. Wild with a strange mixture of fear and curiosity, she looked around her. "Who's there?"

"Awwwk. Who's there?"

The response came from above her head, sounding less frightening and more monotonous than normal speech. Peering up, she tilted her head in the general direction of the sound, but could see nothing out of the ordinary. She shoved away from the desk and sighed. "That's it then. I'm losing my mind."

A loud chirp vibrated from above. The lyrical pitch caught her interest.

"Where are you?" she asked.

Another chirp answered her, followed by her own question floating back toward her. "Where are you?"

The reply came from behind a tattered blanket draped over some sort of dome hanging from a hook on the ceiling. Scooting a chair closer, she ambled on top and reached toward the swinging contraption. Her previous fear disappeared the moment she plucked the blanket away from the cage. "A talking bird."

"Awwwk."

Eyeing the feathered captive behind the golden bars, she let out a large sigh of relief. "Well, this certainly explains a lot."

So. Another poor creature had failed to dodge Du Bois's penchant for acquiring prisoners. How could she have been afraid of this tiny bird? He was small enough to fit in her cupped palms.

She considered the bird a moment longer. He was really quite a beautiful creature, with his multicolored feathers and fascinating little eyes. Green dominated the feathers on his body, and red ran from the top of his head around his neck and down his chest, while a rich blue created a mask of sorts around his eyes. "Hello," she said.

He shifted from foot to foot and lifted his beak high in the air. "Hello," he repeated.

"You're a pretty bird."

He rocked his beak from side to side. "Pretty bird."

Faith became suddenly aware that her time was slipping away. "Would you mind being quiet? I have some thinking to do."

"Awwwk. Get control, girl."

"Precisely. And then I have to get myself out of here."

If it wasn't her imagination, the bird actually winked at her. "Not a chance, honey."

Faith made a face at the jabbering creature. "You sound just like your owner."

He flapped his wings in an excited gesture. "Pretty bird."

Faith clenched her hands into tight, white-knuckled fists. "What am I doing? I'm wasting my time conversing with a stupid bird."

"Pretty bird."

She scrunched her face into a scowl. "*Stupid* bird."

"Pretty bird. Not a chance, honey."

She hesitated, studying the bird with quiet purpose. She'd be a fool to keep up the game, but the creature truly captivated her. What sort of man kept a talking bird locked in a cage? She continued to eye the strange-looking creature, wondering if he was pet or prisoner. Shrugging, she leapt off the chair.

Her plan began formulating clearly in her mind as she flung open the doors of the armoire. Having already mentally selected her choices when she'd peered inside before, she reached for the worn pair of pants first. But the moment her fingers made contact with the rough material, she changed her mind.

Why not teach Du Bois a lesson?

She cocked her head toward the bird and called, "It's not over."

The silly bird didn't disappoint. Flapping his wings, he said, "It's not over. It's not over."

Faith grinned. It was nice to have a bit of encouragement, even if it did come from a talking bird. Widening her smile, she reached into the cabinet and tossed out clothes until she found the most expensive pair of pants and the finest linen shirt among the bunch.

Kicking off her shoes, she stripped down to her chemise, corset, and petticoat. She quickly pulled the shirt over her head, but let out an unladylike oath when it enveloped her completely.

The shifty bird just couldn't let that one get by him. "Dammit."

"Stupid bird," she muttered.

"Pretty bird."

Faith looked at the shirt draping past her knees, wondering what she was going to do.

The bird had an idea. "Dammit."

"Well said, birdie. Two of me could fit in this."

"Awwwk. Get control, girl."

Faith groaned. "Just what I need, a smart-mouthed animal giving me directions. Stupid bird."

"Pretty bird."

She snorted. "Whatever."

Wiggling into the pants, she was once again struck by Du Bois's large size in comparison to her petite frame. Even with the extra layers underneath, she didn't have a chance of filling out his clothing.

Not sure what else to do, she grabbed the shirttails and rolled until she'd made a sort of belt with the extra material. She hiked up the pants and strategically tied a knot in the shirt, securing it below the waistband. She clenched her teeth as she checked that she'd tied the knot tight enough to hold everything in place.

To calm herself, Faith inhaled deeply. The rich scents lingering in the shirt immediately brought to mind the man with the green-eyed gaze and intense manner. She trembled at the thought of his flesh scraping against the same material where hers did now. The sudden fluttering in her belly turned into a hard ball of ice.

She hugged her arms around her middle while one shiver after another passed through her. Would the man's hands feel this soft, or would they feel rough and . . .

"Awwwk. It's not over."

Faith jumped at the remark. "You gave me a fright, you stupid bird."

"Pretty bird."

"Right. I forgot." Dear God, what was happening to her? One night in the company of the dangerous Du Bois and she was reduced to talking like a babbling dimwit to a bird.

"Dammit."

Faith laughed. "Couldn't have said it better myself."

"Pretty bird."

With dramatic enthusiasm, Faith stuck out her tongue at the beast. He sidled from foot to foot, arched his neck like a rooster, and squawked.

Faith rolled her eyes and rushed to the safe, thankful she'd paid close attention to Hank's fingers working the lock. She spun the lock around, clearing it, then proceeded to get down to business. Three turns to the right, two more to the left, a final one to the right and . . .

Click.

The sweetest sound of the evening.

It took both hands to twist the heavy lever and pull the small portal open. She eyed the contents, took only what belonged to her, then pushed the door shut again. She stuffed the money down the shirt, tucking the majority of the stash just above the waistband of the pants.

Feeling contrary, she scribbled a quick note to the owner of the saloon—it was the only proper thing to do after all the hospitality he'd given her—then jumped onto the desk.

"Awwwk. Get control, girl."

"Right. I got it now, birdie."

"It's not over."

She ignored that last remark and concentrated on the rest of her escape. Looking up at the window, she let out a chuckle. She'd scaled too many walls, jumped on and off too many trains, to let a measly little twinkling slab of glass three feet above her head daunt her now.

She tugged the chair on top of the desk, stood on it, and reached upward. Grabbing the window's frame with one hand, she felt around for the opening with the other. Finding the lever, she unlocked the latch and pushed the glass forward until she'd created a substantial slit. Careful to avoid catching the silky material, she threw the bundled dress through the opening.

Her searching bare foot found a toehold in the masonry. Pulling with her arms and pushing with her toes, she raised herself up until she was able to slide her head through the crack of the window. Once she was halfway through the enclosure, she grasped the outside casing and pulled again. One final push with her knee and she was free.

Tumbling to the ground, she used the momentum of the fall to gather her balance. As always, Faith landed on her feet.

Looking up, she tossed a saucy salute toward the window. "This belle won't be dancing for you tonight, Du Bois." She grinned at her own clever pun on words.

A chirp floated through the window. Faith shook her head. "Stupid bird."

"Pretty bird."

Chuckling, she picked up her bundle and took off at a full run. She made it exactly three steps before colliding with a solid mass of silk-encased flesh. "Ommph." The red dress tumbled from her clutches.

She instinctively bent to retrieve the garment, but found herself halted in mid-reach. The suspicious smell of limes and cigars filled her senses as a pair of strong arms snaked out, trapping her in a bold embrace. "It appears, Miss O'Malley, you have yet to learn your lesson."

"Awwwk. It's not over."

The bird's remark, drifting from the window, succinctly stated Faith's very sentiment toward the situation.

Chapter Three

Faith tried to twist free but Du Bois's hold merely tightened. "Be still," he ordered. "Or—"

A feeling of déjà vu quickened in her veins. "You'll have to hurt me?" she finished for him.

He had the audacity to chuckle. "Something like that. You do catch on quickly."

Faith ground her teeth together. She raised her head and looked up at the window she'd just slipped through. How could he have known she'd escape his trap through the tiny opening? Reading her mind a second time in one night, he answered, "I'm fairly observant, Miss O'Malley. I watched you eye that window with the same longing that a land-bound sailor would have for the sea."

Faith cried out her frustration. "How dare you?"

"Honey, I dare because I can."

She automatically stiffened at the way he pronounced "honey" in that bold, masculine, I'm-always-in-charge tone of his. A shiver went skidding across the back of her neck, then moved lower. Her bravado of only seconds before eluded her. She'd certainly underestimated Du Bois's cunning.

A mistake she wouldn't repeat.

Which meant she had to get away. Now. She certainly couldn't allow him to keep her imprisoned in the tiny alleyway where the dim light from the adjacent street made the scene all too intimate.

Du Bois shifted her in his arms, clasping her tighter against his chest. In a low, menacing tone he said, "About the matter of the two thousands dollars that doesn't belong to you . . ."

Unprepared for the tingling sensation in her stomach, Faith panicked. "Let me go."

"Not until you return the money."

She planted both palms against his chest and pushed with all her might. The gesture lengthened the space between them by an entire two inches. Her hammering pulse picked up speed, gnawing at her will to increase the distance even more. "Money? I don't know what you mean."

"So it's to be like that is it? You might want to reconsider your denials in light of your present situation." He easily eliminated the tiny separation she'd orchestrated as he pressed her harder against him. He held her so closely, her breasts crushed against his solid chest. A not entirely unpleasant sensation rippled through her.

Breathing down on her, he added, "As you must be aware, you are in no position to argue with me."

Faith's pulse kicked into an agitated rhythm. "You seem to be under the impression, Du Bois, that you are in control here."

"Now, I wonder where I'd get such an idea. Perhaps because I am in control?"

His smug attitude quickened the fight in her. Calling upon the lessons she'd learned from the friendly old Chinese man at the mining camp outside Cheyenne, she faked to her left then bobbed to the right.

Du Bois pushed her back toward the center.

In answer, she dropped to the ground, managing to surprise him long enough to free herself for a full half second. But Du Bois's swift movements barred further escape with a strong unyielding grip on her upper arm.

"Release me, you oaf."

He gripped both hands on her shoulders and firmly turned her to face him. Their feet shuffled in a bizarre dance of wills. Faith was compelled to reluctantly follow as Du Bois led with his superior strength. He concluded the perplexing waltz once he had her in a position where the only route of escape was through him. He then released his grip from her shoulders and widened his stance, silently communicating his domination of the situation with an arched brow.

"Now. Where were we?" His low, gravelly drawl skidded across her skin, calling to mind the image of a whispered caress.

Faith scowled. "I'm not amused by your manly display of strength. And your attempts at intimidation just won't work on me. Not this time."

His eyes narrowed. "Your attire seems familiar. Strange, isn't it? I don't seem to remember giving you permission to borrow my finest clothes."

Faith lifted her chin. "I'm not afraid of you."

He let out a lusty laugh. "Yes, you are."

Keeping her eyes locked with his, she dodged to her right, then pivoted around him on the left. He shot out a restraining arm. Once again, he physically shifted her so that escape proved troublesome, if not impossible.

"I'm warning you, Du Bois—"

"Ah, dispensing with the Mister, are we?"

Faith sniffed. "Mister implies a gentleman." She trailed

her gaze along his body. "You are no gentleman, regardless of the manner in which you dress."

"In that we agree." Growling, he pulled her back into his embrace, then lifted a hand to her hair, capturing a loose tendril between two fingers. "And since *you* are no lady, am I to assume we can dispense with any further pretense of good manners?"

Faith couldn't make her mind work up a proper response. For a long, stifling moment her captor seemed content to merely stare at the portion of her hair he'd twined between his fingers. Eventually, he took a deep breath and released the curling mass. But then he ran his knuckles across her jaw, a strange look lighting in his eyes.

The shiver that worked its way from the bottom of Faith's toes to the base of her spine was becoming all too familiar. "Release me this instant." She couldn't seem to stop the distress from sounding in her voice.

He stroked her lips with a feather-soft touch.

She twisted her head to the side. "Stop that," she ground through clenched teeth.

Every semblance of the proper gentleman left him as his tone hardened to steel. "I want the money."

"I . . . I don't have the money." Her voice trembled shamefully as she spoke the lie.

"Oh, you don't? Let's see, shall we?" Even in the dim light she could see Du Bois's wicked grin, full of intent. She nearly choked on her gasp as he boldly plunged a hand down the opening of her shirt. She tried to reel away, but he only tightened his hold with the arm that had previously rested lightly against her back.

He paused a moment, his eyes silently daring her to speak, to deny his right to search for what was his. "It seems you've added a bit of weight since we last met."

Faith refused to cower. She held her head high, her mortification buried from his roaming eyes behind a blank stare. She continued to hold his gaze as his hand dipped lower. His fingertips brushed against her breasts, lingering for a fraction of a second before moving farther downward. Faith held her breath, fighting the sigh of wanton pleasure bubbling inside her.

As much as his wordless descent shocked her, her own reaction shamed her. And then her trembles turned into a strange hunger that burned from her cheeks down to her stomach and below.

Du Bois's hand stilled again while his eyes closed to slits. His head drew nearer to hers. Unable to stop the word from tumbling out, she whispered his name. His lips moved closer to hers, his breath a caress on her face. Her heart pounded in anticipation of the kiss, but just before closing the distance, he pushed her away from him, snatching his hand out of her shirt at the same time. She watched in stunned silence as he held up a fistful of loose bills. His booty appeared to be around a hundred dollars.

In that moment, with his reproachful eyes glaring hard at her, Faith realized she'd never truly known humiliation before.

His smile flattened into a grim line. "Mine," he said, waving the money under her nose before stuffing it in one of his pants pockets. "Care to explain yourself?"

"No." How could she? He was prepared to believe she was the lowest kind of woman. And thanks to her strange response to his touch, she could do nothing more than agree.

"Then let me explain it for you." He continued as though she'd given her assent, "From your speech and manner of dress, I can only assume you're an educated woman. And we both know an educated woman in these parts equals a woman with means. Why would such a woman cheat at cards?"

Faith studied the toes of her left foot. "I have my reasons."

"Which are?"

Unable to give her answer now that the time had finally come, she merely shook her head. She tried to bury her despair, but it came lurching out in her words. "You wouldn't understand." For reasons unknown to her, she suddenly wished he *would* understand, and perhaps even offer his help.

She lifted her gaze in time to watch his eyes cloud over with an emotion she couldn't quite name. Disappointment perhaps? "Well, then," he sneered. "That leaves only one explanation for your presence at my tables tonight."

Oh, how she hated that self-righteous tone in his voice. She crossed her arms in front of her. "Do enlighten me."

"Greed."

Faith nearly choked on her response. "Greed? Is that what you think?"

He leaned toward her. "It's what I know."

Needing distance, she placed her palms against his chest and pushed. "Only a greedy person would suspect it in another."

"Meaning?"

"Meaning . . . you seem to take great pleasure in assuming the worst in people. Which merely makes my point."

Du Bois let out an ugly laugh. "What you think of me doesn't matter at the moment. I know firsthand what women like you are all about."

"Making assumptions again?"

"Absolutely. But I find, even as reprehensible as I think your behavior has been, I must compliment you on your, um . . . interesting talents."

Faith sidled to her left. With what seemed very little effort on his part, Du Bois reached out and scooted her back to the right. She sighed in frustration. He bestowed on her a sarcastic grin in return.

"Talents?" she asked at last.

"You speak like a well-bred lady for one."

She strayed to the left, he hauled her back to the right. "You play cards better than most professional gamblers. And lastly, I watched you climb out of that window up there. I must say, you have the finesse of a . . ."

She granted him her most unpleasant smile, the one she reserved for bankers and highborn gentlemen in red silk vests. "Hoyden?"

He inclined his head. "Excellent description. Yes, a hoyden sharp is precisely what you are. Very skilled, I might add."

An idea came to her. She realized if it worked, she could still get away with the money. But before she resorted to the underhanded tactic, she had to try to escape in a fair manner one more time.

She scrambled to her right, but in an instant he pushed her back where she'd stood. Well, then. So be it. "I have one other skill you haven't seen yet," she bragged. "Would you like me to show it to you?"

Without waiting for his answer, she took a step forward. Grasping the sides of his vest, she pulled him to her. She trailed a fingertip along the smooth silk, stunned at the prickling sensation playing havoc with her flesh. Her breathing quickened of its own accord and blood slammed through her veins.

Du Bois's look turned sardonic, but like her own, his breath came in short, quick intakes of air. "I can only imagine just how talented you are."

She allowed him to misunderstand. "Yes. It's a talent as old as man and . . . woman." Was that her voice sounding so husky?

He seemed to visibly get ahold of himself as he captured her roaming hand. "Intriguing, O'Malley. But I must warn you. I like my women willing, soft, and . . . honest."

She wiggled her hand free, then moved it to the back

of his neck. "A paragon of virtue must be quite hard to find in—how did you refer to it? Oh, yes, *these parts*."

"That's true enough."

She played with the hair curling over his collar. His brief tremble sparked an answering response in her own body. Faith never knew she could feel both hot and cold at the same time. She continued to tangle her fingers in his hair.

"Enough." Du Bois wrapped his hand around her wrist, stilling further exploration with gentle pressure. "Since my standards are invariably high, I'm afraid I'm going to have to decline your very tempting offer."

She allowed him to remove her hand from his hair, both thankful and strangely miffed he was the one to stop the game before it had really started. "Coming from you, Du Bois, I consider that quite a compliment."

"Now, why am I not surprised?"

She grimaced. "Because you think you know everything about me. But once more you misunderstand. I wasn't talking about *that* particular skill."

"Oh? Do you cook, sew, ride a horse with great style?"

She smiled. "You seem to find insulting me quite pleasurable. But, alas, you still misunderstand."

His gaze scalded. "Then please, inform me. What wondrous skill do you possess?"

Faith shifted her weight, planting her left foot behind her at an angle. Bending her right knee, she leaned slightly backward. To keep his mind off her new position she toyed with Du Bois's vest.

"You see," she said in a light tone. "When cornered, I fight like I play cards."

His gaze turned suspicious as he braced his hands on both of her shoulders. "You cheat?"

Copying his courteous manner, she smiled. "No. I win."

Just as he set her away from him, she pivoted and raised her right knee in the air. Leading with her heel, she slammed her foot into his stomach, landing the blow exactly as her friend had taught her.

Du Bois doubled over in pain. His howl of outrage wasn't nearly as gratifying as Faith might have predicted. Nevertheless, what was done was done. In the blink of an eye she retrieved her bundled dress and set out, tearing around the corner at neck-breaking speed. She quickened her pace as the bellowed promise to hunt her down like a rabid dog nipped at her heels.

Chapter Four

André charged wordlessly to the back of the saloon. Ignoring the pain in his gut, he released the lock and with a violent shove, plowed into his office. The earsplitting bang of door meeting wall punctuated his foul mood. Unfortunately, the jarring noise did nothing to eliminate the humiliating reality of the last twenty minutes. Not since Pearl ran off with his inheritance could he recall a time he'd suffered so complete a defeat.

Oh, he'd known O'Malley would try to pirate the money and then attempt to steal away in the night. What he hadn't expected was the surprise kick. How could that tiny, delicate woman fire off such a powerful blow?

Shifting his angry gaze around what used to be his once highly organized personal sanctuary, André caved into his fury. "Dammit."

He'd left O'Malley alone for ten minutes and she'd wreaked havoc. Risking a step through the clothes scattered on the floor, he tripped over a delicate, very female slipper. "Hell." He kicked the offensive shoe out of his way, sending it crashing against the desk. The sound of a familiar chirp accompanied his action. He looked up, eyeing the uncovered birdcage with disgust. "Did she leave nothing untouched?"

The bird actually winked at him in return.

"Larkin, you stupid bird—"

"Pretty bird."

André shook his head. "Well, isn't this just . . . perfect."

Larkin rolled his beak around in a circle. "Perfect. Just perfect."

Scrubbing a hand over his face, André swore. "Now, why am I not surprised that hoyden got you to break your wretched two-year silence?"

Larkin flapped his wings. "It's not over."

André swore again, fluently and at length.

Larkin repeated every word, building momentum as he went.

"That does it." Teaching his bird how to talk was just one more insult to add to the long list of other offenses that conniving, bad-mannered, scheming cheat had committed in the last hour. The woman deserved to be locked away for life.

And André planned to ensure that blessed event occurred soon.

"It's not over."

"It is for you, Larkin." André picked up the blanket lying next to his feet. He tossed the cloth on the cage, banishing the chirping bunch of feathers for the night.

Swearing spewed from the cloaked exile. Before André could join in with a choice phrase or two of his own, he spotted a slip of paper propped against the pile of books on his desk. He whipped the note from its perch with as much intensity as he'd used to enter the room moments before.

If the miserable handwriting was any indication, Miss O'Malley had scrawled the words with as little care as she'd given his office. André's irritation only increased as he read her parting jab.

My Dear Mr. Du Bois,
Thank you for your splendid hospitality. But I'm afraid I must decline your offer to remain any longer. I have a much more pressing engagement with your window.
Yours most humbly,
Faith O'Malley

Baring his teeth, André slanted his gaze toward the offensive slab of glass. "Arrogant wench." Crushing the paper in his fist, he stifled the urge to take off after the woman right away. Calling upon composure he couldn't hope to attain, he shut his eyes and released all the air out of his lungs. Rationally, he knew it wouldn't do any good to murder the beautiful charlatan in cold blood. At least, not before he got his and the others' money back.

Dark, ugly thoughts linked together until one emerged over all the others. O'Malley had chosen the wrong saloon, on the wrong evening, to play out her little intrigue.

Five years ago to the day, André had embarked on the greatest debacle of his life—marriage to Pearl LaRue. The events of the last hour had merely added another layer of indignity to his rash, youthful mistake of thinking he could turn a bad woman good.

Perhaps if he'd caught up with Pearl before she'd died in that train wreck, he'd feel less fury, less disgrace. But after three arduous years of searching, the last two conducted by an overpaid Pinkerton, André still didn't know where his wife had hidden the remaining portion of his inheritance. All he knew was that she'd spent the bulk of it in Cripple Creek during the first few months after she'd left him.

And now here he stood, on the night of what would have been his wedding anniversary, facing a far too similar error in judgment. He'd thought he'd learned his lesson with Pearl. What was it about O'Malley, an obvious liar and cheat, that made him want to believe in her? Was it the look of genuine desperation he'd recognized in her startling gaze? Or was it merely the fact that he found her so alluring?

An uncomfortable ache spread through his groin as he realized just how much he'd wanted the woman the way he'd never wanted a woman before. Even now, the titillating thought of O'Malley's sinfully full lips sent renewed hunger slamming through his veins.

A loud rap against the doorjamb knocked André out of his musings.

"Mr. Du Bois. I'm really sorry about this. She . . . I mean, I never thought . . ."

André lifted a hand to stop the stilted flow of words. "I know, Hank. She fooled us both." Remembering the feel of his knuckles sliding against O'Malley's soft skin as he'd plunged in search of the money, André added, "In more ways than one." The tremor that passed through him had nothing to do with anger.

Hank glanced toward the safe and grimaced. "I never would have taken her for . . . for . . ." His voice trailed off again.

The same thought had gnawed at André from the start, but he'd learned long ago that appearances were rarely what they seemed. He shouldn't have been surprised by O'Malley's deception. But he was, and profoundly disappointed too. A chill brushed through him at the unwanted memory of her skilled fingers loitering in his hair. "The world is full of dishonest, people," he said, knowing the words were more for his own benefit than Hank's.

"Yeah, but how'd she do it?"

André lifted a single brow. "I wonder."

"She must have figured out the combination," Hank surmised, obviously unaware of the reason for André's sarcasm. "But that's impossible."

"Really? Maybe she watched your fingers?"

Hank blinked, looking everywhere but at André. The only other sign of his discomfort sounded in his shocked tone. "You knew?"

"I did."

"And you didn't stop her?"

It was André's turn to avoid eye contact, as uneasiness settled. "I tried. She got away."

Hank swore.

The abrupt silence stood in stark contrast to the noise and commotion echoing from the main part of the saloon. In the ensuing hush André realized what he had to do. "I'm going out. As soon as you get an opportunity, switch this safe with the one in my rooms."

Hank nodded.

Before André could leave his office, Hank's voice stopped him. "Wait. Where you headed? In case I need you."

Taking a deep, calming breath, he turned around and said, "I'll be hunting on Hollady Street."

"The Row? You think she's there?"

"It's the most logical place." André allowed the anticipation of his next meeting with O'Malley to swell. "I plan to enjoy every moment it takes to get our money back from that woman."

Hank's brows drew together. "I just had a thought. The others don't know they've been cheated. Word gets out, we'll be an easy mark for every sharp this side of the Mississippi."

The thought had already occurred to André. It was easy enough to fix, with the help of one of his more trusted faro dealers. "Leave that to me. I know just how to handle the situation, with no one the wiser."

"How you going to pay those men back without telling them what Miss O'Malley did tonight?"

André batted away Hank's concern with a contemptuous wave of his hand. "I'll worry about Greene and the others. You just concentrate on switching the safes."

Hank released a quick breath and nodded.

André glanced at the window, then back down to the mess of clothing and books sprinkled on the floor. Sliding his lips into a tight-lipped snarl, he added, "Mark my words, Hank, I'll root our little fox out of her lair before daybreak. And when I'm through with her, she'll be sorry she ever strayed into my saloon."

Hank's smile bowed with the same grim determination André savored in his own heart. "Happy hunting, Boss."

Before bounding up the front steps, Faith stopped a moment to admire the two-story house glowing golden under the street lamp. She couldn't help but smile at the fine job she'd done restoring the old building. After five long years, and two strapping loans, she'd turned the crumbling structure into a respectable brick and stone mansion. The result was finer than any house owned by her fashionable neighbors in the Highlands of North Denver. She'd come a long way from the back streets of mining camps.

In her overzealous efforts to provide more than a roof and bed for the children, no detail had been left untouched. She'd furnished the twelve bedrooms, two sitting rooms, and three parlors with exquisite furniture. She'd hung expensive wallpaper, ordered Oriental rugs straight from Paris, and purchased assorted fineries for every room.

A sudden, ugly dose of conscience whipped through her as an image of André Du Bois, his head lowering toward hers, splintered her thoughts. Just how far had she been willing to go to save Heart House from foreclosure?

The front door opened a crack, saving Faith from further reflection on the consequences of her behavior this evening. Katherine Taylor, the girl she'd left in charge six hours ago, stepped into the light. "Well? What happened?"

Faith skipped up the last three steps. "We did it, Katherine." She pulled the younger girl into a warm hug. "We got all of the money we needed, plus enough extra to finish enlarging the kitchen and dining room."

Katherine pulled back and searched Faith's face. "You got the money? All of it?" Her blue eyes closed to tiny slits. "How'd you get that much money in one night?"

The stab of conscience Faith kept forcing down pounded in her ears. She trembled, fighting the barrage of memories from the evening's events. "I told you to leave it all to me."

As Katherine scanned Faith from head to toe, her features crinkled into a frown. "What happened to Sally's dress?"

Faith held up the red silk bundle. "Plans changed. I had to switch clothes."

"Oh?" Katherine angled her head and peered at Faith, the probing look twisting into a questioning glint. "You didn't do anything unlawful, did you?"

Faith swallowed. No sense in concerning everyone with the full details of the evening. There'd be plenty of time for that later. "We did it, Katherine. We saved Heart House. Now be happy and stop with the questions."

"Oh, I'm thrilled. But why won't you look me in the eyes? I'm almost nineteen, plenty old enough to handle whatever it is you're hiding from me."

To her chagrin, Faith found she couldn't hold Katherine's gaze longer than a second or two. "Don't start making any judgments before you hear the whole story."

"Translation, you did something we're going to both be sorry for."

"I only did what I had to do."

"No, you did more, as always. Look at this place, Faith." Katherine waved her hand in a circle. "None of us could have ever hoped to live in such luxury. Orphanages are usually full of filth, misery, and despair, especially for the likes of us, the unwanted children of prostitutes."

Uncomfortable with the turn of the conversation, Faith grimaced. "I didn't do anything all that special."

"No, you just made a dream come true."

Faith shrugged. "A dream? Maybe. All I know is once my mother moved us to Mattie's brothel, I couldn't wait to get out of that place and bring the rest of the kids with me."

"I know how hard you've worked to make Heart House happen, you wouldn't intentionally jeopardize it by . . ." Katherine's voice trailed off, her gaze as thoughtful as it was concerned. "Are you sure everything's all right?"

Faith looked behind her, suddenly worried they weren't alone. To ensure Du Bois couldn't follow her trail, she'd darted up, down, and across several streets, then doubled back three times. But just in case . . .

"Why don't we go inside for the rest of our conversation?" she suggested.

Katherine nodded, her eyes suddenly haunted. "We're going to keep Heart House, right?" That flash of terror in the younger girl's eyes, the one Faith saw every day when she looked in the mirror, called to the part of her that would do anything to save the orphanage and the children from pain. Unfortunately, her efforts never proved enough. Oh, she could provide a house, material luxuries, and even love, but she had yet to figure out a way to erase the one thing they all shared.

Uncertainty.

Mistrust and fear lived in their gazes, buried in their very souls. Faith had seen the look again tonight, when she'd stared into Du Bois's eyes. Could that have been why she'd come so close to kissing him? The sweet, hot, erasing of pain through a shared moment of pleasure?

Oh, my. Clearly, this wasn't her usual way of thinking. She was a woman who'd vowed chastity, thanks to the harsh reality of her life as the daughter of a pitiful soiled dove who'd killed herself with too much laudanum. After witnessing her mother's destruction, how could Faith have willingly tossed her morals away after one evening in the company of a man?

A breeze kicked up, rustling the bushes lining the porch. The ominous quiver in her heart sent Faith pushing Katherine forward. "Inside. Quick."

Katherine looked over her shoulder. "Are you sure you didn't do anything we'll regret later?"

Fiddling with the knot in Du Bois's shirt, Faith concentrated on the doorjamb. "Of course I'm sure."

Once inside the front parlor, Faith tossed Sally's dress on an exquisite, light blue velvet couch as Katherine moved through the room lighting candles. Faith waited, savoring the moment of serenity that passed through her. How she loved the soft glow of real candlelight and the smell of extinguished matches.

Katherine blew out the last match, turned, and centered her gaze on Faith's bare feet. "What happened to your shoes?"

Faith waved her hand. "You don't want to know."

"Part of that change in plans you mentioned?"

"You could say that."

Katherine shook her head, her voice sounding as though *she* were the wise twenty-five-year-old, rather than Faith. "I think it's time you told me the details of this long story."

Faith didn't answer right away. Instead, she worked the knot in the shirt free and released the money, permitting it to rain onto the floor around her. "This is all you need to know."

Katherine caught her breath inside an audible gasp. She lowered to her knees, touching one bill after another with a delicate caress, as though afraid it would disappear if she handled it improperly.

"It's real."

Tears brimming, she cried, "Oh, Faith. You really did it. I can't believe you pulled it off. Our troubles are over."

Kneeling across from her, Faith scooped up an armful of the money and threw it in the air. But her thoughts clouded as she realized how close she'd come to losing it all. She hadn't expected Du Bois to join the poker game, or her strange physical reaction to him. A thousand little ripples churned in her stomach, reminding her of the weakness she'd discovered in herself, the unthinkable need to respond to a man's touch. She curled a hundred-dollar bill through her fingers, remembering the silky feel of Du Bois's hair flowing through those same fingers.

"All right. What happened? Tell me all of it."

Faith sat back on her heels and eyed Katherine, more a trusted friend than another orphan to clothe and feed. "Well, I went to the saloon as planned. . . ."

Faith stopped in mid-sentence, unsure what to say next. How could she tell Katherine what she'd done tonight? Searching for an explanation she picked up another hundred dollar bill. "I don't know if you should hear this, Katherine. You aren't like the rest of us."

"Of course I am."

Faith made a face. "Your mother only turned to whoring when your father died. She never made you live among it. That alone makes you different. You're educated, too. You went to that prestigious school back East. What was it called?"

"Miss Lindsay's Select School for Young Ladies." Katherine gently pulled the money out of Faith's hand and returned it to the pile between them. "That's in the past. I'm here now, as much a part of this place as you are."

"Not by choice. You'd still be there if they hadn't made you leave when they found out about your mother's profession. Even now, you could get a teaching job somewhere if you wanted to."

Katherine's eyes welled with tears. "I love the children here. I can't imagine leaving. I'd do anything for them."

"As long as it was legal."

"Of course. That goes without saying."

Katherine's answer made it even harder for Faith to explain herself tonight.

"All right. Let's have it, Faith. The truth. You went to the saloon," Katherine prompted. "And?"

Faith bit her bottom lip, searching for the right words. Katherine might have been forced to return to Denver, but she was still a product of her years back East, educated, moral, an example for the others. Would she understand the desperation that had lead Faith to lie, cheat, and steal this evening?

Faith didn't want to find out. Not tonight. "*And* . . . I played cards. I won. That's it."

"No, that's not it. I know that look in your eyes. What else happened? What aren't you telling me?"

Faith shrugged. "Can't we just leave it alone?"

"Don't you think I deserve to hear it all? I've lived with the fear of losing this place just as deeply as you have. Maybe more. Unlike you, I have no skills." A shadow fell across her features. "And nowhere else to go."

"You have an education. You could teach school, like you've taught me. I'm practically a lady. Or at least, can pass for one when I try."

"Who would hire a woman like me, an infamous madam's daughter?" Katherine shook her head. "No, I have nowhere else to go."

Knowing there was no denying the truth, Faith sighed. "I'm sorry."

"I know. Now, save your pity and convince me I have nothing to worry about."

Taking a deep breath, Faith began her tale, but Katherine cut her off almost before she had begun. "Oh, Faith. You lost everything but fifty dollars? And we'd worked so hard raising that thousand."

"Don't worry, it was part of my plan."

Katherine looked at her through squinted eyes. "Go on."

"Then I stacked the deck."

"Oh, Faith, please tell me you didn't cheat."

"I had to. But it gets worse."

"I should have guessed that." Katherine grimaced.

Faith proceeded, only to have Katherine stop her again. "Lord, you got caught?" She drew her lower lip between her teeth. "But now I'm confused. If you got caught, how did you end up with this?" She lifted a handful of money, then let the bills drop one by one.

Faith grabbed a hundred-dollar bill and waved it in the air. "I never admitted to anything. When he locked me in his office—"

Katherine's gaze sharpened. "He?"

"The owner of the saloon, André Du Bois, he's the one who caught me."

"He didn't."

"He did."

Katherine shook her head. "Oh, Faith."

"I got away with the money." She patted her heart and sighed. "But I had to climb out of his office window, hence the change in clothes."

"Oh, Faith."

"Would you stop saying, 'Oh, Faith,' in that resigned tone. You sound like a mother hen."

"Well somebody needs to think clearly here." Katherine pursed her lips. "Tell me more about this André Du Bois."

A shudder quickened Faith's pulse. Du Bois had been the most formidable foe she'd ever encountered, even worse than the banker Prescott. Prescott incited only disdain, while Du Bois called up a mix of emotions that confused her and blunted the edge she usually relied on to help her out of sticky situations. For the first time in her life, Faith had nearly tasted defeat. "I never want to see that man again. He's mean-spirited, nasty, judgmental, arrogant—"

Katherine lifted her brows. "Handsome?"

"You have no idea. Good thing I don't like egotistical, overbearing brutes."

Katherine smirked. "Yeah, a very good thing."

Silence fell between them as each considered the night's events.

Katherine eventually spoke. "Faith?"

"Hmm?"

"Do you think this André Du Bois will let you get away with cheating him?"

She could lie. She could pretend matters weren't as dire as they both knew they were. She did neither. "No."

"Dear God. What are we going to do?"

"There's only one thing we can do. We'll pay off the loan the moment the bank opens in a few hours, before Du Bois can take our money back."

"You mean, the *others'* money."

Faith shrugged. "It's ours now."

"No, it's not."

"This isn't as simple as right and wrong, his or ours. All we have to do is get the money to the bank before Du Bois finds out where I really live."

It was Katherine's turn to sigh. "I don't think it's going be that easy. You've really landed us into the thick of things this time."

Looking at the clock on the mantel, Faith said, "I know. But what else could I do?" She threw up a restraining hand. "Don't answer that."

Katherine sniffed, obvious panic quickening her breathing, worry creasing her brow.

"Stay calm, Katherine. We only have three hours before the bank opens for business. I promise you, I'll be Prescott's first customer. And once Du Bois finds me, it'll be too late."

Katherine moved to the window. "You don't think he followed you home?"

Faith couldn't help but chuckle at that ridiculous notion, until she recalled Du Bois's parting vow to hunt her down. Sobering, she admitted, "Anything's possible. But I don't think he did. I was careful how I made my way home. And"—she rolled her knuckles into a fist and folded it into her other palm—"I kicked him too hard."

"Oh, Faith."

"There you go again. Now, stop this. I know what I did this evening was wrong. But I had to do it. Time has run out. And I promise Du Bois won't be able to find me. I led him to believe . . . well, let's just say he thinks I'm a woman of questionable virtue."

"I shudder to think how he came about that misguided assumption."

Faith curled her lips into a sheepish grin. "I have a feeling he's looking for me right now on the Row."

"You're reckless, that's it. Nothing else explains your behavior this evening." Katherine sighed again. "But I can't fault your courage, or your methods. Given the options, I won't argue that you chose the lesser of two evils."

"The most important point is that we have the money to pay off the loan two whole days early." Faith took a long, deep breath. "Now, enough of this seriousness. Let's wake the children and celebrate our good fortune."

"It's entirely too late."

"No, it's early. The sun will be rising in less than an hour. They'll be awake soon anyway."

Katherine nodded, but she couldn't disguise the anxiety on her face. The look mirrored the feelings Faith had tried to discount since she first stepped into the Dancing Belles saloon.

"Don't worry, Katherine. If Du Bois is looking for me, he's tracking on the wrong side of town. As we speak, he's probably regretting the moment I ever entered his saloon."

"Now *that* I don't doubt."

"Stop your fretting, I have matters completely under control."

Katherine sighed. "Why is it every time you say that we end up in worse trouble than before?"

Chapter Five

Three hours after arriving home with all that lovely money, Faith bypassed the tellers, skirted along the waist-high railing on her left, then charged toward the bank owner's private office. Unwilling to wait for a response to her knock, she turned the knob and pressed forward. "I'm here to discuss my loan."

Thurston P. Prescott III didn't bother looking up as he waved his fleshy hand in bored indifference. "There is nothing more to say, Miss O'Malley. My terms stand."

Outlaw, she wanted to scream. *Cheat*. Just yesterday, he'd adopted that same condescension, then shamelessly called in her loan six months early. No warning. No explanation. Merely the end of all her dreams for the children. Exhaling, Faith forced aside her hostility and coaxed her lips into a pleasant smile. "I have one final item to discuss."

Without lifting his attention to her, Prescott scratched his salt-and-pepper beard. Faith widened her stance, calling upon the patience she'd lost the day before. The constant, even ticking of the mantel clock beat in stark contrast to the banker's furious scribbling. The rich smell of polished mahogany and perfectly aged leather extolled power, ownership.

Faith refused to be intimated. She poked at a stack of papers, sending them scattering onto the floor. "Oh, my, look what I've done."

The banker's head snapped up, frustration knitted across his bushy brows. "I thought I made myself perfectly clear yesterday. You have two more days to come up with the money." He dipped his pen in an inkwell on his left, then dropped his gaze to his paperwork again. "You may go."

Faith squared her shoulders. "This will only take a minute." She tossed out her words in the same girlish tone she'd used to charm Joshua Greene.

A snort filled the air.

"Is that all the response I am to expect?"

Another snort.

Undaunted, Faith let out a small sigh of satisfaction. She plucked the neatly wrapped bundle of money from the hidden pocket in her skirt and placed it on the desk. "Perhaps you'll be interested in what I have to say now."

In one swift movement, Prescott slapped the file closed. His small, sharp eyes hardened. Sputtering, he flung an ugly glare from her face to the money and back again.

Faith granted him her most satisfied grin. "It's all there."

For a moment his gaze filled with pure hatred, but then it cleared of all emotion. "How'd you get this much money in one day?"

At his words, a flicker of conscience ignited, making it no longer possible to escape the truth. She'd lied and cheated to save her orphanage. Silence hung heavy, her guilt clogging her ability to respond right away. With each steady tick of the clock her breathing quickened, her remorse grew. She fought to keep the shame out of her voice. "Does it matter?"

His eyes narrowed, Prescott's voice turned deep with suspicion. "Yes, it does. I won't accept this money until I know it's really yours to give."

Faith sighed. She should have prepared for such a reaction. But she'd been so relieved she'd gotten away from Du Bois with the money, she hadn't thought much further. After convincing Katherine all was well, she'd changed clothes, celebrated with the children, then hurried to the bank.

Tired and more than a little scared, she railed, "Telling you where or how I got this money was not part of our agreement. All you said was that I had to get it." She pointed to the desk, pausing for emphasis. "And there it is."

A succession of loud creaks and groans exploded as Prescott shifted his considerable frame into another position. Resting his elbows on the chair's arms, he steepled his fingers. "Did you steal it?"

Fighting the jerk of shame whipping its way up from her toes, Faith gnawed on her lower lip. Yes, technically she'd stolen the money, but skill had played a role in the evening's events as well. All those days she'd spent playing cards with craggy miners, while her mother conducted business on the other side of camp, had finally proven useful.

"I'll ask just one more time, before I throw you out of my office. Where did you get this money?"

Oh, how she hated that smug accusation in his eyes. A man like Prescott, with his fancy clothes and obscene wealth, exemplified all that threatened her children's chance of a secure future. "Let's just say I have a benefactor."

She flattened her lips into a grim line, suppressing the

sudden urge to smile at the thought of André Du Bois in the role of benefactor. She had no doubt he'd positively go apoplectic if he knew what she'd just claimed. She batted at a stubborn curl falling loose from its pins and bouncing free from her hat. Concentrating on the gesture helped rid her of the disturbing images of the man she'd thwarted just hours before.

Prescott rose from his chair. "Is that right?"

Faith threw her shoulders back, refusing to stir as the banker rounded the desk. She would never let this man see how much she abhorred him and his self-serving attitude that led him to give and take money from the gullible. *Are you any better? Didn't you give and take from the gullible at that poker table last night?* She shook away the disturbing thought with a vigorous toss of her head. As though in hushed reprimand, the wayward tendril slapped her on the cheek.

Barely an inch taller than her, the banker met her gaze eye to eye. "You actually expect me to believe some kind soul gave you nearly two thousand dollars? Your whore friends may help you out on occasion, but I know they don't have that kind of money."

Faith took an involuntary step back as the banker's hot, rancid breath enveloped her. "Is it so hard to comprehend?"

"I find it impossible. No one would give money to you or that . . . *home* . . . of yours. A place filled with illegitimate, insipid bastards." His face inflated with fury. "It's beyond absurd."

Faith recoiled at his callous words. "There are many people in Denver who see the need for my orphanage."

"Prostitutes and whores, yes. Only the shamed mothers of your kind would want a place to discard their brats."

The reality of his words buckled her knees. She had to grasp the side of the desk to steady herself. This man, with his refined Eastern accent and overfilled belly, had never cared about Heart House. "What about your son?" she asked.

Prescott's rage reverberated in his voice. "Don't you ever mention that boy again."

"But I thought you wanted to provide for Michael's future, if not for the others."

"You're wrong."

Hypocrite. Just like the men who'd come to her mother, wanting their pleasure, then cursing her unholy profession once back in their daily lives on the righteous side of Hollady Street. "If that's how you feel, why did you lend me the money in the first place?"

He let out a twisted, bitter laugh. "I knew you could never pay that much money back in time. I gave it to you so you would fail. And then I'd be rid of you and those brats."

He might as well have grasped her heart and squeezed the very life out of it. She shook her head, shunning the weak tears that would proclaim her pain to him. She'd thought Prescott had gladly loaned her the money for his six-year-old son. "It doesn't really matter what you think," she said, realizing the truth as she spoke it. "You signed our agreement. That makes it legal. You can't deny my right to pay off the loan now."

He blinked, his insults held in check for the first time during their one-year association. Smelling victory, Faith clutched her small advantage and pounced. "Take the money and let's be done with this distasteful business."

Prescott stared at the money, hesitating. "Something's not right here." He shook his finger in her face. "I don't know what it is, but I plan to find out."

Faith raised a silent prayer of contrition for the sin she'd committed less than five hours before, hoping God was on her side this morning. She added a heartfelt promise to repent properly once she had the deed to Heart House in her possession. Keeping on the offensive, she continued her attack. "The only part of this that's not right is your behavior. We made a deal. I've lived up to my end of the bargain. And I expect you to keep yours."

Prescott paused. Faith waited, delighting in the defeated look in his eyes.

"I'll have to count the money," he said sullenly.

The taste of victory sweetened in her mouth. "By all means, take your time. My morning is yours."

If his slumped shoulders and grunt were any indication, Faith had saved her orphanage. The snarl spitting threw his teeth as he counted added to her flowering euphoria.

After only a short while, he grumbled again. "It would appear the entire amount is here."

She allowed a full smile to lengthen across her lips. "Try not to sound so disappointed. You've lost, Prescott. And I own Heart House." *I own Heart House.* The thought coiled in her head, making her dizzy with relief. She clenched her jaw shut, silencing the shout of satisfaction begging for release.

"It appears we're through," Prescott said at last.

A happy, tiny giggle slipped out. "Oh, no, not quite. I want the deed, before I leave this morning. And I want you to put in writing that I have no more debt owed to this bank. Or to you."

His grudging look of respect was well worth the risks she'd taken the night before. She merely had to endure a few more tense moments and she'd never have to deal with the banker again.

If only she could be as certain she'd seen the last of André Du Bois. Ever since she'd fled the saloon's back alley, her thoughts had frequently turned to the man's doubled-over image and his vow to hunt her down like a rabid dog. The shiver slinking across her flesh felt entirely too much like a premonition.

* * *

Hours of searching through the streets of Denver had helped André's anger simmer. He'd walked the full length of the Row—Denver's notorious red-light district—but had not discovered O'Malley's crib. Why couldn't he figure out where the slippery woman had disappeared?

The inkling that she wasn't what she seemed thrashed into life, as it had countless times since he'd started the search. Where was she? And more importantly, what could have possibly birthed that look of desperation in those beautiful, expressive eyes?

Perhaps that shifty banker Prescott would have some answers. After just a short time in town, André had discovered the man's uncanny knack for asserting himself into almost every financial transaction in the city. If Faith O'Malley had a debt, Prescott would be involved.

When André entered the bank, the clerk told him he would have to wait his turn to speak with the owner, as Prescott was already conducting business with another customer.

None too happy, André thrust aside his impatience and sat in a chair facing toward the glass-encased office split into three sections by polished, wooden planks. The elegant interior of the bank called to mind his youthful days in New Orleans, before the war and Yankee Occupation had destroyed the opulence in which he'd been born. He knew it was a time that could never be regained, yet the soothing memories of that simpler life flooded his mind, sending a sharp homesickness for his family, and for what might have been, swirling inside.

Unwilling to allow the melancholy he'd banished years ago to return, he diverted his attention back to Prescott's office. At the sight of the woman jerking her chin, André straightened in his chair. "I'll be damned." Dressed in a purple, really very homely, dress, she still managed to catch his attention and hold it fast.

The familiar prickling in his groin churned, confirming

her identity more surely than if she'd turned around to face him. André stood the moment she squared her tiny shoulders and jutted her nose in the air with that defiant fashion he'd endured just hours before.

It was no wonder he hadn't located O'Malley on the Row. The little con had been conducting affairs of a very different kind this morning. Was she starting her own brothel? It would explain the odd, hushed-mouthed reticence of the madams he'd questioned earlier. God, how he wished it weren't true, but what else would explain the need for such a large sum of money? André couldn't bear the thread of disappointment braiding through his mind.

Heavyhearted, he continued to watch her deal with Prescott. She shrugged in response to something the man said, and turned to look out the office. Her gaze roamed the bank in the same calculating manner she'd used to survey his saloon.

André took a step forward, ensuring she saw him the moment her gazed turned in his direction. The instant those big brown eyes met his, he nodded. Her wide-eyed flush prompted him to touch his brow and offer a two-finger salute. She shifted her stance and purposely turned her back to him. Her slight tremble told the true story of her reaction to his presence. Well, now, the morning was indeed looking up.

The time had come to finish their game of chance, with André the victor at last. And he knew just how to orchestrate his triumph.

Chapter Six

After a brief spasm of pure panic and several long minutes of consideration, Faith came to the conclusion that she had no choice but to face the tall, well-dressed bundle of trouble waiting outside Prescott's private office.

The wisest decision would be to confront Du Bois alone, before the banker insinuated himself into the matter. With a quick, uneven sigh, Faith disregarded her anxiety and shoved through to the main foyer. For additional courage, she clutched the two documents Prescott had finally signed in one hand and her favorite parasol in the other. Prepared for the worst, she almost regretted the anticlimactic sensation upon discovering Du Bois's absence.

Capitalizing on her good fortune, she turned toward the back door, but thought better of it at once. When last they'd met, she'd seriously underestimated Du Bois. He most assuredly would be expecting her to exit by way of the empty alley.

Or would he discount the obvious? The apprehension she'd held at bay uncoiled, making her limbs weak. Insisting her brain cooperate, she made her choice. After carefully folding the deed and receipt, she stuffed them into the hidden pocket of her skirt.

Bursting through the bank's entrance, she shuddered as the crisp mountain air chilled her skin. Squinting into the blinding sunlight, she breathed in the fresh pine scent of the late summer morning.

The familiar shiver grazing along her spine had very little to do with the cool breeze lifting the hair off the back of her neck, and a lot to do with the haunting baritone breathing down on her from behind.

"Isn't this a happy coincidence? I say, O'Malley, you do get around."

A choked sigh seemed the most appropriate response, and the only one she could force between her clenched teeth.

Exasperating confidence resonated in his deep tone as moist lips lingered near her ear. "You know, of all the ensembles I've seen you wear, this one is by far the ugliest." She heard the click of boots on the sidewalk as he took a step back.

Flushing, Faith whipped around. Forgetting the difference in their heights, she was taken aback when her gaze engaged nothing more than gold and black-threaded silk. She looked up, and up farther still.

Du Bois's rumble of laughter corralled her to the spot, locking her voice into further silence. He seemed happy enough to continue the one-sided conversation. "Imagine my surprise when I saw you, an accomplished liar and cheat, conducting business with the most notorious banker in Denver."

She hated the way he made the scenario sound like two thieves cavorting with one another. Her throat instantly unclogged. "Insufferable, vulgar, unconscionable—"

"Excellent assessment of your own character, but let's talk about something more pleasant."

"Vermin."

His feral laughter grated. "Well, I wouldn't go that far. You do have a few redeemable qualities."

Sorely tired of the man's veritable lack of self-control when it came to vocalizing his low opinion of her character, Faith tilted her head at a wry angle. "Slinking in the shadows again? Now I wonder why that image continually rings true."

His smile widened. Darn it if her heart didn't skip a beat, and then another. Oh, why couldn't she get ahold of the shivers that poked through her when Du Bois smiled like that?

A single stride devoured the distance between them. Apparently unconcerned with the impropriety of his behavior, he plucked an imaginary speck of dust off her shoulder, then brushed the cloth smooth. "I almost didn't recognize you."

Standing so close, she couldn't help but inhale the masculine scent that wafted from him. Pure male elixir clogged her nose, her lungs, her every thought. Primitive. Pleasing.

My *goodness*.

He swept another, critical gaze across her. "The other dress suited your figure much better." His eyes turned glassy, unreadable, while his gaze continued to roam.

Faith refused to react, but the ripple in her stomach, the one she tried pretending wasn't there, bumped and twirled with zest. One searing look, and the man managed to turn her insides into nothing more substantial than biscuit dough. "To what do I owe this shockingly inappropriate commentary on my attire? Chance? Pure rotten luck?" she asked.

His eyelids took one slow blink, the motion clearing his expression. "Oh, I was out hunting this morning." He laughed, as though he'd just made a remarkably amusing joke. "And my pursuit proved to be really rather simple, in the end." He reached down and tugged on the tendril that had stubbornly refused to cooperate all day. "Why would anyone hide this lovely hair under such a hideous hat?" He released the lock, then ran a lazy finger along the slanted brim.

A sudden memory of that same finger, caressing her lips, sent the first thread of real panic winding through her quivering limbs. There was just too much male in front of her, surrounding her, *devouring* her. Taking a deep breath, Faith nudged his hand away. "You are coarse, the epitome of bad taste."

His amusement twinkled down on her. "Yes."

"You certainly are sure of yourself."

"Just part of my appeal. But let's get to the point. As you know, we have important business to which we must attend."

Of its own accord, her voice lowered to a husky pitch. "We do?"

He idly ran his knuckles along the sleeve of her dress. "I want—" He broke off to take a long, raspy sigh.

Of its own volition, her body strained toward his. He slanted his head, his brow creasing into a frown.

Her voice trembled. "You want?"

He gave his head a violent shake, then abruptly dropped his hand to his side. "What I want is my money."

"*Your* money? I seem to remember three other players at the table."

"All of whom I've since reimbursed." His tone lowered, becoming far more menacing than if he'd raised his voice. "Now. About *my* two-thousand dollars."

Faith shivered, unsure why the gripping sensation circling in her lungs leapt to her heart. "You are becoming quite redundant, Du Bois."

"As are you. So let me make myself perfectly clear. I want the money you cheated from me."

She tried to focus on her parasol as she twirled it in her palm, silently demanding her mind to concentrate on the conversation and not her strange awareness of the big man glaring down on her. "Cheated? What an ugly accusation." There. That sounded perfectly in control.

"So, you're going to play dumb again? What do you suppose Prescott would say if I told him exactly where you got the money to pay off your loan?"

"I don't have a loan."

He fired a disapproving grunt into the charged air between them. "Perhaps not anymore. But I'd wager my saloon that you had a large debt—oh, say, to the tune of two thousand dollars—before you waltzed into Prescott's office this morning."

She couldn't deny it, her hypocrisy only went so far.

"Should I go searching for the papers to prove it?" He tapped his temple. "Let's see, I can only imagine where you've hidden them." He focused on the lace covering her cleavage, looking his fill without an ounce of shame. She was fully aware of the way his breathing quickened, partially because her own breaths skidded from her lungs with the same momentum.

Images of the previous night's search, his hand sliding across the sensitive skin of her breasts, attacked. She tried to steady her voice, to divert her attention away from the memories and sensations he evoked. "Let's say I cheated," she ventured. She cocked her head to one side and hastily added, "For argument's sake, of course."

He folded his arms across his broad chest and pulled a twisted smile. "Of course."

Faith mimicked his sarcasm. "Supposing I did cheat."

"You did."

She shut her eyes for a instant, praying for patience, then waved her hand in dismissal. "We both know you can't allow anyone to discover that a mere woman cheated you, the owner of the most opulent saloon in Denver. Why, your business would be over." She snapped her fingers for emphasis.

"Perhaps I'm more interested in justice than the success of my saloon."

Faith searched his face, measuring, assessing. A grin threatened to emerge, she smothered it. "You're bluffing." When she noticed the way his jaw clenched and how the vein in his neck twitched, she granted the smile full sovereignty. She ran a lone finger along the gold watch fob dangling from his vest. The cold metal heated under her touch. Would Du Bois's skin feel like this? Smooth and cold? Or hot, hard, wonderful? She cleared her throat. "You expect me to believe money and success mean nothing to you? Dressed like this?"

His hand snaked around her wrist, causing her to lift her eyes into cold, threatening ones.

"I want my money."

She let out a squeak as his fingertips moved under the sleeve's cuff, merging the pads to her wrist. The pleasant sensation of her pulse beating against his warm skin alarmed her. "You . . . you're in for grave disappointment, Du Bois. The money is gone. It's now my word against yours."

"Ah, but you forget. I have more than just my word."

"Oh? Your fine manners? Fancy clothes? A talking bird?"

His sneer distorted his handsome features. "My bird is not up for discussion." The light grip against her flesh belied the seething anger she recognized in his features. As he secured his hold lower and stroked the nervous flesh of her palm, she closed her eyes against the pleasure.

His bark startled her lids open. "Pay attention, O'Malley."

She blinked, her thoughts garbled.

"My word against yours is enough. I'm a successful businessman. While you're a—" He halted, allowing the insinuation to settle between them.

Her mind unclogged at the implication, yet she couldn't lift her gaze from the sight of his thumb drawing tiny circles in her palm. As a matter of principle, she refused to be the first to pull away. It had nothing whatsoever to do with the delightful feel of his expert kneading. "You own a saloon, Du Bois. I'm not sure that gives you any particular advantage."

"Let's go find out." He jerked on her hand. The simple motion brought her closer, enough to feel hard male straining against her. And to see tanned, corded neck muscles. And to smell the clean scent of freshly laundered clothing.

"Am I bluffing now?"

Her heart thumped harder at the raw stamp of hunger in his gaze. So. Du Bois wasn't as unaffected as he would like her to think. The fact that he found her as disturbing as she found him made the situation far too personal for her peace of mind. She doubted he knew she could see the secret vulnerability, the silent pain masked behind his desire. It called to the compassion dwelling in her, that same emotion that led her to take care of all the lost souls she found.

Dear God, what was wrong with her? Du Bois was no child seeking asylum. He was a grown man with the power to destroy her and the orphanage. She raised her chin, remembering this fight wasn't hers alone. "I can't imagine you'd willingly involve Prescott in this."

A flash of something that looked suspiciously like respect flickered in his gaze. "And I can't deny that you're a smart woman. That statement alone proves it. But whether or not we involve Prescott is no longer the point here. I plan to get my money back, one way or another."

"Face it, Du Bois. You've lost."

"Have I? I'd like you to look to the other side of the street."

Faith raised her eyebrows. "What game are you playing now?"

"Do it."

"Perhaps if you would release my wrist, I could get a better glimpse?"

He pulled her hand up against his chest. "You'll manage." She watched, stunned, as her traitorous fingers uncurled and her palm flattened into his muscled chest. The sudden desire to follow her hand's lead and mold her body against his caught her off guard.

Frantic, Faith jerked on her hand. He tugged harder in the opposite direction. Momentarily beaten, she pinned him with an insincere grin, then swiveled just enough to eye the sturdy mortar and brick buildings of Market Street.

Unsure what exactly he wanted her to see, she concentrated on the odd variety of people milling about. The teeming streets of Denver had always soothed her. The mix of cowhands, women, merchants, and even gunslingers made Denver the perfect place for anonymity. Often she could walk along this very street, or stroll in front of the Wells Fargo office, and never encounter the glint of disapproval she'd had to endure in the smaller towns and mining camps.

For this alone, she loved Denver.

Du Bois's voice caressed her ear. "See that gentleman dressed in black?"

She gazed at the activity on the street, then focused on several possible candidates. "Well, now, black certainly seems the color of choice these days. Would you like me to look at that tall, lanky one with the black pants, black shirt, and black coat standing to my right? Or that shorter one over there." She jabbed her parasol toward the left side of the street. "With the black pants and black shirt and, surprise, black coat. Or perhaps you mean that one with the black—" She turned back to face him, her eyebrows arched. "Well, you get the idea."

If she wasn't mistaken, she thought she caught Du Bois's lips twitching. "I meant the one with the matching six-shooters and U.S. marshal's badge clipped to his chest. Let's wave, shall we?"

Faith's breath hitched. She was unsure if she was more shocked over the idea of involving a U.S. marshal in their argument, or Du Bois's absurd suggestion to gain his notice by such a juvenile action. "Do what?"

He ignored her question and proceeded to wave. The insipid man had the brass to look superior and masculine performing the outrageous act. "Look, O'Malley, he's waving back."

Resigned, Faith centered her gaze on the man in question. "Yes, I can see that."

Although the marshal was indeed waving, the gesture did nothing to mitigate his intimidating stance—or the threat he posed to Faith. She studied his tall, imposing figure. He'd be almost handsome if he would shave the dark stubble speckling his jaw and if his dark eyes weren't sharp as a hawk's. As it was, he looked harder and more threatening than Du Bois at his worst. "So you know a U.S. marshal. Is that supposed to terrify me?" She didn't add, of course, that it scared her spitless. She had the requisite dry mouth and tongue stuck to the back of her teeth to prove it.

"He's very anxious to meet you. I told him all about your prowess at my poker table last evening."

"How fortuitous for me," Faith managed to mutter.

Du Bois's chuckle sounded much more pleasant than the circumstances warranted. "Now we can either handle this between ourselves or I'll call the marshal over."

She nearly choked on her gasp. "Are you threatening me? That sounds like a threat. I think you're threatening me."

"I am. And you're babbling."

Clamping her mouth shut, she buried her panic behind another painful gasp. "Look, Du Bois, no more games. Even if it was your money—which it wasn't; it was money *I* won—I can't hand it over. I don't have it anymore."

"I thought you might say that. Denial to the end. Well, honey, I've got a plan."

"I'm all astonishment at your foresight."

"You will come to work for me, until the full of your debt is paid."

Faith's heart tumbled to her toes. *Work for him?* She knew saloon owners hired women for only one chore. As timekeeper and money collector for her whoring mother, she'd already endured enough humiliation and fear to last a lifetime. Her pulse jerked as unwanted memories shadowed her ability to tell Du Bois to go to the devil. Never mind that her pride had been stolen years ago. She couldn't hand over her chastity for money.

The remaining scraps of calm disappeared into a tangled heap of sheer hysteria. "I . . . I won't."

"Then you'll go to jail."

No. She couldn't let down the children, now that she'd come this far. She was all they had, and they were all she had. Fresh agony tripped along her spine, making the desire to lash out hard to contain. "You're still bluffing." *Dear God, please let it be so.* "You can't prove anything more to a United States marshal than you can to Prescott."

Andre offered her a glib smile. "Now that's where you're wrong. I may not be able to prove you stacked the deck, or even that you cheated me at my own table. But I can prove you stole the money out of my safe."

Faith had one defense left. Walk away, before her terror froze her to the spot. "I don't think I'll let you blackmail me today."

She turned on her heel, but his hold on her wrist tightened. "Is that right? Well, you don't have much of a choice, now do you?"

She looked up, connecting her stare to his. For countless seconds they wrestled one another in their gazes. "Release me this instant."

Oddly enough, he slowly relinquished his grip. She caught her hand against her side, rubbing her wrist against her hip as though it burned. Considering escape, she glanced over her shoulder. Her gaze immediately united with the marshal's. My goodness, that was one scary man. Especially since he'd moved close enough for her to see the hard scowl contorting his features.

"Remember Hank?"

She turned back to Du Bois, then looked again at the marshal closing in from behind. They might as well have shackled her to the spot. At the moment, she didn't dare run. What would be the point? "Who?"

"Hank. The man who put the money in the safe while you were in my office. When he returned, the safe was wide open but you were gone, and so was the money."

Faith darted her gaze back and forth between Du Bois and the marshal. "Hank didn't see me take the money." Was that her voice sounding so desperate?

"You were the only possible thief. His testimony, along with mine, is enough to get an arrest and a trial."

Her conviction wavered, making her voice shake. "It was my money."

"Now who's redundant? We both know you bottom stacked the deck."

Faith hid her shock behind a blank stare. How could he have possibly detected her method?

As though he were mentally weighing and measuring

her, he rode his gaze all the way down to her toes and back again. "Through the years, I've played against the best. I'll admit you're very good. I can only speculate where you learned such a trick."

"You'll have to forgive my ignorance, but how is it you think I'll admit to cheating in such a dastardly manner?"

He tapped her on the nose. "Because we both know you did."

Faith fought the hysteria kicking against her chest. The same guilt she'd swallowed moments earlier in Prescott's office clawed in her throat, stifling her ability to formulate a believable defense. She couldn't whore for Du Bois. But she couldn't go to jail either. The truth hit like a steam engine out of control.

Her options had run out.

And just as she'd willingly cheated the night before, she would accept this newest turn of misfortune for the children's sake. "You win, Du Bois."

"You'll start tonight?"

She nodded, her eyes large but unwavering.

André tried to harden his heart, but O'Malley's courageous resignation touched a part of him he'd thought dead. He was reminded a second time in an hour of gentler days, when he'd been a fair man. Perhaps he owed O'Malley a chance to explain herself.

He raised his hand, stopping Trey's advance, then touched her shoulder. Her violent flinch cut through him. The notion that this woman had something terrible to hide blasted into his thoughts, making him want to forget why he couldn't trust her.

In spite of his victory, André felt a twinge of guilt. His tone softened, along with his resolve. "I promise you, your position in my saloon will cause you no harm."

She threw him a watery smile and nodded. "Well, if you will excuse me." She sighed. "The time grows late. I have much work to complete before I become . . ." Her voice faltered. "Before I join you at your saloon this evening."

Without another word, she snapped open her parasol, nearly catching André in the face. If he'd moved any slower, he'd be fishing purple silk out of his right eye.

She stepped into the dusty street. Gaining some of her earlier spirit, she spun back to stare into his eyes. "Until tonight?"

André was no fool. "I'll walk you home."

The caged look she'd tried to hide the night before returned. "No. That won't be necessary."

"Yes, it will. After all we've been through, I can't be sure you'll show. And I won't let you slip away again."

She threw her shoulders back. "I always pay my debts."

"I don't trust—"

Her ragged sigh cut him off. "Don't worry, Du Bois. I said I'd show, I'll show. You'll have to believe me."

Dear God, he did believe her, against all he'd learned of her character in the last few hours. Or was there another reason he didn't want to follow her home? Perhaps he didn't want to find out she lived on Hollady Street, that he'd been right about her all along.

For a tense moment, André held her gaze, trying to understand her silent appeal and his own unwillingness to force the issue. "Tonight then. You'll start at dusk."

She released a slow breath. "I'll be there." She turned around again, sidestepping her way through the morning traffic on the busy street. The moment she was out of earshot, Marshal Trey Scott, André's childhood friend and the closest thing to a brother he'd ever had, joined him.

André exhaled. "You know, Trey, I can't help but think something's not right here. What am I missing?"

Trey grinned, looking more like the boy he'd once been than the man who now hunted outlaws with such vengeance he'd earned the nickname Satan's Brother. "That little scene between the two of you was . . . very instructional," Trey said.

André shook his head, trying to clear his thoughts. But he couldn't rid himself of the concern tightening in his chest, concern for a woman who could only be trouble. "It was nothing."

Trey's cracking laugh belied his hard exterior. "Damn, André, I've got eyes. It's my business to notice things. I saw the way she affected you."

André forced down the denial that would be nothing more than a lie. "She's a whore, a master at mesmerizing men."

Trey lifted a single brow, then looked across the street. "That woman is no whore."

"You didn't see her last night."

"No. But I saw the truth today. And so would you, if you'd look past that black fog in your brain. Good God, you must realize Miss O'Malley is nothing like your wife. Pearl was bad through and through. That woman across the street is not."

"She's a cheat."

Trey inclined his head. "Perhaps. But I got a real good look at her a moment ago. I'd stake money at one of your faro tables she's a decent woman in a lot of trouble."

Pressing his lips shut, André held back his response. Trey's conclusion was too close to the one that he'd struggled against ever since he'd first discovered O'Malley cheating at his table. But Pearl had taught him well. And her betrayal made it impossible for him to believe in another woman, especially one who outwardly showed herself to be no better than his wife had been at her lowest.

"I take it she agreed to your proposal?" Trey said.

André nodded, his gut tangling into a tight ball.

"You tell her what she'll be doing to pay off her debt?"

André produced a sheepish grin. "If I'm not mistaken, she thinks she'll be peddling her charms."

"You didn't find it necessary to correct her in that misconception?"

"I did not."

"And you call her a liar and a cheat?"

The stab of guilt returned. "Look, Trey, now that I've finally got that little con right where I want her, I plan to make her thoroughly miserable."

As though hearing the remark, Faith, who had made it safely to the other side of the street, wheeled around to face the two men. After a smug toss of her head, she released a two-finger salute identical to the one André had given her in the bank.

Trey ran a hand over the stubble on his chin, unable to hide his amusement. "I wonder which of you is in more trouble."

Chapter Seven

Faith watched the sun edge behind the western peaks, trailing golden pink fire in its wake. The dusky-hewed gloom added to the bitter taste of defeat on her tongue. If only she had stuck to the house's original design, she wouldn't have needed that extra loan. Now here she stood, months after making the mistake, facing her greatest personal disaster yet.

Drumming nervous fingers against her thigh, she lowered her gaze to the building in front of her. "The Dancing Belles." She read the words aloud, as though the gesture alone would provide a much-needed miracle.

A ribbon of light streamed out of the saloon, beckoning her deeper into the drama she'd set in motion the night before. With a vigorous toss of her head, she flung aside her sorrow.

This was not the time for regrets.

She'd made the choice to cheat on her own. And so she would accept the repercussions alone as well. Just as she always coached the children to face the consequences of their mistakes.

Even as she considered the necessity of her actions tonight, her uneasiness grew. Once through those swinging doors, she would unite her life with the sin that had killed her mother and robbed Faith of a normal childhood. What sort of example did that really make her?

With a gulp, she forced down the bile rising in her throat and moved forward. After two steps she veered right, heading to the large plate-glass window that ran along the front of the gambling establishment.

The clip-clop of horses' hooves and the creaking of wagon wheels mixed with the soft murmurs coming from the few customers inside the saloon. The two-finger picking of a popular Stephen Foster tune added an absurd accompaniment to the sounds of one part of Denver shutting down and another opening for business.

Faith took a deep breath, startled by the absence of the smells she usually associated with bars, stale whiskey, spilled beer, and unwashed floors. Du Bois certainly ran a clean, elegant house.

Her gaze swerved through the saloon, hunting for the tall, overwhelming man who held her ultimate ruin in his hands. The longer she stood looking through the window, the more she realized she couldn't go through with her promise.

Turning to leave, she stopped in mid-stride as her eyes connected with André Du Bois's lazy scrutiny. She wondered how long he'd been behind her, watching her scan the activity in the saloon. The thought sent heat rising to her cheeks.

Out of a perverse need to prove she was not a woman easily frightened, she returned his open perusal. Foregoing propriety, she ran her gaze up and down his tall form. Just as the night before, the simple elegance of his clothing added a measure of sophistication to his chiseled features. The brute had the impertinence to look handsome, calm . . . awake. With the sky a rainbow of color behind him, he looked every bit like her romantic images of a dime-novel hero.

At that whimsical thought, Faith threw her shoulders back, refusing to cower before the man's intimidating presence. Her tone filled with artificial politeness. "Du Bois. Always a dubious pleasure."

He angled his head, peering at the window behind her. "You going to clean those nose prints off the glass before you leave?"

The temperature in her cheeks burned scalding hot. "I wasn't leaving." The lie skidded out of her lips in five halting syllables.

"No?" He raised a cigar to his mouth, tugged a long, slow drag, then blew the choking smoke downwind. "Certainly looked that way to me."

A portion of the truth spilled out of her mouth. "If you must know, I was gathering the courage to walk inside."

Clearly more amused than convinced by her choice of words, he chuckled. "You may be a lot of things, O'Malley, but cowardly is not one of them."

He settled his gaze on her breasts for an inappropriate length of time. Eventually, his eyes roved to her waist, down to her toes, and back to her face. "I see you didn't feel the need to change your clothes from this morning. Didn't I already remark on how revolting I found that dress?"

Faith welcomed the surge of irritation that his arrogance evoked; it was far less confusing than the heat his appraisal had aroused. "You did."

He leaned against the pole behind him and produced a full, stomach-bumping grin. At the memory of that mouth moving toward hers, his eyes filled with sexy intent, Faith almost forgot why she hated the man.

But then he spoke again. "Let me guess. You wore that

ugly purple concoction primarily to irritate me this evening."

"My, my, Du Bois. To use your precise words, you do catch on quickly."

His smile widened, shoving the door to her heart open just a crack. With a blink and a wince, she slammed the tiny slit shut.

"You ready to come inside now?"

Unsure why she couldn't move her gaze away from his face, she continued to stare. She assured the tiny cord of desire pushing against her tense nerves that she really did hate the man. So why this compulsion to catalogue every line, every groove, every feature of his rugged face?

"Let's go, O'Malley. That is, if you're through with your inspection, of course."

"I'm through."

After a long, smothering moment, she realized she still hadn't succeeded in getting her feet to move. Now that the time had arrived, she found she couldn't easily walk into a life of prostitution, no matter how temporary it would be or how badly she wanted to save her orphanage.

Du Bois's scrutiny added to her nervousness. As his eyes moved across her face, her breathing tripped over ragged half breaths. She forced her body to relax, her mind to clear, but nothing could stop her pulse from working itself into a frenzy. She had a sudden, intense need to reach out, pull his head to hers, and sample with him what she would spend the next several months selling to his customers.

Was it true then? Was she a wanton at heart? Or was it this man in particular that had her thinking the kind of lustful thoughts that made her no better than the whore she was to become?

Du Bois withdrew his watch, then made a grand show of releasing the clasp and looking at the time. "Tick-tock, O'Malley."

His sarcasm hurled her into action. "Yes. Yes. I'm coming."

He whisked his hand in a large semicircle. "After you."

She pirouetted, driving her feet forward with sheer will alone. She nearly gained control over her foolish senses, but then Du Bois closed in from behind. His whispered breath, along with the tiny little shove on her backside, sent a delightful chill navigating her spine. "I'll meet you in my office. You remember the way."

With catlike grace, he pivoted around her and trekked toward the staircase leading to the top floor. She stood stationary, strangely beholden to watch him bound up the steps, two at a time. Once he reached the top, he turned and leaned over the balcony. "Go on, O'Malley. Doleful reluctance doesn't suit you." When she still didn't move, he added, "I promise I won't keep you waiting long."

With leaden steps, Faith trudged toward the back of the saloon, all the while searching the empty area on her right. Turning to her left, she passed her gaze over three men playing poker, and linked it with Hank's as he worked behind the bar wiping glasses. Far more than words, his glowering reminded her of the trouble she was in.

Determined to accept defeat with her self-respect intact, she waved a happy greeting. Oddly enough, his expression cleared and he grinned at her in return. Warmed by his response, she allowed a brief smile to linger between them. At his encouraging nod, she walked with renewed confidence toward the setting of the previous night's escapades.

Inside the office, she marveled at the sight before her, scanning the perimeter of the room, registering every nuance of the immaculate interior. All that she'd upset had been put to rights. Even the books were back on the shelves, the chair neatly shoved under the desk.

Seeking another ally, she sauntered toward the birdcage. With quick movements, she positioned the chair directly below her objective and hopped on top. Just as she was about to whip the blanket away, Du Bois's command exploded through the room. "Leave my bird alone."

Startled, Faith twirled around.

Blocking the doorway with his impossibly broad shoulders, Du Bois had the nerve to growl at her again. "Have you no respect for my property? Get off that chair. Now."

She opened her mouth to speak, but promptly lost her balance. Teetering from one foot to another, she waved her arms, praying the momentum would help her regain her balance.

It didn't.

In a final attempt to cushion the majority of her fall, she thrust her hands in front of her.

Du Bois's resigned groan didn't help the situation one bit. He uttered a violent oath and rushed forward, moving quickly enough to catch her around the waist. Thanks to his timely assistance, she avoided certain disaster just as her face careened to a halt mere inches from the floor.

"Well, hell, O'Malley."

Her sentiments exactly.

Chapter Eight

Bent at the waist, her bottom pressed firmly against his midsection, her hands pinned in useless immobility, Faith determined to remain still in Du Bois's light hold. One slip on his part, one pucker on her part, and she'd kiss the wooden plank below her nose.

A masculine chuckle added to her aggravation. "Seems we have an interesting situation here."

The grin in his voice stole any chance of her finding the desire to thank him for his rescue. With more than just her pride inches from crashing into the floor, Faith didn't bother with politeness. "Help me up." She tried not to grit her teeth. "Now."

"You know," he said, "after all we've been through, sort of seems appropriate to leave you . . . dangling."

With her dignity winking at the ceiling, it proved impossible to gain much levity. "You planning to eye my charms all night, Du Bois, or are you going to help me to my feet?"

She didn't like the sound of the grunt that sailed out of him as he adjusted his grip around her middle. Out of reflex, she squirmed.

"I find it necessary to advise you not to move like that. You just might find yourself with a face full of splinters."

She obediently stilled. "Du Bois, I'm warning you."

"Somehow that threat doesn't bother me right at the moment. And now that I have you where I can keep an eye on you, should we discuss the weather, that lovely sunset outside, or your first assignment?"

Faith didn't dare shift, although her muscles screamed from her clenching them too tightly. Using her firm, mother-of-the-house voice, she demanded, "Let me up this instant."

"Ask nicely."

It killed her to add, "Please."

She heard what could only have been another repulsive chuckle.

The man simply had no redeemable quality whatsoever. "Yes, you've made your point," she said. "But my head is filling with blood and I'm getting dizzy."

"Maybe it'll plop some sense into you."

"Du Bois . . ."

With a heavy sigh, he shifted her upright, until her front was flush against his, the band of his arms securing her waist to his. "There. How's that?"

"Unacceptable." Her feet still floated well above the floor. "Put me down. *All* the way down."

He let her slide along his body to the ground, his fingers fanning out on her waist, holding her to him with nothing more than a light touch.

"Better now?"

"I . . ." She lost all ability to breathe as the rest of what she wanted to say vanished from her mind. With a single blink their gazes knotted together. Faith was sure she'd die of apoplexy if she didn't take a breath soon. Too bad her lungs weren't in any sort of mood to cooperate.

Du Bois's features pressed into a frown. "You all right, O'Malley? All the color's draining out of your face."

Her head felt too light to respond. And she seriously doubted the tingling in her legs had anything to do with the aborted disaster of moments before.

His expression clouded with worry. But then something else, something stronger, flashed in his gaze. Longing perhaps? A parallel need grew inside her. And in that shared moment, she longed to remain in his arms forever.

"Honey?"

She tensed at the endearment, instinctively holding back an encouraging smile at the concern softening his eyes. She hadn't realized how safe his grip had felt, a barrier between her and disaster. Until now. Her mind reeled at the feeling of belonging that came with his masculine possession of her waist.

As they stood motionless, silent, she noticed the slight change in his hold, as well as her own growing hunger for more than just the caress of his fingers.

His head inched closer toward hers, intimate intent clear in his expression. She placed her palms against his chest. But instead of pushing him away, her disobedient fingers slid up his vest and tugged gently on his tie. The careless gesture brought him closer. Her senses riveted onto the feel of his heart thudding a passionate staccato near her breasts. In spite of the quiet laughter floating from the saloon, she could hear her short gasps combined with his, a hidden part of her begging to answer the primal call in his gaze.

"May God help us both, O'Malley."

With a rough kick to close the door behind him, he blasted the saloon out of earshot. The force sent the window rattling in its pane, the oil paintings banging against the wall.

The look in his eyes turned watchful. He didn't speak, and yet his silent question was deafening.

"What . . . what, are you doing?" she asked.

A grin pulled at his lips. "Taking what you've promised with those captivating eyes of yours since we first met."

The bold proclamation sent her stomach titling upside down. The realization that he was going to kiss her should have sent terror washing through her, or at the very least, some hint of alarm. But the desire to dissolve against him carried far more authority than her fear. A very female need to join with this man in a primitive mating of lips took hold. She fiddled with his tie, running her fingers around and under the gold pin. His hands clenched against her waist, then began a rhythmic stroking.

A choked sigh tripped out of her lungs and the air filled with her shaky gasps. Peeling her eyes from his, she concentrated only on his lips.

She realized her mistake too late. The craving to take charge, to hurry the inevitable, speared through her. Her heart hadn't forgotten the way this man's smile had stolen a peek behind her well-defended barriers. It urged her to let down her guard with him, even as her brain warned her against such rash actions.

Words of resistance stuck in her throat as a shiver started at her knees, moved up her spine, and ended in a ripple of desire that clouded her mind. Unable to stop herself, she sighed and murmured, "Yes." Unsure what she'd just agreed to, and no longer sure it mattered, she pushed her hips into him.

As she settled deeper into his embrace, his hands smoothed against the small of her back, closing her into the world of sensual pleasure she'd dreaded since childhood. His need, pressed against the bottom of her stomach, reminded her how far they'd already come. It was time to stop.

But why? Why fight this? This bliss, this wondrous

world of feeling? Her soft whimper served as her unspoken permission for him to proceed. Her chest tightened in anticipation.

His fingers stroked with a gentle kneading, then clenched tightly into her hips. "Breathe, Faith." The command was a sensuous nuzzle against her ear.

"I . . . I can't."

Their hearts pounded in unison, signaling their desire, uniting them in a bond of man and woman. When she finally had power over her voice, she said, "I . . . I think you better release me now." It was a valiant effort on her part to stop the unavoidable. But she'd spoken too late, emotion ruled the moment.

Nevertheless, he pulled back, leaving his shadow to darken across her face. His gaze combed hers, searching for something, but she didn't know what. She watched, mesmerized, as his probing eyes feasted on her eyes, her lips, her neck.

No caress could have sparked her need quicker. "I . . . Oh, Lord, help."

His lips curled into a rough grin, his pupils enlarged. "Well said."

Her soft gasp spurred him into action. As he ducked his head, the smell of clean male mingling with tangy citrus knifed through her. The splendid masculine fragrance she would always associate with him settled in her thoughts, creating a memory for all time. Any remaining reluctance sank into a tangled heap underneath her awakening passion.

His lips stilled a hairbreadth away from hers, touching and yet not touching. From the intense look in his eyes, she'd expected a crushing demand. But when he sealed his mouth to hers, his invasion gentled.

His lips skimmed along hers, nipping her trembles into soft murmurs. He trailed the moist tip of his tongue against her pout, while his hand roved up her spine. She whimpered at the pleasure of his fingers finding and then playing with the loose hair flowing along the back of her neck.

How could she possibly defend against such lovely torment? She'd been longing for this coupling with him, and hadn't even known it before now.

Du Bois's tongue slid across her lips again, crumpling her stance and sending her slamming into him. His half growl, half chuckle tickled her cheek, as his hot, moist breath caressed her skin.

"Part your lips, honey."

She willingly did as he requested, only to get the shock of her life. His tongue snaked inside her mouth, brushing against her teeth. With his fingers spread against the small of her back, he pressed her deep into him. His tongue toyed with hers, coaxing a moan from deep within. He tasted of all things dangerous, all things painful and yet sweet. His shallow breathing spirited into her like a forbidden breeze.

A flick of his tongue, a twirling caress, and she was lost. As pleasure emptied into her, surrounded her, she forgot to be afraid.

An onslaught of new feelings stampeded across her heart. Her raging blood pounded desire to the secret spot between her thighs. A hot, tantalizing ache circled inside her stomach as she instinctively met his pulsing stokes, her tongue joining in the sensuous duel.

As the delightful battle slowed, he pulled their union apart, closing her mouth with a gentle lip-to-lip seal. He pressed another kiss across her quivering mouth, then tugged her lower lip between his teeth. Three more times he tasted her, until their breathing merged. All thoughts of time and place stopped as Faith settled into the discovery of André Du Bois.

He loosened his embrace, but didn't release her completely. His hands found previously unknown sites of pleasure while his lips trailed a path along her jaw, down her neck, and back up again. His tongue rolled inside her ear, sending tiny sparks of passion slinking down her spine. The moan that escaped her turned into a violent shudder.

He released her ear after a gentle nip, then dragged a thumb across her brows. "Look at me, O'Malley."

She opened her eyes just as he plucked at a wayward tendril of hair. As his gaze trapped hers, she discovered his eyes were filled with a potent look of pure male arousal. He searched her face, gauging. Then he did something she'd never seen him do before. He surrendered a genuine smile. "Well, now, you can't say that didn't work."

At the bald truth in his words, her head cleared. *Dear, Lord, what had she done?* One kiss and her lustful soul had cheerfully crossed into irrevocable sin. She would be forever unable to return to the bliss of the unknown. Their one embrace proved her a wanton. As reality quelled all thoughts of desire, she did what she should have done before they'd joined so intimately.

She panicked.

She pushed, she pulled, she twisted, she begged. "Get off me."

He smiled deeper, a dreamy vacant look glowing in his eyes. "Is that what you really want?"

"No." She tensed at his snort of laughter. "I mean, yes. Yes, release me."

Faith pushed harder against him. Frantic now, she couldn't pretend she was anything but petrified. He'd made her *feel* and crave and want what she should never have known possible. And, Dear God, she'd adored every moment she'd spent inside his ravishing kiss. "Let me go," she said, pounding on his chest.

André grabbed her attacking wrists. He held her still, staring at her with both bewilderment and delight warring for supremacy in his head. The feel of her pulse slamming against his fingertips created such an exquisite awareness of the bond they'd just shared, he nearly forgot why she was in his office. Then he remembered how she'd cheated him of a small fortune, using nothing more than a few turns of a wrist and a false smile.

Appalled at his lack of control, as much as at her unbridled response, he practically threw her away from him. As he watched her take shallow breaths, her eyes darkened with fear. He'd never seen a woman react like that from a simple kiss. "What is this about? All I did was kiss you."

Doe-sized eyes connected with his. Her trembling was no longer desire filled. And yet her kiss had been one of profound experience, a passionate response to mutual need.

He found himself sorting through his puzzlement, confronted once again with the impossible task of understanding this woman's inconstant, mercurial behavior.

He tried to ignore the tremor in her voice when she asked, "Why did you kiss me?"

Under the circumstances, truth could be his only response. "I wanted to."

"Oh, really? Was that some sort of initiation? A sampling of the goods before you send me out to take care of your customers?"

"Hell, I don't need to sample what countless other men have had already. If I was ever in doubt as to your profession, I'm convinced now." The reality of his words sent a gut-wrenching spasm slicing through him.

She jerked her chin up, eyes blazing. "What do you mean by that?"

"Let's just say, your kiss was very instructive."

She shuddered and hugged her arms around her waist. "Oh? How so?"

"I know you're a woman who uses her charms to get

men to do what you want. Well, I'm telling you now. No kiss, no matter how ravishing, will get me to release you from your debt."

He hadn't realized he'd reached out to caress her cheek until she shoved his hand away. She pulled her palms over her ears and slammed her eyes shut. "I won't listen to you insult my virtue over and over again."

André stifled the urge to pull her back into his embrace and shake her until she admitted he was right. "What virtue? I didn't see any sign of it just a minute ago."

Opening her eyes, she lowered her hands and clenched them into fists. "You can go to hell, Du Bois."

"I may indeed, if we both get lucky."

Chapter Nine

André couldn't fathom what had gotten into the woman. One moment she was succumbing deliciously to his kiss, the next she was claiming offense. And damned if her outrage didn't ring true. And yet her calculated response in his arms, her soft little moans, told him a different story. "Honey, you're no untouched maiden. So why don't we forgo the rest of this pretense? You and I both know that if I didn't have to run a business, we'd be doing a lot more than kissing right now."

And, God help him, he still wanted everything her kiss had promised. He'd never felt such crushing desire, neither in his youth nor during the early days with Pearl. How could he keep away from O'Malley when he'd tasted sheer ecstasy in her arms?

Because she was a cheat, indebted to him for two thousand dollars, and most likely willing to use any means necessary to get out of her obligation. It was a reminder he'd do well to heed.

Her shout brought him back to the matter at hand. "I'm through with your insults. You are ill-bred, do you hear me?"

"My apologies. You are a token of propriety."

"Who gave you permission to judge me?"

"You did, by your very behavior, both last night and just now."

"You don't even know me."

"Oh, I know you. You're a somber-hewed she-devil. A masterful cheat, and a hellion through and through."

Her eyes bored a hole in him. "Well if I'm a hellion, then you're Satan himself. As a matter of fact, you're a rat, a brute—"

He grunted. "Never mind the rest, I get the idea."

She tossed a loose strand of hair out of her face with a violent shake of her head. "I can't think of anything bad enough to call you."

"You seem to be doing just fine."

They stared at one another for five seconds, or perhaps it was five eternities, André wasn't sure which. He raked a hand through his hair, his confusion growing by the minute.

Which was the real O'Malley? he wondered again. Her kiss had held a hint of awakening, a blossoming that suggested first times, that called to mind innocence. He suddenly remembered Trey's words from the morning's incident outside Prescott's bank. Was Trey right? Was he so incapable of seeing past his debacle with Pearl, he couldn't judge another woman fairly? Had his wife colored his perception forever?

O'Malley broke the silence with her sharp words. "You may have blackmailed me into whoring for you, but I won't give it to you for free."

Hearing only the tone of her words, André raised his eyebrows at her angry offense. Especially since it preyed on his increasing confusion. Was she a wolf in sheep's clothing or a sheep in wolf's clothing? Wishing like hell the latter was the truth, he exhaled slowly. "As much as I'm enjoying this interchange, we can't stand here and trade insults all evening."

Her eyes flashed. "Then what do you suggest?"

He leaned toward her. She scooted two steps back, hiding the fact behind a feigned cough. But André noticed the fear underlying her actions. He couldn't explain why that concerned him so much. "Look, O'Malley, I know I should probably apologize for that kiss. But I can't. I won't lie to you and say I regret what just happened."

"It was entirely your fault."

"Oh? I seem to remember you kissing me back with remarkable enthusiasm."

She tried to open her mouth to deny it, but he beat her to it. "Let's just leave it alone for now. We both made a mistake. And I promise, on my part, I won't touch you again."

Her spunk returned with the toss of her chin, the squaring of her shoulders, and the arrogance of her tone. "I plan to hold you to that."

He was so stunned at how quickly her tart spirit had recovered, he didn't dwell on the twinge of remorse he felt at her quick agreement to his vow to stay away from her. "Perhaps we should get you started."

Her eyes widened as she took a deep breath and nodded. Then her shoulders slumped forward.

He picked up the dress he'd tossed to the floor when he'd seen her teetering on the verge of disaster. Ignoring her subdued silence, he shook the crumpled silk until the wrinkles disappeared. "You'll wear this tonight."

Faith angled her head and pointed at the dress. "You want me to wear that?"

He nodded. "Every night, including Sunday."

"But it's so—"

"Respectable?"

"Black."

"It's simple and elegant. All my dealers wear identical dresses to this one."

Her breath caught in her throat and then she turned a remarkable shade of green. "Dealers? As in dealing cards?"

"That's right. I hired you to deal at one of my faro tables. Didn't I mention that to you this morning?" He scratched his chin and frowned. "I'm sure I told you I only hire women to work my tables."

Her stunned expression was almost comical, if he didn't know it for the act that it was. "You hired me to deal cards?"

He shot her an innocent smile. "Didn't I make that clear?"

Faith placed her hands on her hips, thrust out her chest, and tapped her foot. "You know perfectly well you did not. You said nothing other than I had to work off my debt at your saloon. You implied I'd be whoring."

"Then let me make this abundantly clear. I run a fair house, O'Malley, a high-class, respectable establishment for my customers who come here to drink and gamble. Period."

"Then why did you call the saloon The Dancing Belles?" she challenged.

"I don't have to explain myself to you. But if you must know, the name came with the establishment."

"How convenient."

He scowled at her. "You can save your clever insults, I'm not in the mood. While in my employ, you will deal straight. Cheat me, or my customers, and that's the end of it."

Shock ripped through her first, then confusion, then relief. She wouldn't have to whore? It seemed the miracle she'd prayed for had just revealed itself. And although the rat standing before her had deceived her, she couldn't help but accept this happy news with a joyful heart. "I think I understand."

"Good. Let me also add that as a woman in my employ, you will be required to follow a certain set of rules. Break just one and you're fired. At which point I will make sure Marshal Scott takes you to jail immediately."

She sniffed. She should have known he wouldn't make it easy for her. "And what are these rules?"

"No drinking, no drugs, and . . ." He broke off and pinned her with an inflexible look. "No whoring."

"What?"

He took unyielding pleasure in insulting her further. "That's right. You'll have to put your personal business on hold for the next few months. Unless you'd rather hand over the two thousand dollars you stole from me right now."

Faith shook her head in resignation. She'd been so intent on keeping Heart House safe, she hadn't realized how well she had deceived Du Bois about her profession. He actually thought she would rather whore than earn her way fairly. "I'll take the job."

"By the way, did I tell you Marshal Scott will be here later this evening?"

"You don't have to threaten me."

"Oh, but I do. Let's not have any further miscommunication between us. My terms are simple. I'll pay you fifty percent of the house take at your table, but you will never see that money. I'll keep a tally of your earnings in a book, which you may look at any time you wish to ensure I'm keeping an accurate accounting."

There was that arrogant tone she'd grown to hate. "How generous of you."

"I think so."

Faith experienced an overwhelming urge to kick him in the shins.

"Cheer up, O'Malley. Once you earn two thousand dollars, you will be free to leave." His face creased into a hard scowl. "Until that time, you will keep yourself untouched. My dealers are known for their chastity. If I find out you're whoring again, it'll be the end of our agreement."

She loathed the way he judged her so unfairly, offering her the same contempt she'd received too many times in her lifetime. "You don't have to worry about that. You see, I've never—"

"So we understand one another?"

At the inflexibility in his features, she knew she'd waited too long to straighten out his misconception about her profession. She'd deceived the man into believing she was a liar and a whore, willing to do anything for money. The sharp pang in her stomach warned her yet again that she'd landed herself in the middle of her greatest mistake yet. "I understand your terms."

André opened the door, then turned and tossed the dress back at her. Reflexively, she reached out and caught the dress before it tumbled to the floor.

"I'll leave you to change, then join me out in the saloon."

Taking a deep sigh, she nodded. "All right."

He lifted a brow in that contrary way of his, but mercifully chose not to speak again.

She couldn't resist tossing out the last word. "Beast."

He was quick on the uptake. "Hoyden."

In spite of all that had led to this moment, or perhaps because of it, she smiled at the truth in that accusation. "Yes, I am."

Before he banged the door shut, she heard him mutter an oath about a parcel of trouble he certainly didn't need right now.

She knew the feeling.

Chapter Ten

With her limbs still tingling and her mind in turmoil, Faith gaped at the door Du Bois had just slammed shut. Less than an hour before, confronted with her worst nightmare, she'd prayed for a miracle. That miracle had come in a single phrase: *I hired you to deal at one of my faro tables.*

Sorting through the events of the last hour, she worked the black silk of her "uniform" through her fingers.

What type of saloon did Du Bois run? He didn't hire dancing girls. No prostitutes lived on the second floor. Did he really only want women to deal cards for him?

Tapping her finger against her chin, she wondered what he was up to now. The swine had completely misled her into thinking the worst about her intended job duties. From his "Oh, didn't I tell you" remark and cocked eyebrow, she could only guess that he'd enjoyed every moment of her anxiety during his little game of deception.

But hadn't she first deceived him? In an attempt to

protect the children of Heart House, she'd sent the man on a merry chase down Hollady Street, leading him to conclude she was a shady lady seeking money for shady purposes.

Oh, she'd done it for the right reasons, but what a mess she'd made with her good intentions.

Determined to shut out the disturbing events that led to this moment, Faith squeezed her eyes closed. But the memory of Du Bois's moist, soul-stealing kiss and the sweet taste of his tongue nuzzling hers brought back the delicious shivers she couldn't ignore.

Why had she allowed him to kiss her when she'd known she couldn't possibly see it through to its logical conclusion? She'd blamed him for the embrace, yet both of them knew she'd wanted him to kiss her—she'd practically asked him to kiss her.

Licking the very lips that had turned her into the kind of woman she'd dreaded most, she realized too late her mistake. She'd allowed a kiss to transform an arrogant saloon owner into a man who set her blood boiling.

She'd never expected to be tempted by the seductive pull toward something grittier, something . . . sinful. If a simple kiss could evoke such feelings in her, what would an intimate skin-to-skin embrace do?

Faith shook her head and pounded a fist against her thigh. She could *not* think like this. Kisses lead to sex. And sex led to disaster.

The memory of the countless sweaty men, who'd paid their money, then lain with her mother, should have been enough to quell any silly romantic notions Faith might have had about sex.

Dirty, nasty, filthy. That's what she knew of intimate relations between a man and a woman. But would it be different with Du Bois? Would it be special?

Like his kiss?

A resurgence of heat pooled between her legs. What

was happening to her? One simple joining of her lips with his and she'd lost her common sense.

At least facing the man again wouldn't be a problem. Dealing faro would demand her complete concentration. She wouldn't even have to acknowledge him. Unless he chose to be her case keeper, conveniently keeping watch over her while he counted cards for the players.

"He wouldn't dare."

Oh, yes, he would. Especially if she kept him waiting much longer. With grim determination, she quickly stripped off the plain dress she'd worn to spite Du Bois and stepped into the elegant black gown.

As she pulled the garment over her shoulders and fastened it closed, her breath caught in her throat. The dress was a perfect fit. She sighed, releasing some of the built-up tension in her neck, then spun toward the mirror standing next to the armoire.

She barely recognized the stranger that stared back at her. Was it just the refinement of the black silk, or did Du Bois's kiss have something to do with the alterations she now saw in her reflection? "Well, what do you know."

"Awwwk. Know, know. What do you know?"

Faith grinned, welcoming the distraction from her disturbing thoughts of Du Bois and his far-too-disturbing kiss.

She angled her head up toward the birdcage. Disaster had been inches away the last time she'd approached the intriguing little bird. Should she take the risk again?

"What do you know?"

Mind made up, she hopped back on the chair and dragged away a corner of the blanket. Peering underneath, she said, "Hello."

The colorful little guy shook his beak in greeting. "Hello. What do you know."

Faith widened her smile. "What have you been up to since we last met?"

"Pretty bird."

"You still trying to convince me of that?"

He flapped his wing. "Pretty bird."

Amused, Faith shook her head. The children would love this bird. Maybe she'd get them one like it, as a peace offering for failing to tuck them into bed the nights she had to work at the Dancing Belles.

Her heart sank at the memory of the sullen, terrified faces as she'd kissed each of them good night. The children were very conscious of any change in their routine. In a world where many of them had been unable to rely on anything, they took great comfort and security in the regular, dependable schedule of the orphanage. And Faith leaving in the evening to go to work set them to worrying.

Katherine had promised to read them an extra story before bed to help quiet their jittery nerves, and Faith had every confidence in the young woman's capability in caring for the children. But the nervous antics of the orphans had only served to highlight to Faith the magnitude of trouble in which she'd landed herself and Heart House.

Johnny, a boy who had just come to the orphanage only a few months ago, had been frantic, as though he knew exactly where she was headed and what she planned to do. At the age of twelve, he'd seen too much of the ugly side of life thanks to his prostitute mother, whose money went to feeding her opium addiction instead of her son.

Only time and a lot of love could heal Johnny's unseen wounds. At least tonight Faith would return with her promise intact that all would be well. Perhaps if she brought him a bird one night soon, he'd accept that she wasn't living the life of his mother.

She'd have to remember to ask Du Bois where she could find such an odd creature. Or maybe he'd give her this one. He couldn't possibly be that attached to the little fellow.

"Awwwk. Pretty bird."

Faith giggled. "Yes, I think we've established that." Knowing she'd stalled long enough, she offered the farewell she gave the younger orphans every evening before extinguishing their lanterns. "Night, night."

Allowing the blanket to drop from her fingers, Faith bounded to the floor. She nudged the chair out of her way, smoothed her hands down her skirt, and forced back the last of her uneasiness.

It was silly to worry any further. She could manage whatever came her way. She always had. And she could surely handle a certain arrogant, way-too-big-for-his-britches saloon owner.

After all, he was just a man.

Shoulders back, attitude adjusted, she twisted the door handle and prepared to face the consequences of her actions the previous evening.

The first thing Faith noticed as she entered the saloon was the noise. Laughter, shouting, and piano music created a chaotic harmony. The two bartenders poured drinks as fast as they could. The stale smell of smoke filled her nostrils, while the air, already a foggy haze, stung her eyes into blinking watery orbs.

The sights, sounds, and smells of a typical saloon could not dispel the opulence and cleanliness that set this place apart. Every expensive fixture sparkled; every glass and bottle behind the bar shined. The wealth and power emanating throughout the décor reminded her just what a man like André Du Bois held dear.

It would be well worth her sanity to keep that in mind.

As though compelled by her thoughts of him, Faith connected gazes with the saloon owner himself. From across the room, his eyes held hers, sending her heart trembling inside her chest.

A lopsided smirk tugged his lips into a captivating angle, calling to mind all the unholy sensations he'd drawn from deep within her. Her knees froze, then suddenly gave out. She had the presence of mind to reach out and steady herself on the edge of the bar just in time to prevent herself from collapsing to the ground.

Well. She'd fooled herself into thinking André Du Bois was *just* another man. He was unlike any man she'd ever known, capable of making her feel the frightening thrill of forbidden desire.

What gave him the right to do this to her? Before tonight she'd been a woman who could handle any challenge thrown her way. Now, clutching white knuckles to the bar, she had a sick feeling that this time she'd met her match.

With far more attentiveness than he'd like, André followed O'Malley's progress through the saloon. He'd known the exact moment when she'd exited his office, perhaps because he'd fixed his gaze on the door for the last twenty minutes.

Ever since their shared embrace, he'd been unable to concentrate on anything or anyone other than Faith O'Malley. He'd waved off Hank, ignored his customers, and set out to find a quiet spot to think. As he'd silently considered all that had happened, he'd almost convinced himself that what they'd shared had been merely a kiss. But he knew better. They'd captured something profoundly deeper.

And dammit, he was heading right down the same path as the night when he'd made the ill-conceived decision to marry Pearl LaRue and save her from herself.

What a fool he'd been those five years ago. As he'd stood in front of the preacher, reciting his vows, he hadn't even considered that Pearl might have liked her role as temptress to everything male, had enjoyed taking money in return for her favors.

Was O'Malley the same? He'd learned the hard way that a man couldn't change a woman's heart, or her desires. But O'Malley's very real display of panic after their kiss made him reconsider his opinion of her.

Watching her, he suddenly wished she was exactly what she looked like now: a brave young woman caught in a series of unfortunate mistakes, yet willing to see the consequences of her actions through to the end.

Well, hell. He was *not* starting to like O'Malley. Absolutely not. André broke eye contact with O'Malley, wishing he could sever her from his thoughts as easily. As he surveyed the activity in the saloon, it didn't take him long to notice how the men stared at O'Malley as though she were ripe for the taking.

And why not?

There she stood, more magnificent in that black dress than a body had a right to be. Glowing, radiant. She had the look of frailty and strength, innocence and secrets untold—a powerful combination a man could hardly ignore. Even now, André wanted to wrap her in his embrace and protect her from the bad things in this world. His gut twisted tighter and in that moment, he knew he should have never hired her to pay off her debt.

The situation had trouble written all over it.

As if events were determined to prove him right, a young cowboy, carrying trail dust on his boots and more fuzz than beard on his chin, staggered toward O'Malley. His broad-brimmed hat covered his eyes until he tilted it back to get a better look at her. A deep spark of anger ignited inside André as the kid looked away from her face and leered at her chest.

Seemingly unaware of the notice she'd drawn, she jerked her shoulders at something the kid said to her. She slowly turned to look at him, then shook her head and took a step back. He closed the distance, but Faith stepped back again.

André released a hiss. *Trouble*, all right.

He caught Hank's eye, then cocked his head in the direction of O'Malley and her unwanted admirer. Hank nodded and set out from the opposite side of the room. André made it to the bar in a matter of seconds, Hank covering ground just as quickly.

Ignoring O'Malley for the moment, André focused his attention on the kid. Tall and lanky, he reeked of too much liquor and week-old horse sweat. André knew he could take the kid with a single punch, but he didn't allow brawling in the saloon, so he would settle the matter without a fight. Clearing his throat, he said, "Got something on your mind, kid?"

The boy ignored him, and continued to stare at O'Malley as though she was the answer to all his dreams. André decided a fight wouldn't be such a bad idea. As a matter of fact, he relished the notion.

Lowering his voice to a menacing rumble, he said, "Miss O'Malley is here to work the tables. Find someone else to talk to."

The boy looked ready to argue, until Hank sidled up on the other side of him. Obviously realizing he was outsized and outnumbered, the kid gulped. "I was just getting acquainted."

André mustered up some of his famous self-control. "Looked like you wanted to do more than get acquainted."

The kid shrugged. "Thought I might purchase her services, was all."

André caught the soft gasp from O'Malley, and his conscience got the best of him. On more than one occasion, he'd accused her of lacking virtue. Now, as the ugly suggestion came from another man's mouth, pure rage sliced through his gut.

Too angry to consider where the rage came from, he growled out a warning. "She's not here for that sort of entertainment." He closed his hand into a fist. "See that you remember that."

Before the boy could respond, Hank grabbed his arm and escorted him away. "I'll handle it from here, Mr. Du Bois."

André looked down at his tight fist and blinked. "Right."

Forcing his anger to ebb, he waited for Hank and the kid to work their way out of earshot before turning to O'Malley. As he looked into her whisky-hued eyes, some unnamed emotion clogged his ability to speak. She looked even more beautiful close up.

The dress added a touch of refinement to her already graceful form. He took a deep breath, and the lilac fragrance that was hers alone rose above the stench of stale smoke and liquor. Sudden tenderness gripped his heart, and he had to stifle the urge to brush his lips against her forehead. "The dress suits you."

Her gaze snapped to his. "Did you just give me a compliment?"

He enjoyed the shock flashing in her eyes. It added to the image of innocence that unfolded a little more each time they met. He finally accepted that he wanted, *needed*, her to be as innocent as she looked now. And it scared the hell out of him. But not enough to stop him from adding, "You look lovely."

Clearly confused, she said, "I don't know how to respond."

He grinned down at her. "A simple thank-you will work for me."

She lowered her head, smoothed the skirt with shaking fingers, then raised her gaze to his again. He liked the way she looked him directly in the eyes.

"Thank you," she whispered.

He suddenly wanted to shock her again, replace that slight smile of delight quivering on her lips with a hard kiss. But as before, he restrained himself. "Let's get you started at one of the tables."

She shot a glance to her left, where the cowboy who'd just harassed her stood and placed his first bet. A line of worry creased her brow as she nibbled on her lower lip. André pointed to the faro table on the opposite side of the room from the kid. "I want you to work with Rose tonight."

She nodded, a sigh of relief slipping through her lips. He couldn't explain why the sound warmed him so much. Or why the sudden feeling of possessiveness felt damn good.

Trouble.

No doubt about it. Faith O'Malley was pure trouble.

Chapter Eleven

For the next few days, life at the Dancing Belles fell into a routine. As he'd done every evening since opening, André surveyed the interaction between his employees and customers from the back of the saloon. He drank in the finely honed rhythm and waited for the surge of pride that came with ownership. Unfortunately, this night the sights and sounds didn't bring their usual satisfaction.

Why wasn't he content?

And why couldn't he shake the notion that something was missing? The longer he beheld the workings of what had become his home, the more a strange sense of disquiet tugged at him. It was as though tonight, instead of seeing the fruits of his hard work, he saw just another saloon.

His gaze continued to rove, pausing at the faro table closest to the door.

O'Malley.

The now-familiar jerk of his pulse was just as unwelcome as the last time he'd experienced the sensation, and the time before that. As she flashed a full smile at one of her customers, possessiveness knifed through his heart. Dammit. The woman had spent far too much time in his head already. He wasn't about to allow her to continue making him crazy just because she smiled at the men placing bets at her table.

Determined to concentrate on anything other than his growing awareness of Faith O'Malley, he shifted his gaze back to the bar. Despite his valiant efforts, his thoughts wandered back to the woman. With a sigh, he gave in and returned his gaze to her table. His heart made that strange kicking beat before settling into a rapid tap-tap.

What was it that drew him to her? She'd shown up for work every night since they'd come to their agreement, and he had yet to get used to her presence. If he were a wise man he'd discover her secret, the one that kept her silent whenever he questioned her at length as to what she'd done with his money.

Perhaps if he knew the truth, she'd no longer have this power over him. In the hopes of finding out something, anything, he'd attempted to walk her home. But each time he'd offered, she'd found an excuse to keep him away.

He knew he could have insisted, could have forced the issue, but he hadn't. He'd rather remain in ignorance than discover he'd been right about her from the start. And since she always came to work, punctual and ready to do her best, he didn't really need to know more.

The man standing next to him pounded him on the back, gaining his full attention. "When you gonna quit gaping at the woman and offer me some of that fine Kentucky bourbon you keep stashed in your office?"

André snapped his gaze to his friend. "I wasn't gaping at Miss O'Malley, Trey."

"Right. But you knew exactly who I was talking about, now didn't you?"

André frowned. The man was in serious need of a punch in the face. "You want the bourbon or not?"

"I want."

"Then shut up and follow me." A moment later André shoved into his office, the other man following on his heels.

Trey shouldered the door shut, then folded his arms across his chest and leaned back against it. "I see you convinced the little vixen the error of her ways. Can't help but notice how she's been a model of hard work and effort these last three nights."

André snorted. "She's shown. That's what matters."

"Seems to be catching on to her duties well enough. And the male customers certainly seem to like losing their money at her table." André bristled at the sarcastic goading in Trey's voice. "What do you think?"

"Subtlety never was one of your finer points."

Trey tossed his hulking frame into an empty chair. "So I've been told."

André opened the bottom right-hand drawer and pulled out a bottle of bourbon and two glasses. He pointed to a wooden box on the table next the Trey. "Grab me a cigar."

"Sure thing."

After exchanging one of the glasses for the cigar, André propped his leg against the desk. Half-sitting, half-standing, he lit a match and puffed until smoke surged into his mouth.

Trey took a large gulp, making André wince at the waste of fine liquor that was supposed to be savored, not choked back like cheap whiskey. "Have you no decency?" André asked.

Trey pretended not to hear and took another, bigger gulp before settling into the conversation. "You never did tell me what Miss O'Malley said when you told her she'd be dealing faro instead of whoring."

André lifted a shoulder. "I don't really remember what she said." The lie slid easily through his lips. Hell, he remembered everything about that first night of her employ, including the embrace they'd shared. Her response to his kiss was not something a man could easily forget.

Trey chuckled. "She was pretty angry, I take it?"

"She was flat out relieved." And damned if her reaction didn't still warm him clear through to his soul. André felt the betraying smile on his lips just before he realized it was too late to hide it from the other man.

Trey's eyes narrowed. "You got something you want to tell me?"

"No."

"You sure about that? Don't want to share with me why you haven't bothered finding out more information about our little fugitive? Or why you won't let me do it either?"

"No."

"Don't want to tell me why the poor little dear couldn't look you straight in the eye that first evening, or why she keeps sliding glances toward you when you aren't gawking at her?"

To hell with decency. André downed the entire glass of bourbon in one swig and filled up the tumbler again. "She doesn't *glance*, she scowls."

"You noticed that too?"

André swore. "I'm warning you, Trey."

Trey lifted his palm toward him. "I get it. Change the subject or get out."

"And here I thought you'd lost all signs of being a perceptive man."

Trey fiddled with his glass, holding it up to the light and twirling it around until a rainbow of color shot into the air between them. "Lead crystal?"

"Imported from Ireland."

Frowning, Trey continued to shoot ribbons of color into the room. "You've certainly left nothing to chance."

The comment wasn't what he'd expected, but André knew his friend well enough to know there was more. "What's your point?"

"Who said there was a point?"

Answering the rhetorical question was beneath them both, so André waited.

Trey leaned forward, his face serious as he gathered his thoughts. "Over the last five years I've traveled across most of the West. And your saloon has no rival, except maybe in San Francisco. But even there, I'm not so sure."

"I planned it that way."

Trey settled back into the chair. "Why go to so much expense?"

Knowing where Trey was headed, André wanted to tell the bastard to go to hell, but since Trey would find too much comfort in obliging him, he kept silent. At Trey's unrelenting stare, he eventually pulled the cigar away. "Does it matter why?"

"You know it does."

Studying the contents of his glass, André swirled the amber liquid around. "Why ask when you already know the answer?"

It was Trey's turn to swear. "Pearl? Is she the reason for all this opulence?" He spat the woman's name as a curse.

Stunned at his friend's lack of understanding, André gulped down more of the bourbon. "Hell, Trey. This has nothing to do with Pearl. How could you, of all people, ask me that?"

"Then why don't you tell me what this does have to do with."

"You should understand. Especially after what we went through back in Louisiana."

Trey cocked his head. "You still riding that horse? That was fourteen years ago."

"Look, Trey—"

Trey cut him off. "No, you look, Andre. Look real hard around you and tell me what you see."

Without looking up, André placed his glass on the desk. "I don't have to look around to know that I like what I have here."

"Well, I don't."

Quelling his temper was becoming harder for André by the second. But nothing would come of a fight, so he took another slow drag off his cigar. "Do I look like a man who cares what you, or anybody else, thinks?"

Trey snorted and went on as though André hadn't spoken. "Sure, I see shocking displays of wealth everywhere I look. But what I really see are just things."

"That's right. I have things. *Nice* things, like what those Yankee bastards stole from me, from us." André paused for a moment, then dug deep into the bitterness rooted inside his soul. "As firstborn sons, our futures were secure. We were destined to be planters, like our fathers and their fathers and their fathers before them. Then the war came and we lost *everything*."

"So did a lot of people. But we had it better than most. We had food. And friendship. None of that has changed."

André stifled the shudder rising out of his bitterness over all that might have been. "Do you know what I remember of New Orleans after Yankee Occupation?"

Trey lifted a shoulder. "All right, it wasn't easy, I'll give you that. But there were good times too. We found amusement where we could."

The snarl that slid from his lips felt too damn good for André not to experience a hint of concern. Perhaps bitterness was becoming more a part of him than he'd realized. "Poverty is all I remember. And I *never* want to taste it again."

Trey twirled the glass in his palm, studying it as though it was a complicated puzzle waiting to be solved. "I'd say you're a long way from poverty, my friend."

"That's right. I have wealth. And a future."

"Dammit, André, the more things you have, the more you have to lose." An old sadness marred his features. "If the war and the years after it taught me anything, they taught me that."

"What do you know about it? You own a pair of six-shooters, a tin star, and a horse."

"I . . . know."

The whispered response cut deep, and André flinched at the realization of his insensitivity toward his friend's loss. At what they'd both lost with a single rifle shot. "Look, I'm sorry. I didn't mean—"

Cutting him off, Trey shook his head and purposely focused on the previous conversation. "The people that come with all these *things* aren't real. They're sharps, professional gamblers, and women of questionable virtue, the sort that only want what you can give them. There's no future here."

"I'll never be poor again. That's my future."

"I find it necessary to point out that you said that once before. And then you met Pearl."

"Pearl might have run off with my first fortune, but no one will ever steal from me again."

Trey leaned forward, the look of a shrewd lawman blazing in his eyes. "Including a little minx who managed to swindle a lively sum right out from under your nose."

"Especially her."

Emptying the last of his bourbon, Trey placed the glass on the table to his right. "You know, André, if you weren't so hell-bent on comparing the two women, you'd see that your O'Malley is different from Pearl." He searched André's face with the same resolve he used to get answers when criminals weren't talking. "But I'd say you already know a lot about their differences."

"They're exactly the same."

"Oh? I noticed how you watched O'Malley tonight."

André hated that smug tone. "How did I watch her?"

"Like you can't stop thinking about her, can't stop wondering what it would be like to know her better."

"You saw all that?"

"And more." Trey laughed. "Like it or not, whenever she walks into the saloon, you look at her as if she's the only person in the room."

"She's a cheat. And if I do look at her more than anyone else, it's simply because I'm keeping an eye on her."

"Now you're lying to me *and* to yourself."

"Faith O'Malley can't be trusted. Didn't she prove that the other night at my poker table?"

"She's definitely clever. And wily—"

"So we agree."

Trey frowned. "No. She's also a woman of integrity."

"All of a sudden you know her so well?"

"I've watched her too."

André pretended the spasm of white-hot jealousy was just a trick of his imagination. "Have you now?"

"I'd stake my life that she stole that money for a good reason. Have you even asked her why she needed it?"

"I asked. That first night in the alley."

"What'd she say?"

"She didn't say. She just stared at her toes."

Sniffing, Trey said, "Knowing you, I'm sure you made it real easy for her to trust you with the truth."

"Meaning?"

"Ask her again."

André swallowed back a quick retort. Trey had no understanding of women like O'Malley since the only woman he'd truly known had been pure and sweet, made to share his life with him. Trey was comparing her to the wrong woman. "I don't need to ask her anything," André said. "She cheated me and three of my customers out of two thousand dollars. It doesn't matter why."

"If you really thought that, she'd be in jail right now. Deep down, you know I'm right." Trey gave him a single nod. "Yep. She had a good reason."

"I see you're determined to defend her." And there went that spasm again. It was *not* jealousy. André just hated to be told he was wrong, that was all.

Trey started to open his mouth, seemingly rethought his words, then started again. "Hasn't she shown up every night to honor her debt to you? That says a lot about her character."

"You're putting more into her actions than there is."

"Not just me. You let her go that first afternoon outside the bank because you knew she'd show up here."

André snarled. "When did you become a mind reader?"

"It's my job to read people, and to make quick judgments. As far as Faith O'Malley goes, I'd say she needs your protection, not your lack of trust."

André didn't like what Trey said, didn't like that he desperately wanted to believe his friend was right about O'Malley. He hadn't realized how tired he'd become of meeting disreputable characters, tired of always keeping his guard up, tired of trusting so few. The part of him that wanted to believe in O'Malley warred with the part of him that needed to shun all she appeared to be.

Under the circumstances he did the only thing he could. He attacked Trey. "You sit there and have the gall to tell me O'Malley needs protection? What do you know about it? All you know is vengeance. Ever since the Sherwood gang killed Laurette, you've lived for nothing else."

Trey slammed a fist into his palm. "She was my wife."

"And she was my sister."

Trey's shoulder's slumped and he sank farther into the chair. "We've been through this too many times to start again."

"I miss her too, Trey."

"Then leave it alone."

André choked down his own pain. What he had to say was too important to hold back the words any longer. "I can't. If she knew what you'd become, her heart would break. It's been eight years. Let go of the past."

Bitterness filled the other man's eyes. "Like you?"

André didn't have an answer to that. Hell, Trey was right. He hadn't let go of the past any more than his brother-in-law had. In this, they were the same.

Unable to find the words to soothe Trey's grief, André watched helplessly as the man rose from his chair and went to the mantel. As though he didn't realize what he was doing, Trey's touch gentled the moment his finger ran along the frame surrounding the photograph of Laurette. "We weren't talking about me anyway."

Trey pulled his hand to his side, clenching his fingers into a tight fist. After a moment he turned back to face André, all expression cleared from his eyes. This was familiar ground for them. Both were too filled with pain to continue discussing the woman they'd each loved too much and lost too soon.

"We were talking about that lady-hoyden of yours."

Though prepared for the change of subject, André flinched. "What about her?"

"Take your own advice and move on. Become again the man who once married the wrong woman for the mere sake of saving her from herself. Stop letting money mean so much."

The need for honesty overruled any desire to defend himself. "It's not about the money."

"Then let O'Malley out of her debt to you. Let her have that money free and clear."

André thought hard about Trey's suggestion. Hell, it wasn't the first time he'd thought about it. Ever since he'd pulled the little beauty into his arms and discovered she held secrets in her lips that called to a part of him no woman had ever touched, he'd considered letting the matter drop. But something in him, the part the Yankees had pillaged and Pearl had helped destroy, couldn't give into those desires. One earth-shattering kiss didn't mean O'Malley was worth the trouble of trusting again.

A knock interrupted his thoughts. Grateful for the distraction, André called out, "Enter."

The door cracked opened and a very lovely head spilled through the tiny opening. "I need to talk to you, Du Bois."

Just for a moment, André allowed himself to enjoy the rush of pleasure elevating his body temperature at O'Malley's habit of looking him straight in the eye. He barely managed to stop the sarcastic grin he reserved for her alone from graduating into an actual smile. "Come in, O'Malley. We were just discussing you."

She wrinkled her nose at him. "We?"

André indicated Trey with a nod of his head.

She took a step forward, then halted as her eyes focused on the U.S. marshal's badge. She shook her head. "I'm sure what I have to say can wait. I'll just leave you two alone."

She backed out of the room, but André pressed forward until he could see her lingering outside the doorway. "I said come in, O'Malley. It's long past time you officially met the esteemed marshal."

As she popped her head back into the room, her wary eyes filled with frustration. "I'd rather not tonight."

André reached out, clasped her arm, and urged her back inside. "All the more reason for me to insist."

She batted his hand away, but reluctantly trudged forward. "Perhaps another time?"

"Now works for me."

The flash of alarm in her eyes made all the agony he'd suffered since he'd first met the vixen much easier to swallow.

Now for a little fun.

Chapter Twelve

The last thing Faith had expected when she'd knocked on Du Bois's door was to encounter the U.S. marshal's large person. Over the last three days her avoidance of the lawman had been near flawless, a work of artistry and manipulation that would appall dear Katherine, but made Faith rather proud. She might have thought of a way to continue avoiding this inevitable meeting but for Du Bois's disdainful behavior. When she considered his performance of only seconds before, ill-mannered was the word that came to mind.

With perhaps more frustration than sense, she pushed aside care and strode into his office with her best imitation of nobility. Hands on hips, she stared down her upturned nose. "Look, Du Bois, I get what you're doing." She threw a scowl at the marshal, then turned back around. "Let's forget the charade tonight. We both know if you wanted to send me to jail, you would have done it by now."

The marshal laughed outright. "Well, now. Beautiful *and* smart."

Over her shoulder, Du Bois sneered at his friend, but aimed his words at her. "If you're so confident you know what I will or will *not* do, why bother coming back to work every night?"

She lifted her nose higher and sniffed. "I always pay my debts."

"Hate to say it, André, but I told you."

André cut the marshal another hard glare. "Shut up, Trey."

Faith bit back her own suggestion as to what the marshal could do with his opinions. Staggering as the notion seemed, for once she and Du Bois were in complete agreement. The last thing she needed right now was an interfering U.S. marshal.

"So, what did you want again?" Du Bois asked her.

"Since the customers are dwindling, Rose thought it might be a good idea if I left for the evening. She told me to ask you first."

André just stared at her, a grin twitching at the corner of his lips.

When she realized he wasn't going to answer her, Faith sighed. "Is that a yes or a no?"

He released a smug smile, allowing it to grow into full, arrogant completion. She wanted to wipe that grin off his face far more than she wanted his answer. She raised her hand and stepped forward.

His grin widened. "Kind of quick to temper, aren't you?"

It was a darn shame that sexy grin took the punch right out of her anger. She waved her raised hand in the air. "I'll take that as a yes."

"Not so fast. It's a 'I'll have to think about it.' "

In the face of that brash smile, it was certainly understandable that her patience would run out. Tired and cranky, she was more than willing to tell a certain saloon owner and his pesky U.S. marshal friend what she thought of them both.

All night, they'd watched her from their usual vantage point in the back. She'd tried not to notice them, but the two together were hard not to notice. If a girl were the romantic sort—which, of course, Faith was not—she might entertain fanciful notions about such a pair. There was the dark and brooding one, the marshal's badge adding a hint of respectability to his roguish good looks.

And the other?

As she eyed Du Bois now, she realized he was equally as handsome as his friend, but his refined elegance made him appear much more intimidating. And it frightened her. Never before had a man borne so much authority over her emotions. To her mortification, she couldn't keep the shake out of her voice. "How about just giving me your answer. Can I go or not?"

"You bank out with Hank?"

"Yes."

"All square with Rose?"

"What game are you playing now, Du Bois? Why don't you just say what you really want?"

His eyes narrowed and his lips crushed into a hard, thin line. "You mean other than my money returned, the exact location where you live, and a simple explanation as to why you felt the need to swindle a large enough sum of money to finance a small war?"

She lifted a single eyebrow. Holding his arrogant, forceful, and entirely too attractive stare, she asked, "Oh, is that all?"

"No." Visibly relaxing, he curled his lips toward that thrilling smile again. "I could use another shot of whiskey."

She hated how he could so easily defuse a situation, making all her lovely anger just disappear. She tried desperately not to return his smile. Like a dog on point, she made her request for a third time. "It's real simple. Either I go home now or not. Make the decision."

She'd forgotten all about the other man in the room until a choked bark of laughter caught her attention. She swung a disapproving glare at him just as he swallowed a devilish grin behind a grunt.

"Something funny?" she asked.

The marshal shook his head. "No, ma'am. Just enjoying the show."

"Then keep out of this."

He nodded. "Whatever the lady says."

She stifled the urge to walk over to the brute and kick him in the shins. Turning back to Du Bois, she started tapping her foot. "Well?"

Throwing his hands in the air, he said to her with mock politeness, "Seems I've been remiss in my duties as your host this evening."

She eyed him with a wary, rapidly beating heart. That smile glaring at her was about to make her forget she couldn't stand the man. "Now what are you up to?"

Du Bois grabbed her hand, and tugged her deeper into the room. "Like I said before, you've never *officially* meet U.S. Marshal Trey Scott."

She tried to tug her hand free. "Perhaps I don't want to meet him."

"Sure you do."

She tugged again, but he pulled her closer until they stood inches apart. His scent filled her head, making her dizzy with a longing she couldn't accept.

She knew she could give into the little voice inside her head urging her to mold her body against his and be done with it. Right now, she could reach up and tug his head toward hers, finally discovering whether the kiss they'd shared had been real or just a figment of her imagination. She did neither. In an attempt to harden her defenses against him, she fired off insults. "You are the most foolish, self-deluded, bullheaded, rude man I know."

"There you go again, complimenting me with your fine words."

She poked a finger against his chest. "A swine, that's what you are."

"You're too kind really." He leaned over her and dropped his voice to a sensual whisper. "Watch out, O'Malley, you might turn my head."

"I'm completely unimpressed with your clever responses, Du Bois." This time as she tugged, André released her and she spun to leave. Unfortunately, she found herself eye to eye with a shiny badge that had "U.S. Marshal" branded in the metal.

Strange. Even though the man towered over her, she wasn't at all scared. And she experienced none of the confusing emotions that overtook her whenever Du Bois got this close to her. She looked up, and up some more, before she finally noticed that the marshal's grin made him appear almost boyish.

Maybe her absence of fear was due to lack of sleep, or maybe it was that very likable smile. Or maybe it was simply because he'd shaved off the dark stubble from the day before, and wore only a black mustache.

"It's a real pleasure to finally meet you, Miss O'Malley." His voice was a deep, soothing bass rumbling in his chest.

She stared at him for a long moment, unsure if he was telling the truth or playing a game with her. But he winked at her, and she finally returned his smile. "You too, Marshal."

"Call me Trey."

"Yes. I think I'd like that."

From behind her André growled. "You're done for the evening, O'Malley."

She spun around. Forgetting for a moment what she'd

come into the office for in the first place, she scrunched her eyebrows together. "What?"

"You may go home now."

"I . . . Now wait a minute. Why you letting me go all of a sudden?"

Du Bois's gaze didn't meet her eyes. "It's been a long day."

The marshal's offer confused her even more. "I'll escort you home, Miss O'Malley."

Faith turned back around. "You? No . . ." She quickly gained control of her spinning thoughts. "No, that won't be necessary. I can—"

Du Bois took a step forward, trapping her from behind. A snarl crackled out of him, his hot breath rushing across the back of her neck. She could smell the fight in him. "*I'll* escort her."

The marshal took a step closer, cutting her off from the front. "You have a saloon to run, André. It would be my pleasure to assist you." He looked down at Faith. "It wouldn't be a hardship."

Too much musky, hulking male surrounded her. Her insides started to tremble, alerting Faith to the fact that the man behind her was far too close and the man in front of her was far too unfamiliar for this intimacy. She thrust out her palms, landing one on each of their chests, and tried to push around them, but Du Bois placed a restraining hand on her shoulder. "I said I'd do it. That's the end of it."

Faith looked from one to the other. Deciding the marshal was the less lethal of the two she took a tiny, hair-breadth step closer to Trey.

She could feel his words rumbling in the air as he spoke. "Not a problem," Trey said. "I was leaving anyway."

Du Bois's anger wrapped around her, and oddly enough, it warmed her through. "I insist."

"Oh, well." Trey shrugged. "If you insist."

Faith tried to interrupt, but they kept talking as though she was no longer in the room.

"I do," André said.

Trey shrugged again.

"Then it's settled."

Not for Faith.

She couldn't afford either man to know where she lived. Prescott had taught her well. Men with money and power couldn't be trusted. The children's safety demanded they never find out about the orphanage, at least not until she was no longer indebted to Du Bois.

She watched, measuring, as the two stood glaring at one another, neither moving. They were playing some sort of game with one another. She'd seen a similar scene just this afternoon when two of the older boys had fought over a toy.

She didn't much like the idea that she might be of no more value than a toy, but she didn't have time to think about that now. In case they thought she approved of either of them winning, she voiced her own opinion of the matter. "As much as I appreciate all this chivalry. I can get home on my own—"

A stream of swearing from behind the blanket cut off her argument. The words were so vile, a craggy old miner would blush. The disagreement forgotten for a moment, all three turned to the cage. The marshal burst out laughing, Du Bois grinned, but Faith remarked on the outrageous creature first. "Nice bird you have there, Du Bois."

At least he had the grace to look somewhat humiliated. But then he shot her a sarcastic look. "You should know, you taught him how to speak," André said.

"Awwwk. Pretty bird."

She pointed to the cage. "I taught him *that*."

More cussing erupted, the bird's words coming out in a tone that sounded exactly like his owner's.

Faith angled her head and directed her finger at Du Bois. "Wonder who taught him that."

"It is a wonder." The remark came from Trey, who couldn't stop laughing.

Faith shook her head. "And to think, I was going to ask you to give him to me for the chil—" She caught herself just in time and clamped her lips shut.

"Give what for who?"

She quickly backed away, arms up, palms out, but landed straight in a solid bunch of U.S. marshal muscle and flesh. "Nothing. I misspoke," she said.

"Tell me, dammit. You said you wanted me to give him to you. Why do you want Larkin?"

"Larkin?"

He nodded toward the swear-spewing blanket. "The bird."

"Oh, the bird."

Trey placed his hands on her shoulders and gently nudged her forward. "Well, if you'll excuse me I'll leave you two to argue this one on your own."

The marshal's departure didn't register until the door clicked shut. One thought superseded all others. She was alone with Du Bois. For the first time since he'd kissed her three days before. Trying to gain some semblance of control over her hammering pulse, she blew out a slow breath. She opened her mouth to continue the conversation, but for the life of her couldn't remember what they'd been talking about.

Everything was forgotten, except the fact that here she stood. Alone. With Du Bois. And he was looking exceptionally handsome in a gray vest, crisp striped shirt, and red tie.

His expression changed, turning into something both frightening and exciting in its intensity. Oh, she knew what would happen next.

André Du Bois was going to kiss her again.

Chapter Thirteen

Expecting an invasion of sensual demands, Faith braced for attack. But as Du Bois's eyes darkened to a stormy green, the emptiness inside her opened again, beckoning him to fill it as he had three days before.

As though understanding the command of her heart, he moved a step closer. She gulped his spicy scent into her lungs, and suddenly her daily burden of raising twenty-one children alone turned into a thousand-pound weight on her heart. If only she could find a moment's relief, just this once.

A rush of contentment surged through her blood as he reached around her and spanned his fingers against the small of her back. She waited, holding her breath.

Afraid she wouldn't be able to stop from begging for more, she prayed he wouldn't touch his lips to hers. In the next breath her prayer tumbled into the hope that he would do exactly that.

Adding to her agitation, he didn't release her or kiss

her right away. Instead, he pulled her closer, then took a loose tendril falling across her cheek and roped it around his finger. "You have beautiful hair, O'Malley." He was standing so close, his words fell across her cheek like a warm, welcomed caress.

His already turbulent gaze filled with a longing her soul recognized. "I don't think this is a good idea," she said.

He continued to stare at the hair wrapped around his finger. "Probably not."

He let the tendril bounce free, and the storm clouds faded from his gaze. He leaned forward and planted a gentle kiss on her . . . *forehead.*

Shocked, her mind wrestled between relief and disappointment. Before she could decide which of the two emotions bothered her most, he gave her cheek a sweet, almost tender tap, tap with his finger.

"You look tired," he said.

Oh, my.

She knew how to defend against lust, desire, even sexual determination. But how could she hold out against such sweet affection? He wasn't supposed to like her or worry about her. That would mean they could become friends. And then . . .

Her eyes started watering. Big, fat tears threatened to spill down her cheeks. She blinked rapidly, desperately trying to gain some control over her strange reaction to his simple gesture of concern.

He skimmed his gaze across her face, and his eyes narrowed. "You're not getting emotional on me?"

And to think, she'd almost allowed herself a moment to believe they could become friends. Swiping the back of her hand across her cheek, she flicked him a look. "I'll try to restrain myself."

His eyes continued to dance with soft emotion as he caressed her bottom lip with his fingertip. "I knew I could count on you." She couldn't manage to speak past the wonderful burst of sensations his finger evoked inside her.

After a moment, he asked, "How much sleep are you getting?"

"Enough." For one insane moment she wanted to share the strain of her schedule, and her fear of losing the orphanage, with him. But the part of her that had survived too many years alone couldn't give into such a weak desire.

Gentling his touch further, he traced his fingertip along the curve of her cheek into the shadows below her eye. "Now, why don't I believe you?"

Even though she heard the twinge of sarcasm in his voice, she couldn't muster her usual antagonism, and that scared her. She had to remember why she didn't like this man. Or she would fall into his arms and beg for the atonement his kiss would bring. She blurted out the first thing that came to mind. "Can I have your bird?"

"No."

His quick response cut through the remainder of her ambivalence. "Very kind of you to spend so much time considering."

His grin switched into the smile that turned her legs into nothing more substantial than cooked gelatin. "Always willing to oblige," he said.

She locked her knees to keep from falling. "Why can't I have the bird?"

"Tell me why you want him."

She pushed out of his embrace, but kept her gaze pinned to the third button of his shirt. "I like him. He'd make a good pet."

Placing his finger under her chin, he applied enough pressure to force her to look him in the eye. "You know, O'Malley, telling little lies leads to telling bigger ones."

She wrenched her chin free from his grasp. "I told you the truth."

"Not all of it."

"Can I have the bird or not?"

"Tell me the real reason you want him first. Then maybe I'll consider it."

She swallowed three times, and each time the beating of her heart grew louder in her ears. "Well, that settles it then. I won't be taking a bird with me tonight."

"O'Malley—"

She elbowed around him, then tossed a saucy salute as she swung open the door. "I'll be heading home now. Enjoy the rest of your evening."

"Wait a moment, and I'll escort you."

She looked over her shoulder and saw that he was closing in fast. "No." She increased her pace. "That won't be necessary."

Two strides and he came alongside her. "Bad things can happen to a woman alone on the strcets this time of night."

The vanity in his tone stopped her retreat. Placing her hands on her hips, she said, "I can take care of myself."

His lips smoothed into that conceited smile she hated so much. "You overestimate your strength."

"Watch out, your paranoia might be mistaken for caring."

He threw his head back and laughed. Darn it if the gesture didn't look wonderful on him. "All right, O'Malley, you win. I won't see you home." He tilted his head forward. "*This* time."

Wondering why he'd given in so quickly, Faith eyed his broad back as he strode ahead of her. He pushed open the swinging door, turned, and swept his hand in a large semi-circle. "See you tomorrow evening."

When she didn't move right away, he came back to her side, took her arm, and steered her toward the exit. "Good night, O'Malley."

Her feet started moving while her jaw opened, closed, opened again, then finally snapped shut. "Oh, all right,

Du Bois, I'll play along." She forced her most insincere smile onto her lips, then passed through the doorway. "*This* time."

"O'Malley," he called after her.

She didn't bother turning around. "What now?"

"Don't forget the rules of your position here."

She threw him a scowl over her shoulder. "I wouldn't dream of it."

As she sauntered down the street, André feasted on the glorious picture her swishing hips made.

Unable to take his eyes off her, he motioned for Hank to join him.

"Yeah, Boss?"

"You know what to do."

Hank looked down the street and straightened. "You want me to follow her all the way home, or partway like last time?"

Just like the last three evenings when he'd given the order, André couldn't understand his sudden reluctance to send Hank on the errand. Hell, he wanted to know where O'Malley lived. But what if he found out he'd been right about her all along? Then again, what if Trey was right, and André had misjudged her?

One way or another, the time had come to end the mystery. "Follow her the whole way."

A shadow rode in her wake. Out of the corner of her eye, Faith watched a hulking form dart in and then back out of the alley immediately to her left.

Hank. He'd followed her ever since she'd first left the Dancing Belles saloon. She'd like to think Du Bois had sent him for her protection. But she knew better. From his parting reminder, she figured he just wanted to find out whether or not she was breaking his rules.

That brief glimpse of concern must have been an illusion. Shaking off a sudden wave of melancholy, she considered her options. She could lose Hank easy enough. Sure, he was big and scary on first sight, but under all that gruffness and muscle lay a gentle heart. With a little charm she could get Hank to talk. Why not find out what Du Bois was really up to?

Heading down the next alley, she withdrew deep into the shadows. Hank entered a moment after her. Tentatively looking around, he leaned to his right and squinted into the inky black. Shaking his head, he squinted harder and continued forward.

Faith waited until he was directly next to her. "Looking for me?"

The sound of Hank's holler sent a swirl of guilt coursing through her brain. "Hank," she whispered. "It's me, Faith." When he didn't calm down right away, she reached out to touch his sleeve.

With the petulance she'd witnessed in very young boys, Hank pushed her hand away. "That was *not* funny, Miss O'Malley."

"I know. I'm sorry."

"What are you doing slinking in the dark?"

"Waiting for you."

"You knew I was following you?"

"You're sort of hard to miss." She touched his sleeve again. Although his arm continued to shake, this time he didn't push her hand away. For his benefit, she said, "It's a little spooky, don't you think? I can't see my own shadow. Let's get out of here?"

He instantly turned and started out. Once they were back in the full light of the street, she asked, "Why are you following me?"

"Just doing my job."

"I figured that. But why?"

Hank gave her a sympathetic smile. "As much as I like you, Miss O'Malley, I can't tell you any more than I already have."

"If it's for my protection . . . ?" She paused, waiting for him to affirm or deny the suggestion, but old tight-lipped Hank pretended grave interest in his right thumbnail. His silence confirmed her suspicions that Du Bois wasn't in the least worried about her safety.

So, the tenderness, the concern had been an illusion.

After another moment she softened her tone and dripped sugar into the air. "You really won't tell me why you're here?"

"I can't."

A little more sugar. "Not even a hint?"

Nothing.

"Hank, please?"

He sighed. "Miss O'Malley, I like you. Really. Even when you did all that fancy cardplaying the other night, I thought you were something special. But I work for Mr. Du Bois. And he doesn't trust you."

She couldn't keep the bitter taste of disappointment from filling her mouth. "Does he trust anyone?"

Hank looked down the street, as though checking to see if anyone was listening. "Sure. Just not . . ."

"Me."

"No, it's not you in particular. It's all women." He looked behind him again. "And believe me, he has a good reason not to trust your sort."

Faith tried not to feel wounded by his choice of words, but she'd long since accepted that to Du Bois and Hank she was just another woman of questionable virtue. Disheartened, she lowered her lashes to hide the hurt.

Hank must have seen something of her humiliation. "Oh, no. I didn't mean it like that. I meant he doesn't trust women, period."

A small portion of her sadness lifted. "Why not?"

Hank slammed his mouth shut and shook his head.

Now that the subject had been broached, Faith

couldn't let the matter drop. "If you must follow me home, can't you at least tell me the rest?"

"I already said too much."

"You know, I have my own reasons for not wanting Du Bois to know where I live."

Hank blew out a puff of air. "I have to follow you anyway."

"I always show up for work, don't I?" she asked.

"Can't argue with that."

"And I work hard when I'm there."

"Of course you do."

She lifted an eyebrow. "Seems silly that you follow me home. What difference could it possibly make?"

"It's not that Mr. Du Bois doesn't think you'll show for work, he just wants to know—" Hank cut his own words off, scowled and pointed a finger at her. "Oh, no, you don't."

Think, Faith. *Think*. She hated manipulating this big, kind man, but she had to protect the children. "No one would have to know that you didn't follow me home."

"I would know. And that means Mr. Du Bois would figure it out eventually. He's like that."

"What if you accidentally lost me?"

Hank rubbed his chin. "No. That could never happen."

Before he had time to consider the possibility further, Faith darted down the alley again. After a few hundred feet a wooden fence blocked her passage to the other side. With considerable reaching, a good toehold, and a solid jump, she scrambled over the barrier.

Hank's bark of shock and thudding pursuit motivated her feet to lift themselves faster off the ground. She sped around the next corner, then wove her way through two other streets. After a few more turns Faith checked behind her. When she realized Hank wasn't following her, she slowed her pace and sighed. But guilt reared quickly.

She'd like to think she and Hank had become friends, although she couldn't count on it.

For now, she had to operate on the assumption that both Hank and his boss were threats to Heart House. Perhaps she'd played a rotten trick, but in the end, she'd managed to protect her children for another night.

Chapter Fourteen

As André went about the business of the day, he still couldn't fathom how Hank had lost O'Malley the evening before. Although he knew the woman was crafty, something about Hank's story didn't make sense. Had Hank lost her intentionally?

That would mean the two had become friends. At the notion a quiet, damning jolt of jealousy burned through André's soul. He wondered how long he could continue pretending he wasn't growing attached to O'Malley.

The answer was painfully obvious.

Not long enough.

Well, the game was over and the time had come to find out exactly who she was and where she lived. André would ask the one man who knew the truth—Thurston P. Prescott III. And if the banker wouldn't cooperate, André would introduce him to Trey before he left town at the end of the week. Amazing the plethora of information a tin star could get out of an otherwise silent source.

Now that he'd decided to take action, André was anxious to be done with the whole ugly affair. Unfortunately, before he could question Prescott, he had to check in at Mattie's first.

All week long he'd a bad feeling about one of his dealers. Julia had left early three nights in a row, with the obvious lie of not feeling well. God, he hoped he didn't find the girl working for the famous madam again. As much as he'd hate to do it, if Julia had broken the rules, he would fire her. If for no other reason, he'd have to release her for the sake of the other women who wanted to make the change permanently.

His gut told him Julia had lapsed. And his gut was never wrong. Except once. Even now, he couldn't squelch the onslaught of painful memories over his wife's betrayal and subsequent self-destruction. Till the end of his days, he'd never understand what made a woman like Pearl indulge in a style of life that she'd hated as much as she'd craved.

Well, it was too late to save Pearl. He just hoped it wasn't too late to help Julia.

Clutching the red dress to her chest, Faith walked along the upstairs hallway of the parlor house. She stopped at the end of the corridor, shifted the neatly folded garment to one arm, and knocked on the closed door. "Sally, it's me, Faith. I've come to return your dress."

As she waited for an answer, Mattie Silks sauntered down the hall after her. "Faith, dear, I don't think she's up for visitors. She had a bad bout of coughing this morning."

"Her tuberculosis again? Why didn't you tell me this when I first arrived?"

Mattie shrugged. "It's none of my concern. As long as

that lunger does her job in the evenings, I don't care what she does during the day."

Choked with anger, Faith took a long, hard look at the petite madam. Pretty and plump, the cold-hearted woman had the audacity to wear a cross, studded with diamonds. Faith's anger boiled deeper as she realized the expensive piece of jewelry had been purchased with the money Mattie had earned off her girls.

Faith strained to keep the fury out of her voice. "How could you not care? Sally's been with you for years. And that lovely accent of hers brings in the fancy men *and* their money."

"I run a business, not a charity house like you." Mattie giggled at her pun on words. "Oh, that's funny."

Faith looked at the dress in her hands, sickened at the sinful deeds that had been committed to pay for it. Mattie drove all her girls hard, literally enslaving them with her demand that they work every evening in expensive dresses supplied with their own money.

Mattie's eyes turned shrewd as she reached out and touched Faith's shoulder. "You've got it all wrong. This life isn't all bad. You just have to look at it from the proper perspective."

"Don't forget who you're talking to. I know all about this kind of life."

Undaunted, Mattie continued. "Well, if you ever get tired of taking care of other women's mistakes, I could use a girl like you." Her gaze took in Faith's hair, her face, and all of her body. "You'd bring in the fancy money too."

Feeling as though she'd been undressed right on the spot, Faith shuddered and stepped out from under Mattie's touch. "I've told you a hundred times. I'm not interested."

"The offer's always open."

"I said no."

"If you change your mind . . ."

"I won't." Faith turned back to the closed door. Knocking again, she said, "Sally, open up." Coughing erupted in answer. Hating to ask but not having much of a choice, Faith turned back to Mattie. "Would you unlock this door, please?"

Like a dog with a bone, Mattie continued the previous conversation. "Sally won't be around much longer. You could take her place. She has the best room in the house."

In an attempt to gather her patience, Faith squeezed her eyes shut for a moment. "Just open the door."

Mattie shook her finger inches from Faith's face. "Rude, that's what you are. I should kick you out of here."

Faith sniffed. "But you won't. Like it or not, you need me. I keep you in business."

"How you figure that?"

"I care for your *boarders* when they get into trouble, and I keep their children so they can come back to work for you. You'd be out of half your income if it weren't for me."

"I'd manage." Mattie unlocked the door, leaned against the opposite wall, and flashed a false smile. "By the way, a man came around a few days ago asking about you."

Faith looked sharply at the madam, her hand frozen on the door handle.

Mattie plucked at her handkerchief. "Handsome devil, that one."

Choking back a nervous groan, Faith asked, "You get his name?"

Considerable cleavage jiggled as Mattie laughed. "Oh, I'd like to get more than that. I bet he's one hot ride."

Faith bit her bottom lip so hard, the tinny taste of blood touched her tongue. "Mattie, please."

"Honestly, you are such a prude."

"His name?"

Smiling an I-got-you-now smile, the madam paused before speaking again. "It was that new saloon owner, André Du Bois."

Faith searched Mattie's face. Afraid she might hear something awful, but determined to know the truth, she had to ask, "What did you tell him?"

Mattie fired her own question in response. "What does he want with you?"

"It's personal. And I'd rather you not tell him how you know me."

Mattie rolled her eyes. "I'm not stupid. I don't want anyone to know I have dealings with *you*."

Faith's hold on good manners snapped. Entirely too many people had toyed with her lately. She couldn't help but offer a bit of it in return. "Wouldn't want that, now would we?" At Mattie's horror-stricken face, Faith sighed. "Don't worry. I'm always discreet."

"As am I."

"Since we understand one another, I'd like to check on Sally now."

Mattie moved aside. "You better watch out, girl. André Du Bois isn't like most men."

Faith didn't need the madam telling her something she already knew.

"If he wants to find you, he'll find you."

Hearing the truth spoken so casually, Faith could only nod her head and agree.

André consulted the large double doors outside the fancy parlor house, hoping once again that Julia hadn't gone back to work for the buxom madam. True, Mattie ran the most elegant parlor house in town, but a bordello was still a bordello.

Pushing open the door, he stepped into the gaudy foyer and strode into the main parlor. Though nothing in particular assaulted his sensibilities, everything about the chosen décor was too much. Alone, each piece of furniture and the various adornments could almost pass for tasteful. But together, the red velvet divans, the paintings, the gold fixtures, and the bold wallpaper defined bad taste.

As with the decor, Mattie Silks overdid everything. She only served champagne, and her girls dressed in the height of Parisian fashion. As André surveyed the interior with a critical heart, a twinge of conscience got to him. Here he stood, judging the woman for the very offense Trey had accused him of the night before.

Ignoring the possibility that he had anything in common with the madam, André nodded to the notorious bouncer walking toward him. "Jack."

"Du Bois."

"Mattie around?"

Jack smiled, the diamond in his tooth twinkling under the soft lantern light that glowed day and night. "She's not talking to you. Not since you stole Julia, Rose, *and* Lizzie right out from under her nose like that."

Shrugging, André pulled out a fifty-dollar bill. "Tell her it's important."

Jack grunted while quickly palming the money. "She won't like it."

"Just get her."

Moments later Mattie Silks sauntered toward him, taking her time and striking a pose every fifth or sixth step. Carrying a flute of champagne, she wore an immovable smile on her face. With her hips swaying, cleavage bouncing, and face painted, André decided she looked older than her reported twenty-nine years.

Stopping close enough for him to get a whiff of her cheap perfume, she offered her cheek. Out of politeness, André leaned down and touched his lips to the plump curve, the taste of grease and pungent roses slipping into his mouth.

In the next second, he found he couldn't prevent his

mind from comparing Mattie's offensive smell to O'Malley's soft, pleasing scent. Shaking his head, he stepped back and offered his usual greeting. "You're looking well."

"Don't you use those sweet words on me." Tapping him on the chin, she added, "I'm still mad at you, André Du Bois."

"I know."

"You've stolen a total of five of my best girls. And for what?"

"A better choice, a clean life where they can make money without whoring."

Mattie sidled to the nearest chair and hitched her hip against one of the arms. "Such an ugly word. I like to consider my girls as entertainers."

"Rose and Lizzie are happy."

"Ha. You make them wear dreary black."

"They aren't complaining," he said.

"*Yet*. But they will, just like Gretchen and Patsy."

André didn't bother commenting on the two girls he'd lost.

"So, what brings you here this morning?" she asked.

"You mean afternoon. The sun rose hours ago, Mattie."

"You will call me Madame Silks."

André inclined his head, trying not to laugh at the way she attempted to pronounce the word like the French, but failed horribly. "It's pronounced Ma*dame*."

Mattie relaxed into a sexy pose, her tone full of affection. "You are the most rude, impolite man I know."

André grinned. "That's why you love me."

Without taking her eyes off him, she took a long, slow sip from her glass. "We should go into business, the two of us. With your brains and my looks, we'd make a fortune."

"I'm not looking to go into the whore business. I'm looking to get women out of it."

With her free hand, she tossed her curls. "So they can deal at your tables? You fool yourself, my dear. You offer them little more than I do. One sin for another?"

"I give them a better living than what you give them. That's why they leave you and come to me."

He had to hand it to her. Though she visibly stiffened at what fell just short of an insult, none of her outrage showed on her face. "I should throw you out of here," she said.

"Probably." André edged toward her, glancing at the staircase. "But you like me too much to send me away yet."

Fanning herself with her hand, she sighed. "You're a devil. Pity I like devils so much. So, what can I do for you?"

"I'm looking for a woman."

"I have several."

"Not that kind."

She rode her gaze up his pants leg, and stopped just below his belt buckle. "Maybe I'll break a rule or two and take care of you myself."

"Not today."

"You are a man of phenomenal willpower."

Tired of the game, André shifted his weight from one foot to the other. "Let's get to the point. I'm looking for Julia."

Her eyes darted to the staircase, then back to him. She couldn't quite hide the satisfaction in her smile. "Julia?" she asked.

"She's here, isn't she? I see it in that smug smile. You got her back."

"I don't know what you mean?"

"Let's make this simple. I want to know if Julia is still one of my dealers."

"You know, André. This is the second time in less than

a week you've come looking for a woman. Having a hard time keeping track of your girls?"

"I was looking for Faith O'Malley for a very different reason."

"Personal reasons?"

"You could say that."

Mattie locked her eyes with his, interest fringing the edges of her gaze. "I knew you had a secret. But I never thought it was . . . *that*." A giggle danced from her lips.

"You know O'Malley?"

After a final searching glance of his face, her expression cleared. "Now I didn't say that I did, or that I didn't."

This was far too familiar territory. He'd gotten this exact behavior from every other madam on the Row. "I get it. You know her, but you won't tell me you know her."

"My, you are a smart man."

"What is it about that woman that keeps all you . . . *ladies* silent? Does she have something on you? Is she a blackmailer?"

"Faith? You must be joking."

"So you do know her. Is she a crib girl?"

"You mean to tell me you really don't know what she does and why?"

André took another step toward Mattie, using the difference in their heights to make his point. "You plan to continue playing this game, or are you going to solve this mystery for me?"

Calmly, she took another sip of her champagne. "You're going to have to find this one out on your own, you arrogant brute." She tapped a finger on his chin. "It'll serve you right for stealing my Rose and Lizzie with promises of legitimacy." She giggled as if she'd just made a marvelous joke. "But at least I have Ju—" Covering her mouth with two fingers, she fluttered her lashes. "Oops, it almost slipped."

"I knew it. Julia is here."

"Of course she is, silly man. You can't change a woman like her. I predict Rose and Lizzie will be back as well."

Clenching his hands into fists, André swallowed his disappointment. "Don't count on it."

Dammit. He'd lost another woman to the allure of fine clothes, expensive champagne and the illusion of glamour. Three in one month. Well, Julia was the last. As long as he owned a means to save these women, he'd fight like hell to keep the rest straight. *Especially* Rose and Lizzie.

"Oh, look. I've upset you." As she rose to her full height, she pressed her palm against his broad chest and pushed him back a step. "But you're in luck. Since I'm feeling generous this afternoon, I'll give you a little hint about your Faith."

Not trusting himself to speak, André held his breath.

"You're looking in the wrong places. She's not on the Row."

His heart soared. Could Trey have been right about O'Malley? "You mean, she's not a—"

"Oh, you have the right idea. Sort of. Well, not really, at least not the complete right idea."

André felt the muscles in his jaw tighten, and his nerves stretched to near snapping. "Could you confuse me any more?"

"I could, but like I said, I'm feeling generous this morning."

"Afternoon. It's early afternoon, Mattie."

Jack came up from behind Mattie and whispered in her ear. She shook her head violently. "No, not now." She flicked a sideways glance at André. "Just keep her in her room until I'm through here."

"Julia?" André insisted.

Pretending confusion, Mattie cocked her head to the left. "Julia, Faith, which one were you looking for again?"

"Either. Both."

A crash and a wail shot out from a back room. Mattie grasped André's arm and directed him toward the door. "So good to see you. We'll have to do this again sometime." At the sound of another crash, Mattie released her hold. "Jack, please show Mr. Du Bois the way out."

Mattie was already hustling off in the direction of the commotion by the time André asked, "What's the hurry?" Knowing the question fell on deaf ears, he turned to go. But as a familiar voice washed over him, he spun back around.

"Mattie, Jack, where are you? I need some fresh water for Sa—"

Unable to stop himself, André steered his gaze toward the staircase. In the instant his eyes locked with Faith O'Malley's, he knew he'd never before experienced true torment until now.

The reality of how close he'd come to losing his objectivity—again—over a woman—again—struck him to the core. For days he'd hoped. For days he'd put off finding concrete answers. But now he had to face the truth.

Faith O'Malley was a whore.

In one word he managed to convey all the anger, the pain, and the disappointment he felt. "You."

Wide-eyed, O'Malley continued to stare at him, unmoving. A heartbeat passed before her guarded look changed to shock.

Refusing to accept that any of the emotions flitting across her face warranted consideration, he attacked. "Dammit all to hell, I knew it."

Just as she opened her mouth to respond, Jack took his arm and physically escorted André to the front door. Too stunned to fight, André went willingly.

Chapter Fifteen

Faith watched Jack shove Du Bois out the front entrance, trying to grasp the fact that he was here, of all places, in Mattie's bordello. One moment she was searching for water, and the next, her whole life had pitched into a tangled heap of regret.

Just remembering the look in Du Bois's eyes, the condemnation and disappointment, sent a shiver inching along her spine.

All her lies, all her deceptions, had caught up with her in a single moment of recognition. Instant conclusions had been drawn as silent accusations had glared out of Du Bois's gaze and straight into her shattered heart.

What did she expect? a tiny voice chided. She'd intentionally misled him, coaxed him to assume the worst. And judging from his stern expression, she realized just how successful her deception had proved to be. She doubted she would ever be able to change his opinion of her.

Part of her wanted to tell him the truth, to tell him about the orphanage. But could she risk the children's welfare? Would he understand her mission? She wanted desperately to believe he would.

Not that it would change his opinion of her. Her attempt to keep him away from Heart House had gone far beyond a misunderstanding. If she revealed the extent of her fabrications now, it would only prove to him she was more of a liar than he'd previously believed.

And she realized that of all the people she wanted to have a good opinion of her, André Du Bois was the one who mattered most.

Feeling sick to her stomach, Faith returned to Sally's room. Pouring a fresh glass of water, she forced her mind to concentrate on spending time with her friend and not the disaster her own life had become.

Taking in the other woman's ragged appearance, Faith's heart began to ache even more. Sally had lost her luster far too quickly over the last few months. Illness had eaten away her youthful beauty and renowned curves. Her once vibrant red hair now hung in shredded clumps along her gaunt face, a testimony to the hidden difficulties of life in a brothel.

Saddened with the hopelessness of Sally's lot, Faith handed the water to her.

After taking a quick sip, Sally set the glass on the bedside table. "You all right, Faith? You look like you've seen a ghost."

The question brought back the reality of the last few minutes, and the memory of Du Bois's stunned censure. "Worse."

Sally leaned back into the pillows Faith had propped up earlier and raised her eyebrows. "Oh?"

Overwhelmed with hopelessness, Faith buried her face in her hands. "Oh, Sally, I've really made a mess of things."

Sally patted an empty spot on her bed. "Come. Tell me what it is you've done. It couldn't be as bad as you say. You're too good to do anything too terrible."

Faith sighed. She looked at the woman, whose recent years had been filled with the horrors of a life Faith couldn't begin to understand. "Sally, what led you to take up a life as a . . . a, I mean . . ."

"A whore?"

Faith cringed.

"It's all right. I know what I am."

"Why, why do you do it?"

Sally rolled a cigarette as she talked. "I didn't plan to become a whore, if that's what you mean. I came to Denver looking for a new life."

Faith interrupted her. "You're not going to smoke that?"

Not quite meeting her gaze, Sally shook her head. "I just like the feel of it in my fingers."

"All right. Go on with your story."

"I had to leave England. I couldn't stay because of the man my father had betrothed me to. He was this simply wretched marquis, a hundred years old if a day. I was only sixteen at the time, and no one would listen to my pleas, except my twin brother. But he couldn't sway my father."

"So you left?"

"I had a little money and a lot of dreams." She lit the cigarette and took a deep pull of smoke into her lungs. Her hands shook just before another fit of coughing racked through her entire body.

Faith moved to snatch the cigarette out of her fingers. "Give me that. You told me you weren't going to smoke it. Honestly, you're like one of the kids. Do you want to die?"

"I am dying."

Faith closed her eyes against the truth. But Sally couldn't hide her swollen eyes, the bruise on her left cheek, or her blackened nails. The legacy of her chosen life. "Is there anyone I should contact for you?"

Sally shook her head. "No, I'm already dead to my family." She reached out to Faith. "Stop looking so sad. If you cry, I will too."

A lone tear trickled out of Faith's eyes, followed by another and another. "Oh, Sally. I can't help it."

Sally blinked. "For what it's worth, there were good parts of my life too."

"Would you stop talking like you're already dead?"

She gave Faith a shaky smile. "It's the truth of things. But don't pity me. I had nice clothes, as fine as anything I wore back in London. And I had all the luxuries. So, I had to give pleasure to men. It wasn't all that bad."

"Really?"

"Sometimes it was even fun. I just made sure I never fell in love with any of them. Now that would have been disastrous."

Faith's heart plummeted. The truth of Sally's proclamation hit her full force. Lord help her, she couldn't have gone and done something that disastrous, could she? But if she listened to the part of her soul that had begun dying an agonizing death from the moment she'd looked into Du Bois's condemning eyes, she knew she had.

"What's happened, Faith? Please say you haven't agreed to work for Mattie? You aren't ready."

"No, no." And before she knew it, her story spilled from her lips. She told everything about her encounters with Du Bois, including the two kisses.

Sally looked at her for a moment. "What's the name of this saloon owner?"

"André Du Bois?"

"Oh, Faith. Not him."

"You've heard of Du Bois?"

"Who hasn't? The girls around here call him St. André. From what I've heard, he's not like most men."

The same words Mattie had used. "No, he's not. But he's no saint. He's arrogant, rude, impolite . . . I could go on, but I think you get the picture."

Sally sat up, placed her hands on Faith's shoulders, and shook her. "Now you listen to me. Only a woman ignorant of the war we all fight would neglect to put on battle armor."

"I don't understand."

Collapsing back on the bed, Sally exhaled. "I'm telling you to beware, Faith," Sally said. "It's for your own good. You're going to end up like the rest of us. I see it in your eyes. These feelings you have for André, those are what kill women like us."

Faith bristled. "I'm not like you."

The pity in Sally's eyes hurt more than any accusation she could have leveled at Faith. "You're the daughter of a whore. What do you think that means?"

Shaking her head violently, Faith wailed from the injustice of her reality. "I'm not like my mother. I'm *not*."

"Maybe not. But you can never be a part of normal society either. You may not live our life, but you're as much a part of it as I am."

"I haven't even had sex. Ever."

"*Yet*. But if you allow your feelings for André to do your thinking for you, you will."

Remembering the glorious sensations just his kiss had provoked, she reached up and touched her lips. "Would it . . . would it be so bad?"

Sally pulled Faith's hand away from her lips and squeezed. "It would be wonderful."

"Then why not do it?" Oh, God, help her. Was she truly considering such a thing?

Sally sighed. "Because once you have sex the first time, every other time after that gets easier. You'll no longer have blissful ignorance. And you won't be special anymore."

"What are you saying?"

"If you don't want to end up like me, keep yourself pure. Cover yourself with the invisible armor of chastity."

"You talk as though we're in battle."

"As women in a world ruled by men, we are. The only weapon we have is chastity."

Faith didn't know what to believe anymore. Sally sounded so . . . convinced. Faith had always counted herself lucky that she had made a life for herself and the children in this so-called man's world. But did that mean she had truly broken free from the sins of her mother?

Or was she doomed, as Sally suggested?

"Oh, look at me," said Sally, "I'm scaring you and I don't mean to. Listen to your heart, Faith. Hear what it tells you about who you are and what you really desire. If anyone can be accepted into respectable society, it's you."

Faith didn't have to listen to her heart. She already knew what her heart wanted—the impossible.

Her heart wanted André Du Bois.

Chapter Sixteen

As day inched into night, dragging a ribbon of blues, pinks, and purples behind it, Faith approached the Dancing Belles for what she expected was her last time ever. Pure dread sliced through her and a chill crept down her back from the cool breeze kicking toward the mountains. The wind tugged bits of her hair free from its knot.

She stopped along the street to view the distant peaks, hoping to gather comfort from their snowcapped beauty. Instead, her heart grew heavier.

Having spent the last three hours coming to terms with her unrequited feelings for Du Bois, she'd gotten a glimpse of the future that lay before her. Like a barren cloud blowing over dry land, promising much but producing nothing, any chance of earning his respect had disappeared in that one moment of recognition at Mattie's brothel.

The soft glow of light and low murmurs flowing from the saloon compelled her forward in a strange, mesmer-

izing summons of welcome. As she entered, Hank came to her side. "Mr. Du Bois wants to speak with you in his office."

"Thank you."

"Just doing my job." His accompanying scowl warned her he hadn't yet forgiven her for the trick she'd played on him in the alley. In serious need of a friend, she touched his hand to keep him by her side. "Hank, I'm sorry about last night. I know you won't believe this, but I had to do it."

A myriad of emotions waltzed across his features before his lips cracked into a tentative smile. "I understand."

"I'm glad. One day, I'll explain it all."

"When you're ready."

Well, at least she'd healed one rift. "Thank you for understanding."

His face reddened. "Now go on," he urged. "He won't bite."

"I wish I had your confidence."

He nudged her forward. "You're better off facing him sooner rather than later."

If only that were true. As the closed door loomed ahead of her, two concerns grappled against one another. The first was her worry over losing her job. What would she do if Du Bois fired her, and then demanded she pay back the money she'd stolen from him? If he found out about Heart House, would he give her an ultimatum and threaten to shut her down as Prescott had tried to do?

As nerve-racking as she found that possibility, another—more selfish—concern rose to the top of her fears. How could she face Du Bois, knowing the feelings she had for him were too strong to deny? And how could she keep from begging him to kiss her, begging him to feel for her a tiny portion of what she felt for him?

With each step, she sent up a silent prayer for courage, but she doubted God listened with a sympathetic ear.

She'd done enough in the last few weeks to ensure that the Lord had turned away from her for good. Overly aware of how very alone and scared she'd suddenly become, Faith rolled her trembling fingers into a fist, then knocked twice on Du Bois's office door.

"Enter."

A wave of white-hot terror slithered through her chest as she entered the room.

With his attention riveted on one of the photographs on the mantle, Du Bois didn't turn around. "Shut the door."

She did as he commanded, and waited for him to face her. But when he eventually turned and met her gaze, she wished he'd kept his back to her a little while longer. Although his expression held little emotion, his clenched jaw and the muscle ticking in the side of his neck told of the battle that raged inside him.

"I see you wore the black dress." He spoke in a near whisper, but the underlining anger in his tone shouted to her across the space between them.

"I've come to work."

As he skimmed his gaze over her, the expression in his eyes changed, suddenly shattering, as though the world had let him down one too many times.

Heart hammering, head whirling, she could hardly keep from rushing forward and pulling him into her arms. She suddenly wanted to soothe his agony, and perhaps end a little of hers as well. Staring at him now, feeling his pain as though it were her own, she could deny the truth no longer: She loved him. And like a dangerous reef that shipwrecked the mightiest of boats, she knew her love for this man could easily destroy her.

As his eyes held hers, silently communicating the full extent of his disappointment, her soul died a silent death—one she feared was the first of many more to come.

His voice lunged into the stiff tension between them. "Do you remember the rules of our deal?"

"No drinking. No drugs. No whoring." She was surprised at how clear and strong her words came out.

"And yet you're here tonight after what happened this afternoon."

"Yes."

He searched her face, and his eyebrows drew together as though he puzzled over what to say next. She returned his stare, silently willing him to believe in her just this once.

"Ask me, André." It was the first time she'd ever used his given name, and she recognized the intimacy it drew them toward. "Ask me what I was doing at Mattie's." Her heartache raised her voice to a higher tone. "Then ask me how I'm acquainted with her."

His eyes roamed over her face. The longing and the pain and the depth of raging emotions in his gaze silenced her ability to speak further. "I don't want to know why you were there," he said. "God help us both, I don't want to know." He moved quickly and wrapped his fingers around her shoulders. With one great tug, he pulled her in his arms. "Don't you understand? I *can't* know."

"But it's not—"

His mouth swallowed the rest of her words. Unlike any they'd shared before, this kiss was filled with pure, hot, furious need. His lips moved across hers, demanding her full participation and filling her with his uncontrolled passion. Her responding need matched his, even as she could taste the rage on his lips, feel the disappointment washing through him.

For weeks she'd held back her own anger, blaming herself for her predicament. But now her anger at him exploded inside her desire. How she wanted to rant at him for his lack of understanding and inability to see that she wasn't what she'd led him to believe. Couldn't he tell she was different from the women Mattie employed?

Needing to cry out her frustration, she parted her lips, but he thrust his tongue inside. They dueled with one another between shallow snatches of air. She couldn't deny the craving in his kiss, or the returning ache that grew in her. The longing for this man to fill her lonely heart fought against her anger.

Hot, hard passion battled against her equally intense rage, threatening to suffocate her. André's arms loosened their grip, but his kiss deepened. He spanned his hands against her lower back and drew her hard against him. She could feel his need straining toward her. Her hands clenched against his shoulders as she ground her hips into him in a primal, instinctual answer to his body's demands.

This was not a pleasant kiss, nor was it just a physical joining. It held more intimacy than she'd ever imagined possible between a man and woman. Her very soul understood this man, better now than ever before. As deep as her anger went, she wanted to soothe the pain she heard crying out in his kiss.

He suddenly went still and tried to draw away from her, but she wouldn't let him. Not yet. Not until she showed him that she was more than the woman he'd met that first night at his poker table. She moved her hands to cup his face and put all her answers to his unspoken questions in her kiss. After a moment, she softened her hold and gently touched her lips to his temple, then let him go.

Breathing hard, he stared at her. She stared back, watching, waiting. Raking a hand through his hair, he swore. "God, O'Malley, I don't know what—"

Faith pressed a finger against his lips. Whatever he planned to say, she wasn't ready to hear it.

He drew back, turned, and walked again to the mantel. He ran his hand along the frame of a single photograph, as though drawing strength from the gesture.

With his attention focused elsewhere, she let her eyes delight in the sight of him. With her anger now spent, her love swelled in her heart, and she catalogued all that had happened during their kiss.

Though he didn't know it, André Du Bois had just given her a precious gift. Before meeting him, she'd thought intimacy between a man and woman was dirty and sinful. But now she knew love could make touching and kissing and sharing of one's body with another beautiful. No matter what happened next, she would always be grateful to him.

"Why were you at Mattie's?"

Faith took a deep breath, hoping the right words would tumble from her lips. "I had to return the dress I borrowed from one of her girls." When he didn't respond, she explained further. "The red dress I wore that first night we met wasn't mine."

He spun around and shot her a chill look, clearly unwilling to believe her. "You weren't carrying a dress when I saw you."

"I was looking for water." His raised eyebrow was enough of a question. "Sally, the girl who loaned me the dress, has tuberculosis. When you saw me on the stairs, she'd just had a fit of coughing. I wanted to get some water to help soothe her throat."

André's heart pitched at her words while a twisted, ruthless spark of hope rode him hard. She'd been nursing a sick woman? Was the explanation of her presence in the brothel so simple? "Do you work for Mattie?"

"No."

He had to know the rest, had to ask. "Are you a whore?"

She smiled at him, relief in her eyes and something else, something he couldn't name, didn't want to name just yet.

"No," she said. "I'm not a whore."

"Were you ever?"

Her smile deepened, as if she'd been waiting to have her say for a very long time. "*Never.*"

"Then how do you know Mattie?"

A shadow darkened across her features, but in the next instant she threw her shoulders back and looked him directly in the eye. "Before she died, my mother worked for Mattie."

"Your mother? Was she—"

"Yes. She was a whore. Which makes me the daughter of a whore." Her voice hitched, but she maintained unrelenting eye contact with him. "I spent most of my childhood traveling from mining camp to mining camp, wherever men were willing to pay for my mother's time. Eventually, she got tired of traveling, so she went to work for Mattie."

"Faith, I . . . Oh, God."

He speared shaky fingers through her hair, but she pushed away from his touch. "So while you were kicking your heels at fancy balls and banquets, I was keeping time and collecting money for my mother."

When she stopped speaking, she wrapped her arms around her middle and shivered. André reached out to touch her, but she shook her head and held up a hand to stop his pursuit. "Don't." She crossed three steps to her left. "We have to finish this. Now."

As much as he wanted to never speak on the topic again, he knew she was right. His next question was the hardest to ask. "If you weren't trying to get money to start a brothel, then what?"

She gave him a blank look. "Is that what you thought? That I needed money for a brothel?"

"What else could you have needed that much money for?" As soon as he spoke his thoughts aloud, he finally understood their absurdity. He'd measured her against his wife because he'd been afraid. O'Malley had stepped into his saloon and stolen his breath the moment he'd laid eyes on her. He'd lost trust in his own objectivity years before. So, instead of sorting through his initial impressions of her, he'd assumed the worst.

Her next words stamped across his guilty conscience. "There are a lot of things money can buy other than a brothel."

She had every right to her anger, but he wasn't through. He had to know the rest. "Then why did you need the money?"

"Because Pres—" She broke off, her brows drawing together before her expression closed inside itself. "I can't tell you. There are others who could be hurt if you decided to close Hear—if you decided to stop me now."

"But I saw you at the bank by yourself. Who else is involved?"

Her features were fierce, her voice determined. "The loan was mine."

André didn't understand her reluctance to tell him the whole truth. What could she possibly be hiding? "If the loan was yours, then how is this not your secret to tell?"

She opened her mouth to speak, then promptly shut it. "We made a deal, Du Bois. I've stuck to my end, you *must* stick to yours."

Her vehemence stunned him. Had others let her down so badly that she couldn't trust *his* word? "Faith, secrets and deceptions are the same as lies. Truth is always the best. Haven't you learned that yet?"

"You don't understand."

"Trust me."

She laughed at him. "You want me trust you?"

"Would it be that hard?"

"Oh, let's see. There's the way you instantly assumed I could only need the money for a brothel. You suppose something like that might hold me back?"

He cringed. "I was wrong. And I'm sorry."

"I could also remind you of the countless little threats you've made in the last few weeks. For instance, the ones involving a certain U.S. marshal come immediately to mind."

"You played your part in this deception as well. What was I supposed to think? If I'm not mistaken, O'Malley, you wanted me to think you lived on the Row. Or am I wrong?"

She had the cheek to break eye contact with him. "All right, I'll give you that."

"So we start clean," he decided.

It was her turn to play the skeptic. "Oh? How do we do that? Even now, can you honestly tell me you believe I've had nothing but good intentions in all this?"

"I'm no hypocrite. I won't pretend it hasn't crossed my mind that if you had nothing bad to hide, you'd tell me the truth."

She threw her hands in the air, then snapped him a glare. "And you want me to trust you?"

"I'm not the one who keeps secrets," he said.

"Oh, is that a fact? Then you want to tell me why you don't trust women? Or why you so readily and instantly assumed I was a prostitute, without once asking me if it were true? You can't expect trust unless you're willing to give it as well."

He couldn't deny the truth in what she said. "All I know is that nothing good comes from deception. What are you hiding?"

"Please, don't keep asking the same questions."

"I have to."

She started pacing, throwing him a piercing look every other step. "Would you settle for a compromise?"

He tucked his hands inside his pants pockets. "A compromise?"

"Yeah, you know, it's when each person gives a little, and both get something back in return."

"Oh, I know what it is. I've just never done it before."

She smiled at that, then shook her head. "Right."

"So what's this compromise you have in mind?"

She grazed him with another penetrating look. Under the circumstances, he supposed she had every right to be leery of him, but knowing it and accepting it were two different things.

"Here's how it would work," she said. "Once I pay off the rest of the money I owe you, I'll tell you everything."

As though really seeing her for the first time, he realized that if O'Malley said she would tell him the truth eventually, she would.

From the beginning, he'd measured her against Pearl, all the while refusing to admit that O'Malley just might have a good reason for her behavior. He suddenly remembered the silent desperation underlying her actions on that first night. He'd denied it then, put it down to the honed skills of a professional sharp. But now he realized her despair had been real. Something terrible had led her to his saloon. He knew it as surely as he knew his own name. "All right, O'Malley. I won't ask any more questions." At her sigh of satisfaction, he added, "For now."

Not in the least discouraged, she relaxed her face into a smile. "So, you finally accept that I'm not a prostitute?"

How could he believe anything else, when the evidence had been in front of him all along? "Yes."

"And I'm not fired?"

"Not tonight."

She touched his sleeve. "Thank you."

He covered her hand with his. Overcome with the sudden urge to pull her into his arms and kiss her again, he blew out a hiss. "Ready to deal some faro?"

Her delicious grin sent damning heat curling in his loins.

Chapter Seventeen

Over the course of the next few weeks, Faith's days settled into a pleasant routine. She worked at the orphanage, visited an increasingly ailing Sally every afternoon, then dealt faro at the Dancing Belles in the evening. Though on the verge of near exhaustion, she'd never felt happier in her life. And she knew the source of her joy.

André Du Bois.

No longer her enemy, he was now a person to her, with worries and burdens and flaws. And instead of finding fault with his imperfections, she realized that her love and admiration had only deepened day by day.

As she spread flour on the chopping board and pressed out more dough, she glanced at the clock on the table to her left. Only a few more hours and she'd see him again. A rush of anticipation tingled along her spine.

What had happened to her restraint? A single thought of the handsome saloon owner, and she was getting all shaky and quivery inside. She fought to concentrate on making her pies, but her thoughts kept wandering back to the last time she'd been alone with Du Bois.

Giving up the battle, she allowed images of their first and last kiss to play with one another in her mind. Both times Du Bois's lips had been hot, demanding, and fearfully exciting. She pressed a flour-tipped finger against her trembling mouth as thousands of little pinpricks knifed through her stomach. She licked away the white powder, and a shiver marched across her chest.

Though he'd not touched her again, there were times when he looked at her in a way that had her burning up from the inside out. One day soon, she hoped he'd follow through with all those silent promises he hurled at her.

She looked forward to the day when there would be no more debt between them, no more secrets. On countless occasions she'd opened her mouth to tell him the truth about Heart House, but each time something in her had halted her confession. Perhaps it was the habit of caution, or simple fear, but she could never quite find the words to tell him about the orphanage.

If she told him the truth, would he finally kiss her again? A very selfish part of her wanted it to be that simple. But she'd learned her lesson well, thanks to Thurston P. Prescott III. Twenty-one children and one near adult needed her. And until she was certain of their safety, she had to maintain her silence.

Kneading the dough a bit harder than necessary, Faith sighed. Why couldn't she have met Du Bois under different circumstances? No matter what Sally said, Faith sensed that her feelings for the saloon owner were special, different, and *good*. After a week of arguing, Sally had finally stopped warning Faith to keep her chastity. Now, the other woman just cautioned her to be careful.

But Faith didn't want be careful anymore. For once in her life, she didn't want to be responsible. She wanted to toss aside caution and discover for herself the ecstasy that Du Bois's kisses pledged to her.

The back door burst open, jarring her out of the glorious daydreams of kisses and heated touches. "Faith, come quick, Katherine just hit a home run."

As Faith stared down at the grimacing little girl, pure delight filled her. The very idea of prim and proper Katherine whacking a ball hard enough to hit it over the backyard fence was quite a thought indeed. "Maggie, are you certain of this?"

"Yes, darn it. I saw it with my own eyes." She pointed to her left. "Look for yourself."

Faith wiped her hands on her apron and glanced out the window above the sink. Half the kids were jumping up and down, screaming and carrying on in childish enthusiasm. The other half looked positively bleak. They slapped leather gloves against their legs or scuffed toes in the sand. "Well, what do you know. She finally did it." Faith watched Katherine skip from one base to the next, taking her time, giggling all the way.

Maggie tugged on Faith's hand. "Hurry, Faith. The Hawks need you, or else those awful Panthers will beat us again."

Faith smiled to herself. Baseball. Who'd have thought that one tiny suggestion to try out a new game would end in success with the children? As a whole, they were all still a little fuzzy on the rules, but they had a good time anyway. And that's what mattered most.

Maggie tugged harder. "You can't let us down when we need you the most."

Faith wouldn't dream of letting the children down. *Ever*. If that meant playing a game of baseball, or continuing her silence with Du Bois, then so be it. "I'll be right out. Just let me finish this pie and put it in the oven first."

Maggie looked out the window and gasped. "She's almost all the way around the bases." Shifting from foot to foot, the little girl snorted in impatience. "Hurry up, will ya?"

Faith hurried.

André turned to Trey as they walked down Ogden Street, unsure what words to use to stop his friend from making a big mistake. He went for the direct approach. "You'll send word if it turns out Brock Sherwood and his gang really are holed up in that shack outside Cripple Creek?"

Trey nodded, his gaze set on the mountains in the distance.

Drawing to a stop, André waited for Trey to turn back and focus his gaze on him. "You sure you don't want me to come with you?"

Trey shook his head. "This is my quest."

"I want justice served too."

Curling his lips into a sneer, Trey ground out his words. "Justice? Hell, after what they did to Laurette, I don't want justice. I want vengeance."

Sick of the same argument André slammed his clenched fist into his palm. "It won't bring her back."

"Easy for you to say. You weren't the one who got her killed."

How could he convince his brother-in-law that Laurette's death wasn't his fault? "Trey, you couldn't have known—"

"Don't say it again, André. I've heard it too many times. We both know I wasn't there to protect her."

André didn't like the unbending look he saw in his friend's eyes. It meant trouble. "Maybe I should come with you after all."

"You'll only get in the way. Besides, you have issues of your own to settle."

"Nothing is as important as this."

Trey lifted his eyebrows. "I think so. You and Miss O'Malley have to finish what you started."

"Now isn't the time to discuss O'Malley."

"It's the exact time to talk about her." The bitterness in Trey's eyes softened. "When this is over, I want a niece or nephew to spoil. You and that fiery cardsharp can give me that."

Though his gut rippled in anticipation at his friend's words, André knew Trey was trying to divert his thoughts. "Trey, you can't win this one. You have to find peace in Laurette's memory. I have. You can too."

"Now that I know where Sherwood is hiding, it's time I settled it once and for all."

André swore over the familiar wave of helplessness marching through him. "There's nothing I can say to talk you out of this?"

"I'm leaving in an hour." Trey's gaze hardened again. "*Alone*. And you're going to stay here and find out what Miss O'Malley is hiding. I'll wager she's going to surprise the hell out of you."

Before André could respond, Trey slapped him on the back. "Take care, my friend." Without another word he turned on his heel and charged down the street toward the jail.

Knowing his words would fall on deaf ears, André didn't bother following after Trey. Perhaps his friend was right, perhaps it was time for him to settle the score. One way or another.

After a few moments of pause, André continued on his own path toward the bank. Heavy-hearted, he allowed his head to fill with the business that lay ahead of him. He liked taking care of his own financial affairs. Pearl had once convinced him to take on a manager, and he'd ended up broke.

Never again.

He joined in the mingling crowds on the streets, the

hurried energy soothing away his frustration. He liked the personality of Denver in the day. The honest people milling about reminded him of better times, simpler times. Here he saw life. Real life. Full of hard, honest work.

With the clean scent of pine riding along the breeze that skimmed his face, André experienced pure contentment. He didn't particularly miss Louisiana or the South, but he missed his family and his life before poverty had stolen his youthful innocence. At heart, André was a man of strong family bonds, which was why Trey's destructive quest concerned him.

But was he any different from his brother-in-law? His need for wealth, and the drive for the security that came with it had hardened his heart as sure as Trey's quest to avenge Laurette's death had hardened his.

André couldn't say exactly when he'd lost a handle on his own perspective. Perhaps when he'd made the mistake of marrying Pearl. Her death had freed him legally, but he hadn't been the same since.

His frequent contact with O'Malley had begun to change him, though. And now he realized he wanted to change, wanted to become the man he was before poverty, before Pearl—before bitterness had raked through his soul.

He was so focused on his thoughts, he failed to watch his steps. Swerving, he barely avoided colliding into a small child running straight for him. Unfortunately, in his attempt to miss the first kid, he ran into another.

The second boy tipped forward, fell hard into him, then leaned back. "Sorry, sir," he muttered, keeping his eyes cemented to André's waistcoat.

"My fault entirely," André said, gazing down at a bent head of black curls just as he felt the whisper of a touch against his vest.

"Sorry again, sir." The boy shrugged away. The quick flick of triumph in the kid's expression was all it took for

André to figure out what had just happened.

As the boy swaggered off, André reached out and grabbed him by the shirt collar. "Not so fast. I want a word with you."

The kid pulled hard to free himself, but André had too firm a hold for escape. Out of the corner of his eye, André caught sight of a smaller boy lingering just out of reach. He took a step closer, dragging his captive with him. Just as he was about to clutch the other child, a holler erupted, "Run, Michael."

Michael dodged André's grasp and took off at a gallop. At least André had the presence of mind to keep his grip around the older of the two. Hauling the kid around to face him, he said, "I think you have something of mine."

"No, sir. I . . . I don't have anything of yours." His eyes darted across the street, searching, gauging.

André was in no mood to play games with a young thief a third his size and weight. "Hand it over."

"I don't know what you mean."

André made sure the look on his face squelched any desire for the kid to continue denying his crime. "Yes, you do."

Shoulders slumped, the boy nodded. Pulling André's wallet from his pocket, he said, "I . . . I'm sorry, mister. I don't ever do this sort of thing. Well, not anymore. It's just, we need the money. And you looked like you wouldn't miss it."

Although the kid's gaze was never at rest, André caught a glimpse of the desperation there. Strangely, his thoughts jumped to O'Malley and the similar look she'd had that first night in his office. This time he would ask the questions he hadn't asked of her. He started with the simple. "What's your name?"

"Johnny. Look, mister. We didn't mean any harm."

André followed Johnny's glance across the street. "We? As in you and that other boy over there?"

"Yeah, but we didn't need the money for ourselves. We did it for—" Johnny sighed. "Oh, boy. I'm in big trouble now." He gave André an imploring look. "Please let me go. I don't want her to find out about this."

Patience thin, André snarled through gritted teeth. "Her?" he prompted.

Shaking his head vigorously, Johnny sighed. "Well, not really a her. I mean, she needed the money, but not for herself. For the orphanage."

Again, the kid stopped his explanations without giving a complete answer. André tried not to bark out his next question. "What orphanage?"

"Heart House. Where we live."

"So, the orphanage needs money?"

The swift bunching of muscles under his hand warned André what the kid planned. "I wouldn't try it."

Johnny tried it.

André tightened his grip, making it harder for the kid to move.

"You're not going to let me go, are you?"

Placing his free hand firmly on a bony shoulder, André shook his head. "Not till I get more answers. I want to know about this orphanage."

Johnny sighed again. "A few weeks ago, I heard Faith tell Katherine she had to get two thousand dollars or we'd lose Heart House."

At the familiar name and the exact amount a certain card cheat owed him, André's gut twisted. Everything else forgotten, he moved a step closer to the kid and pressed for more answers. "You just say Faith?"

The kid kept talking, suddenly spewing words out as fast as they could come. "Yeah. Faith. She's the reason I have a home now. She's the nicest lady I know." A dark sadness flicked in his features. "But she's working too hard. Every night she goes somewhere and stays till real late. She's promised me she's not doing what Momma did, but she's always so tired. Like Momma was before she died." Tears filled the boy's eyes, but he kept them from spilling with a few hard blinks. Thrusting out his chest, he continued. "I don't want Faith dying like Momma. And I don't want to go back on the streets again like after Momma died."

André recognized the fear, the underlying despair. It was too similar to behavior of a certain hoyden exactly three weeks, six days, and nine hours ago. Not that he was counting. "This Faith you mentioned, she about this tall?" André placed his hand in the air at chest height. "Real pretty, with dark hair and big brown eyes?"

"Yeah, that's her. You know her?"

An ugly thought rushed to the top of the others. "She teach you how to pick pockets?"

The kid's eyes got as big as billiard balls. "Oh, no. Hey, you're not gonna tell her what I did. She'll have my hide if she finds out."

Suddenly André's head couldn't quite take it all in fast enough. An orphanage, a loan, and Faith O'Malley. It didn't make any sense, and yet it all made perfect sense. "Let's go."

"Where you taking me?"

"Home. It's time I saw this . . . Heart House."

"Oh, no. I'm not going there with you. Not till you promise not to tell Faith what I did."

André wasn't about to bargain with a twelve-year old pickpocketing scamp. When he caught sight of the other little boy peering around a building across the street, he roped his fingers around Johnny's arm and started out. "We'll just follow your little friend over there."

Johnny pulled back, dug in his heels, using his full body weight for leverage. "You can't tell on Michael too. He's already in trouble for running away last week."

That got André's attention. "Is it so bad at this orphanage that you have to run away?"

"Oh, no, he didn't mean to run away. Not really. He just kind of got lost, looking for his dad."

"Seems reasonable."

Johnny missed the sarcasm in André's tone. "Yeah, that's what I said. But Faith made Michael promise not to ever come to this side of town again. She'll get all sad and gloomy if she finds out he came with me today. Then she'll give us both that 'I'm really disappointed in you' lecture."

"She will, huh?" Seemed like a pretty good punishment to André. And he'd known O'Malley long enough to remember how particularly moving her 'I'm disappointed in you' lecture could be. She'd given it to him twice in the past week. Once after he'd argued with Trey over Laurette, and the other after he'd yelled at Hank, for what he couldn't remember now.

"Please, mister, that's the worst. I'd rather take a whipping. But she never whips me, says that wouldn't teach me anything."

André found himself silently commending her approach. Not quite sure why he did it, he started bargaining with the kid after all. "Tell you what. Take me to the orphanage and I won't tell on Michael."

"Promise?"

"You have my word."

Johnny looked hard at him, searching his face with the shrewdness of a man twice his age. André held his glare, allowing the kid as much time as he needed. "All right. It's a deal."

André lifted his hand from Johnny's shoulder, but kept hold of his shirt collar. "Before I completely release you, I must point out that I'm bigger and faster than you."

A hint of respect whisked across Johnny's features. "In other words, don't try anything foolish?"

"Exactly."

André let go of the collar. Prepared for the break, he caught Johnny by the neck in two strides.

Johnny slid him a sheepish grin. "Just checking."

André grinned back. Recognizing a lot of himself in the crafty move, he slapped the boy on the back, then looped his arm across his shoulder. "Wouldn't have expected anything less." After a few blocks of silence, he asked, "This Faith you mentioned. What's she got to do with the orphanage?"

The boy's grin widened. "Oh, she's the owner."

Chapter Eighteen

After making a diving catch, Faith jumped up with the ball secure inside her glove. Waving her hand in the air, she laughed. "Got it." With the sound of her team's cheers ringing in her ears, she laughed louder.

She simply loved baseball, mostly because it gave all the children an opportunity to play. When she'd first read about the game in the Denver newspaper, she'd sent for the rules, knowing it would be perfect for the children.

She'd been right.

As the other team took the field between innings, she did a quick head count. Noticing two were missing, she asked, "Anyone know where Michael and Johnny went?"

Maggie spoke up. "Sure, they went to—" One of the other kids elbowed her silent, then finished her sentence for her. "We don't know where they went."

Maggie's scowl told otherwise.

Faith lifted her brows. "Oh? No idea, hmm."

"None."

Sighing, Faith began to worry. It would take a powerful lure to draw Michael and Johnny away from a baseball game, and that probably meant trouble.

Just then, as though conjured by her thoughts, Michael came tearing around the front of the house, glancing nervously over his shoulder. When his gaze landed on Faith, he skidded to a halt and walked slowly, head hung low. She waited until he stopped in front of her. "Want to tell me where you were?" she asked.

Michael shook his head.

Faith knelt in front of him and ran a hand across his forehead, smoothing his face free of hair. "You might as well tell me. I'll find out eventually."

Michael shuddered. "I was with Johnny. We didn't mean to get into trouble."

A shocked gasp slipped out before she could stop it. "Trouble? What happened?" She looked over his shoulder, peering toward the front gate. "And where's Johnny?"

"I didn't want to leave him, honest. But he told me to run when he got caught."

Oh, Lord, not again. "Caught? Doing what?"

Michael clamped his lips shut and dug his foot in the dirt.

Faith relented, knowing she'd get nothing more out of him for now. She just hoped he hadn't tried to go to the bank to see his father again. On her deathbed, Michael's mother had foolishly told him the name of his father, perhaps in the hope Prescott would do the right thing. The banker had denied the truth, but Michael had persisted. The last time he'd confronted his father, Prescott had nearly gone mad with rage, calling Michael filthy names before kicking him out of the building.

For that alone, Faith hated the man.

The sound of voices chattering in the distance, captured her attention. She looked over Michael's shoulder again, her heart sinking at the sight before her. "Oh, no."

Of all the people she might have expected, she never once thought she'd see André Du Bois tugging a very reluctant Johnny behind him. Her first instinct was to hide, to pretend she knew neither man nor boy. But when her eyes met Du Bois's steady gaze, she knew the secrets between them were at an end.

Sighing, she slowly stood, and ruffled Michael's hair. "Go on, you can play on Katherine's team." She sent him forward with a tiny shove on his back, then waved her hand in a circle, motioning to Katherine to continue the game without her.

Katherine looked at her with a questioning expression. Faith cocked her head in the direction of Du Bois and Johnny. Katherine's eyes widened, but she quickly composed herself. "All right, kids. Whose turn is it to hit?"

Once the game began again, Faith trudged toward the white picket fence. As she crossed the yard, she never moved her gaze from Du Bois's. Fighting for composure and courage, she pushed her hair away from her face, then took several gulps of air.

As she opened the gate, Johnny burst into a run, launching himself into her arms. "Please don't be mad at me, Faith." Tears trickled down his cheeks, each one hitching her breath. She couldn't remember the boy ever crying, not even the night she'd rescued him from jail. "I was only trying to help," he said.

Putting Du Bois out of her mind for a moment, Faith concentrated only on Johnny. She held the boy tight against her and rubbed her hand down his hair. "What's this all about? I've never seen you so upset. What's happened?"

A strangled sob was his answer.

She pulled away and bent down, searching his face. "Are you hurt?"

A curt snort sounded from above her. "He's not hurt."

Faith snapped her gaze to Du Bois. "What did you do to Johnny?"

"I'll let him tell you the story."

She reached behind her and pried the boy's hands from her waist. "Johnny?"

The boy wailed and threw himself in her arms again.

Faith patted his back. "What's all this?" She cut Du Bois another hard look. "Did this man hurt you?"

Johnny shook his head. "No. I . . . I stole his wallet."

Of all the scenarios she'd expected, this was the one she dreaded most. With a finger under his chin, she lifted his gaze to hers. "You what?"

He sniffed. "I picked his pocket."

"Oh, Johnny. You didn't. We talked about this."

"I know. Faith, please don't give me 'the lecture.' "

Her heart thumped in her chest, a deep sense of defeat riding against her nerves. In the past months she'd tried to teach Johnny right from wrong. She'd failed. "I don't understand. You couldn't have needed the money." She attempted to keep the hurt out of her voice, but at the sight of his grimace, she knew she hadn't.

"I did it for you." Johnny's pathetic grimace sent the first twinges of guilt through her. "*You* needed the money. I heard you tell Katherine all about the loan."

Oh, God, no. "You heard?"

"I couldn't sleep one night. I went to the front parlor, but I heard you and Katherine coming so I hid in the fireplace. I didn't mean to listen."

She'd never guessed one of the children would overhear. It had been so late that night when she'd confessed her problems to Katherine. "Oh, Johnny. I'm sorry."

Johnny sobbed again. "I heard you say you might lose Heart House. I couldn't let that happen."

"Oh, honey, you needn't think about things like that. It's my job to do all the worrying."

Johnny didn't seem to hear her. "But you have to go to work every night. Like Momma did."

"I'm not doing . . . *that*. I promise."

"Then why do you look so tired all the time?"

She pulled him back into her embrace. "I'm not that tired. Look at me, Johnny. You don't ever have to worry about money while you're here with me. From now on, you get to be just a kid."

Johnny shook his head, regret and hope working against each other on his young face. "I don't know how to be a kid."

Faith didn't have a ready response. She understood far too well, and yet words eluded her. For the first time, she looked up at Du Bois. The sympathy in his gaze gave her the courage to say, "I don't think I know either." She sighed. "But we'll figure it out together." Her heart filled with determination. "I *promise*. Now, I think the first thing to do is to go join the others in the game." At just that moment, Maggie slid into third base. "Looks like the Hawks might catch up. Why don't you go take my place?"

Johnny stuck his bony chest out. "I'll hit a home run, I promise."

"All right then." Before she sent him away, Faith smiled and ruffled his hair. And for the first time since he'd come to Heart House, Johnny didn't shrug away from her gesture of affection.

It was a start. With the resiliency of youth, Johnny swiped a hand across his face and bound toward the game in progress.

For a moment, she just watched as Johnny ran to the group and slapped his fellow teammates on the back, soaking in all of their youthful energy.

"You going to keep pretending I'm not here?"

"What a wonderful idea," she said, keeping her attention on the game. "No one could ever accuse you of lacking insight."

"You're not afraid to look at me, are you?"

"I'm no coward."

She hated the hint of laughter she heard woven inside his tone. "Didn't say that you were."

Faith swallowed. She'd told Johnny she'd handle things. Now she had to make good on that promise. "I think we'd better go inside for our talk."

André nodded, knowing he could hold back his questions that long.

"Follow me," she said.

Out of a strange perverse need to watch this woman squirm, he delighted in the tremor in her voice. "What a wonderful idea. I'm curious to see the inside of your home. The one I assume I helped pay for."

She spun around then, a swathe of fear turning her eyes a liquid brown. But with a single blink, her eyes reflected only sheer determination and a look that said she wouldn't allow him to intimidate her. Watching her glaring at him, he decided that he liked this woman riled. And he planned to rile her good. "I'll let you lead the way."

"How very much the gentleman you are."

"It's amazing the talents I have whenever it suits."

She snarled at him. He grinned. Sniffing, she turned abruptly and made her way to a row of stairs leading to the front door. With interest, he noted the immaculate lawn, the flowers and shrubs planted in tidy rows. Everywhere he looked he saw order and charm and warmth and beauty. He hadn't seen quite this much concentration on the tiny details that turned a house into a home since his boyhood days in Louisiana. Even the brick looked clean and cared for.

Crossing the threshold, he was greeted with the familiar smells of his childhood. The tangy odor of the soot from the fireplace mingled with the lemon wax from the floors. The lingering aroma of fresh-baked pies transported him back in time twenty years. For a brief moment André expected to see his nanny, Minnie, barking orders at the rest of the house servants. A sudden wave of grief made his voice harsh. "This doesn't look like any of the orphanages I've ever seen."

"Well, now. There you go again, Du Bois, pretending to be all smart and savvy. Careful, someone might mistake you for an observant man."

He relished the growl in her tone. It matched his mood. "Imagine the scandal."

She continued forward, leading him into a fancy parlor. He studied the room's furnishings, still amazed at both the luxury and the warmth that surrounded him. "Definitely not your typical orphanage."

"This isn't just an orphanage. It's a baby farm. Where prostitutes leave their—" She broke off and swallowed, obviously unable to say the word.

"Mistakes?" he offered.

"Such an ugly word for innocent souls, don't you think?"

"Yes. I do."

She turned and looked at him then, the sadness in her eyes touching the lost little boy in him he'd thought dead. In that moment they crossed into new territory, where shared pain met compassion.

He took his time looking at her, feasting on her beauty as he hadn't allowed himself to do for three weeks. He'd been afraid to look at her, afraid he'd want her anyway, knowing she'd lied and cheated him. Because he had wanted to believe in her, despite what his head and logic had dictated.

"Tell me about this place. Help me to understand."

"I," she opened her mouth, shut it, then tried again. "It's simple, really. I take in unwanted children of whores. I provide them a home and the chance for a secure future."

"So that's why none of the madams would help me find you."

She grimaced. "Probably. In a way, I keep them in business. The mothers of most of these kids pay me a monthly fee to keep their children here."

He took her hand in his, squeezed gently. "Is that how you get the money to fund this place?"

She linked her gaze with his, holding him with the intensity of her stare. "Partly. But it's not enough. It's never enough." She dropped her gaze to the ground. "I want the best for the kids."

As he silently studied Faith's bent head, André saw the true beauty in her. The kind that came from a heart, which sacrificed everything for children no one else wanted.

He released her hands so he could lift her chin. Searching her features, he noticed the dark circles, the lines of fatigue dancing across her face. In that moment he understood Johnny's desire to pick his pocket, to protect the woman who had cared enough to give him a home.

But this home had been built on deceit and cheating. He had to remember that, or else he might find himself doing something foolish. Like falling in love with Faith O'Malley.

Confusion battled with the compassion inside his head. "Let me see if I understand this. You took out a loan with Prescott for this place." He looked around, drank in the opulence. Touched a vase, a crystal ornament, a porcelain pitcher. "Don't you think you overreached necessity a little?"

Faith circled her gaze around the room. "Perhaps. All right, yes. But these kids are special. Most of their mothers and *all* of their fathers don't want them. Well, I do. And I want them to have the good things in life, all the comforts they couldn't have otherwise."

He didn't know which was worse, his understanding or

his anger at her recklessness. "What if you had lost them?" The ramifications were astounding.

Little lines connected between her eyebrows. "I don't know what you mean?"

"What if you had failed that night at my poker table? What if someone else had caught you cheating, and called you out?" His gut twisted at the many possibilities, the sheer magnitude of the foolish risk she'd taken that night. "What would these children have done if you'd ended up broke? Or worse? You could have ended up dead." The very idea sucked the air out of his lungs.

"I would never fail these kids."

The veins on his neck threatened to pop open from the strain of keeping his voice level. "What if sheer determination isn't enough?" Her insulted glare only added to his fury. "I know from experience, O'Malley. No one can handle all their problems alone. There's always something bigger than you."

"You make it sound as though my ultimate defeat is inevitable." She unleashed her fury in her next statement. "Well, you're wrong."

"Oh? What if something happens to you?"

She turned her back to him. "Most of these kids come here already knowing how to survive on their own."

"How? By picking pockets?"

Her shoulders flinched. "I didn't teach Johnny how to do that."

"Maybe not. But haven't you taught him that the end justifies the means."

"I'm trying to teach him and the rest of the children to never give up, no matter what the obstacles."

"Oh, I get it. As long as everything turns out all right, then do what it takes to survive?"

"Yes. No." She threw her hands in the air and twirled to face him. She jutted an angry finger in the air. "You're intentionally making this more complicated than it is."

"I know what I know. Three weeks ago, you sat at my table, desperate. You made the decision to cheat, then justified it because of the children. How close am I?"

"You're making it sound ugly."

"I'm making it sound the way it is. You're teaching these kids to cheat if they can't get what they want honestly."

Her lips pulled into a tight knot, and color drained out of her cheeks. "How dare you judge me. You have no idea what it's like to be poor."

"I know a lot more than you imagine. And like it or not, I have a stake in this now."

She lifted her chin, her eyes scattering flames at him. "You have no say here."

He leaned forward. "Last I counted, I still own one thousand, five hundred dollars worth of this house."

"I'm paying you back, every penny."

As angry with her as he was at the moment, the offer sailed out of his mouth shocking him. "What if I say I don't want you to pay me back? What if I say I want to help?"

"I . . . no." Her expression closed. "I won't accept your help."

"Why?"

"How can I teach the children the importance of facing the consequences of their actions if I don't do so myself? That would make me a hypocrite."

"Do they know you cheated to get the money?"

"No."

"Then I don't understand—"

"*I* know. If I take money from you, how could I possibly expect them to live up to a standard I can't meet on my own with no one watching me?"

"Even if the pace is killing you?"

"I can handle myself."

"No, you can't. Johnny saw what's happening to you,

and it terrified him enough to go out and steal. I see it too. You're nearly dead on your feet. You're pushing too hard, just to make the point that you can take care of everything alone. What if you aren't as alone as you think? What if I'm here now?"

She shook her head, tears welling in her eyes. "If I take money from you, all I've done is taught the children to accept charity. How will that help them?"

He crossed the divide between them and linked his fingers with hers, as though he could will her to understand the meaning of what he was trying to do for her, for himself. Hell, he barely understood his actions. He regarded the whole situation with a mixture of emotions running the spectrum from pure rage to compassion. "Perhaps, if you let me help you, it will teach them to accept gifts when freely given to them."

"Nothing is free."

He paused, considering what to do next. Maybe her refusal was for the best, at least for now. Maybe he should allow her to continue working for him. What better way to keep an eye on her, protect her from making any further foolish decisions? And he could always fiddle with the numbers, give her a bigger percentage of her earnings than before.

"All right, O'Malley. If you're so hell-bent on running yourself into the grave, I won't stand in your way."

Tired, dull brown eyes rose to look at him. Pain etched lines into her smooth complexion, while storm clouds of confusion circled in her gaze. "I have to finish what I started."

"All right. Just answer me this. Why didn't you tell me you needed the money for this house?"

In answer Faith grabbed his sleeve, pulling him toward a window overlooking the yard where the children played. "Look at them."

He did. Watching Michael make it safely to first base

with Johnny jumping up and down, shouting encouragement, he marveled at their youth and vigor. It brought back happy memories of his own childhood.

Memories she'd never had as a child.

He turned to her, as understanding slapped him in the head. "You wanted to protect them, give them what you didn't have yourself."

"Yes, including an opportunity to go to a regular school, like normal school children. Thanks to Katherine's tutoring, most of the older kids are ready."

"You've done a lot for them."

"Not enough. And there will always be threats."

"Life is full of uncertainty."

"That's not what I mean." In a halting tone, she told him about Prescott and his attempt to shut the doors of Heart House by calling in her loan a full six months early. "So you see, there are people in Denver that don't want me to succeed." I couldn't trust you. Or rely on the fact that you wouldn't try to shut me down too."

"I wouldn't have."

She nodded. "I realize that now, but when we first met, you weren't very . . . understanding."

"You didn't make it easy."

"I know."

He watched her look out the window at the children again, her affection for them obvious. And then he knew the truth. "You would have done anything for them."

"Yes."

"Even work as a who—"

He felt the shudder pass through her as though it had started in his own body. "*Yes.*"

He couldn't bear the thought that she would willingly sleep with men, any men, for the sake of the children. And if she had, would that make her noble or something . . . vile? He'd be a liar if he said he understood what could lead her to accept such a fate. He had to think, had to sort through his emotions alone. "I think I better go now."

Faith bristled, ready to defend her actions, explain her reasons to him, until she spied the hint of confusion in his gaze. She knew it made her a coward, but she decided to let him work through the matter on his own.

As they moved into the hallway, she took two steps to meet every one of his. She liked the way he walked, in the same way he conquered life—with conviction.

At the front door, she stopped, waiting for him to speak. As the tension grew with the silence, she didn't think she'd ever been more aware of another human being than she was of this big, clean-smelling, well-dressed man. He leaned toward her, but instead of molding his lips to hers, he brushed his mouth against the slope of her cheek, then moved to her forehead.

It was the second time he'd kissed her like that. And this time she discovered just how much she hated it.

"Until tonight, O'Malley."

Chapter Nineteen

André stood on the fringes of the nightly activity, watching O'Malley work the faro table with her usual style and finesse. Already she'd become his best dealer, managing to deal squarely and yet charming her customers into playing much longer than they should.

She had that way about her.

For two days André had avoided her, speaking to her only when necessary or when she spoke first. He still hadn't sorted through the secrets he'd discovered about her and her orphanage. But as hard as he tried to hold on to his anger over the sheer recklessness of her desperate actions to pay off her loan, he couldn't.

Though he didn't approve of her methods, he understood why she'd cheated. And he admired her determination to accept the consequences of her mistakes. Even if the pace was killing her. He narrowed his eyes, gauging her visible fatigue. Exhaustion was etched in her features, weariness circled in her eyes. He could no longer deny the desire to alleviate her suffering.

If she'd let him.

Joining the crowd around her table, he waited, watching. Shoulders slumped, she looked ready to keel over. He studied the case keeper, judging that Faith was about halfway through the deck. Although it would only be a short while before she finished this round, the night was far from over.

A spasm of compassion moved across his soul. Instead of worrying about his own need to understand her actions, he should have tried harder to end the debt between them, thereby giving her relief from the grueling schedule she forced upon herself.

Inching around to the back of the table, he whispered into her ear. "This is your last deal for now. Before you shuffle the next deck, come talk to me. I'll be by the stairs."

She nodded, not breaking her momentum or concentration. André suddenly wanted to ruffle her, wipe that serious expression off her face. Whether he replaced it with anger, passion, or laughter, he didn't much care. But replace it he would.

Treading toward the stairs, he made idle conversation along the way. When Faith eventually joined him, he knew what to say. "Larkin is ready to go home."

"Home?"

He kept his expression bland. "I want to give him to the children."

"Last time I asked, your refusal was quite adamant." She angled her head and let out a snort. "What are you up to now?"

"Who says I'm up to anything?" He tweaked her nose. "Honestly, O'Malley, you're so suspicious."

"You've practically ignored me for two days, and suddenly you're generosity itself. Why the sudden change of heart?"

He liked the miffed look playing across her features. So, she'd missed him these last two days. "Larkin needs more attention than I can give him."

She considered him for a moment, tucked her arms around her waist, and sighed. "All right. The children will love him. Thank you, I'll take him." Her smile blinded him.

He realized he would do anything to see that smile of hers directed at him always. "He's upstairs. Why don't we go get him, and you can leave early."

Her smile disappeared and she stilled his progress with a skeptical glare. "Special favors? I thought we talked about this already. I work off my debts."

"It's just for tonight. Tomorrow I'll expect you to work your full shift."

Reaching for her, he looped her arm in the crook of his. "I'll show you where he is."

After quietly accompanying him up the first two stairs, she stopped and pulled away from him. "Why do I get the feeling you have another reason for taking me upstairs?" Her gaze reflected uncertainty.

In an attempt to cut through the tension, he wiggled his eyebrows at her. "Maybe I do."

Her gasp and instant flash of excitement disappeared inside a deliberate blink. "Du Bois, no, I can't. I've never . . ."

He pressed a finger against her lips. "I know, O'Malley. I didn't mean that."

She gave him a quelling look that could move the dead to confession.

"Okay, so maybe I *thought* about it. But, no, I won't try anything."

She started up again, dragging him forward with her. "Good."

He finished the thought. "Anything, that is, that you don't want me to try."

Huffing, she lifted her eyes to the ceiling. "Du Bois, I'm warning you."

He mimicked her irritated tone. "Is that a yes or a no?"

She turned on her heel and with intentional caution, walked down one step at a time. "I think I'll wait downstairs."

He hopped down after her. "Come on, O'Malley." Moving alongside her, he placed his hand on her arm. "I won't touch you."

Nodding, she started up the stairs again.

"Unless, of course, you want me to."

Faith sniffed. Halting again, she wondered how long he'd keep to his promise. Looking into his pleading eyes, she knew her answer.

Until she asked him otherwise.

He gave her that devilish grin that had her reaching to the banister to steady herself.

"All right," he said. "I'll fess up. Larkin is in my office. I'm luring you to my rooms to insist you lie down and get some sleep."

Her voice croaked. "*Sleep?*"

"Yes, which is something you're not getting enough of. Come on, don't argue. Let me entice you up to my rooms with the promise of a soft bed and a softer pillow. How's that sound?"

She was too tired to lie. "Like heaven."

"Tempted, are you?"

She blinked. "Not at all."

"Come on, I promise to keep my randy hands to myself."

Not taking any chances, she darted down the stairs, then rushed over to where Hank stood surveying the saloon. She whispered her request in his ear. He gave her a vigorous nod in answer.

Relieved, she started back to the second floor. Du Bois bounded after her, a scowl marring his handsome face. "What did you say to Hank?"

It was her turn to waggle her eyebrows. "If you don't keep to your promise, I'll scream. And then Hank will be up here in two seconds flat."

"Is that right? Think you've charmed him?"

She lifted a shoulder. "We understand one another."

"Ever since you talked him into not following you home the other night?"

That got her attention. "What makes you think I would do something like that?"

Once they reached the landing, he stopped to look at her. "Just a wild guess."

Before she could think up a quick retort, he took her arm, steered her down the hallway, and stopped at the first door on their right. With a flick of his wrist he turned the knob and guided her into the large suite.

As she walked forward, the decidedly masculine smells of coffee, cigars, and lime mingled with the fresh scent of clean linens. Furnished with fancy mahogany furniture and decorated in dark blue velvet, the luxurious room left no doubt as to Du Bois's priorities. He was a man concerned with good taste, success, and wealth.

Turning in a slow circle, she breathed in deeply. The intimacy of the situation suddenly struck her. She was alone with Du Bois in his bedroom. Assailed by his familiar scent, surrounded by some of his most personal possessions, she felt her awareness of a man she already thought about more often than she should jump to a new level. All her senses were tuned to his slightest movement. Trying to bring her mind back into focus, she barked out an insult. "And you had the nerve to criticize my choice in decor?"

His answering chuckle made it all the harder to keep

her head clear. "They say it takes a very black pot to see the black of the kettle."

Self-deprecation? From Du Bois?

Her gaze continued to wander, drinking greedily of the comfort calling to her to stretch out and rest, if only for a short time. Du Bois placed a palm against her back and urged her toward the large four-poster bed in the middle of the room. "Go on, lie down. I'll come wake you in a little while and escort you home."

Seduced by the look of the soft pillows, she stared longingly at the bed. "No. If I'm through for the night, I should go home now. There's plenty of work still to do there."

"All the more reason to rest first. Go on, O'Malley. Don't make me force you."

She spun around to tell him what she thought of his idea, but he'd already slipped out of the room.

The click of the door punctuated his exit.

She looked around surreptitiously, as though someone might be watching her. Realizing she truly was alone, she grinned in delight, threw her hands in the air, and vaulted on top of the bed. Bouncing, she resisted the urge to fall back and sleep through the next eternity.

First she wanted comfort, without the confines of silk and stiff taffeta. Exercising considerable willpower, she crawled back off the bed to remove her dress and corset.

As she stripped down to her chemise, curiosity warred with fatigue. Promising her tired body rest, she explored the room quickly. When she eyed an armoire identical to the piece in the downstairs office, she couldn't resist further inspection. Flinging open the doors, she discovered more of Du Bois's clothing, similar to the shirts and pants she'd rummaged through the first night she'd come to the Dancing Belles.

In that moment her resolve overcame her fear and she stripped the rest of her clothing off. As she dressed in one of Du Bois's shirts, his smell merged with hers, sending a hot lick of fire through her veins.

With trembling fingers working the buttons, trepidation replaced her resolve. What was she doing? She'd fought this decision all her life. Perhaps she was just tired of waffling, and perhaps it was something more.

With the battle raging inside her, she roamed the room, forcing her heartbeat to calm while perversely enjoying the heat of desire riding her hard.

The bed beckoned. Her agitation forgotten, she drifted across the floor and climbed on the bed. Settling under a blanket, she allowed the fierce wave of excitement to weave her pounding blood into every fiber of her body.

Oh, yes, *this* was going to be good.

Chapter Twenty

André stood in the doorway of his room, watching Faith sleep. Cuddled in his bed, she looked as though she belonged there. He'd never had a woman upstairs, much less in his bed. But with her head pillowed against her arm she looked . . . *perfect.*

As he drank in her lovely form, his heart hammered against his chest. She'd stripped out of her dress and corset—now how he was supposed to keep his mind off that particular fact, he couldn't say—and borrowed one of his shirts.

She was one bold, audacious woman. And probably had no idea what such an act would do to a man who found keeping his hands to himself already an impossible battle.

Or did she?

Her delectable form lay in a highly unladylike position. Her limbs tangled in the blanket, one creamy leg kicked free from the confusion, bare to the middle of her thigh.

Unable to move his gaze away from the flesh gleaming at him, he felt his fingers itch to touch and explore the smooth expanse of skin.

He swallowed hard and entered the room. Turning, he clicked the door locked and pressed his forehead against the wood. "Just wake her up, then be on your way," he muttered.

Fine advice for a man of iron will, which he was most definitely not. Determined to refrain from touching her, he swung back around, stepped toward the bed, and looked his fill.

His body strained toward her; he longed to climb in bed and take her in his arms, to ease the ache that had ridden hard over him since meeting her. Hell, at least she snored. And she made enough noise to wake the people in the boardinghouse three blocks away. He tried hard to concentrate on that little flaw: unfortunately, instead of bothering him, it weakened his resolve.

He continued to watch her, gauging his next move. The woman slept with as much abandon as she went through her waking life. Passionate, larger than life, Faith O'Malley had the courage of eight sailors fighting a hurricane in a two-man boat.

And André Du Bois was a fool.

She was just a woman, dammit, a woman who cheated and schemed to get her way, who recklessly put the lives of innocent children on the line. And yet, even before he'd known about the orphanage, he'd already concluded that Faith O'Malley was a woman unlike any he'd ever known.

He loved her humor, her courage, her willingness to accept her mistakes and see them through.

Ah, hell. He loved her.

And it was nothing like anything he'd ever felt before. Not even the emotions he'd had for Pearl could match this all-consuming longing to be with O'Malley through the good times and the bad.

He wanted to protect her, keep the world from hurting her any further. But he also wanted to laugh with her, fight with her, and let her smooth his cares away as well. Now, with his emotions bursting, he wanted to bury himself inside her.

But he wouldn't do it.

Because he knew what that could do to her. The reality of her childhood had left her scared of intimacy, for good reason. God, how he wanted to heal her scars, show her the wonderful reality of intimacy with a man who loved her. He vowed that he would get her to trust him before he took her with him into the world of pleasure he knew they alone could share.

No longer a man of mighty will, he reached out and touched her cheek, running a knuckle along the soft arc. She moaned in her sleep, smiled, and then giggled. But she didn't wake.

"Faith, honey. It's time to get up."

Another soft squeak, a sigh, and another smile. And then a violent kick that sent the blanket higher up her leg.

Right. Now, how was he supposed to keep his promise when she looked so damn tantalizing? "Faith?" He rubbed his hand down her arm.

"Mmmm."

"Come on, honey."

She snorted—she actually snorted—then rolled to the other side of the bed.

An interesting predicament. He could either walk around to the other side of the bed or climb across. Not much of a decision, when he was growing harder by the second. Since his life's blood pulsed, already demanding quick, hard release, why not prolong the agony a little longer?

Since she was dressed in nothing more than his shirt, a thin linen barrier between his touch and her naked flesh, André wondered who would protect *him* from *her*.

Most definitely *not* good.

He couldn't keep his hand from shaking. Swallowing, he edged onto the bed and stretched his hand along the slope of her back. The warmth of sleep shimmered out of her, igniting a fire in his veins. Restraint made his voice harsh. "Faith? Wake up."

She arched her back into his touch and moaned her pleasure as he caressed.

"You're not making this easy for me."

She mumbled something in response. It sounded like she'd said "sleepy," but he couldn't quite make it out. He continued to stroke her back, and the curve of her hip, drawing from her little puffs of delight.

Out of nowhere, the image of O'Malley's instant fear the first time he'd kissed her screamed across his brain, stilling his advance. He looked at his hand, silently cursing his lusty soul and his lack of restraint. He hadn't kept his promise. But if he remembered correctly, he'd only promised to keep his hands off her *if* that was what she wanted.

He tentatively ran his fingertip down the line of her neck, tracing further along her spine and curving across her ribs. As she smiled and moved closer to him, he decided she definitely wanted his touch. "All right then. You asked for it, O'Malley."

He leaned forward and nuzzled his nose into the hollow of her neck, just below her ear. Her soft lilac scent filled his senses and something happened to him, something he'd never before experienced.

He lost control.

He roped his arm around her waist and tugged her against his need. She sighed and curled into him, wiggling her hips into his.

God, he'd never gotten this hard.

"Only a kiss, honey. That's all I want." He'd become quite the liar.

Needing relief, he rode his hand lower, to the bottom of her belly, and pressed her hard against him. She moaned, and squirmed deeper into his embrace. The thin barrier of clothing between them seemed ten inches thick. He wanted to rip off her shirt, pull his pants down, and drive into her.

But he also wanted to go slowly, to savor each moment with her, to give her exquisite pleasure.

He concentrated on her neck, hoping he'd find a way to forget about her tight little butt squirming against him. He twirled his tongue along the smooth column, tasting her cool, slightly salty skin.

Faith squeezed her eyes shut, refusing to surface from the loveliest dream of her life. Never had she felt so excited and yet safe and peaceful all at once. The odd emotions sliced around in her head, making her nearly lose the fight to stay alert. She remembered needing sleep, and Du Bois insisting she go to his room, his bed, for a rest. Imagine that, a rest in the middle of the evening. How absurd, decadent, and incredibly wonderful.

But now she suddenly didn't want to doze, she wanted something else. In her sleep-filled brain she realized she was getting that something else right now. And, oh, it was marvelous. She couldn't help but release a moan of pleasure, and then another. Arching her back, she reveled in the protective, slick warmth cuddling against her.

Wait a minute. Warmth couldn't cuddle. Oh, my, it felt too good to question it. Heat licked between her legs, pooling in a restless, unsettling pleasure. She reached down to help relieve the ache, and came in contact with a big masculine hand traveling along her belly.

She didn't experience even a moment of fear, or doubt. She knew who that hand belonged to, knew who was behind her. And as another moan tore through her, she accepted the truth. Her heart had been waiting for this moment since the first time she'd stared at him across a poker table.

And right now, she wanted what he had to give her. All of it. His hand stilled under hers and she sighed. "Don't stop," she whispered, her boldness shocking her as much as her lack of fear. "Please."

Moist, hot lips whispered into her ear. "Good evening, O'Malley. You sleep well?"

"I don't want to talk right now."

His tongue nipped her lobe. "You sure?"

A shiver sped through her. "Oh, yes."

"No fear?"

She kneaded his hand, then rubbed her palm against his knuckles. "No fear, no regret."

His fingers caressed her ribs, then wrapped around her breast. "I want you, Faith." His tremble knifed through her. "I need you. Now."

"I . . . you. You'll have to show me what to do. I don't know what to do."

He pressed a smile against her shoulder. "I know. For now, just relax." He trailed his lips along the top of her arm. "And enjoy."

He continued to run his tongue along her neck, nipping occasionally at the tender flesh. She pressed her head backward, twisting so he could have full access to her throat.

"What do I have to do?"

"Don't think."

"I can't anyway."

His chuckle rumbled against her bare flesh. "Then let me lead for a while." He massaged her shoulders and tickled her skin with feather-light kisses. "Just ease back into me."

"I don't think I could get any more relaxed."

He chuckled again, sounding very male and satisfied. "Good. Now turn over and kiss me."

"Thought you'd never ask." She rolled onto her back and gazed up at him. He lay on his side, up on one elbow, and stared down at her. They looked hard at one another, each demanding total honesty. A smile crossed her lips. His expression changed, softening, and she said, "I like the warmth in your eyes."

"Oh?"

She reached up and ran her fingertip along his left eyebrow. "You look as though you like me."

"I do. I think I always have."

She smiled, and her heart filled with joy. "I know."

He lowered his head toward hers. "Too much talking."

She accepted his kiss, this time with her eyes open, her heart prepared for whatever came next. His kiss was filled with such tenderness, a tear trickled out of her eye.

With a satisfied moan, she felt him shift above her.

As his tongue toyed with hers, she fully accepted the power he had over her. Just as she gave into her trembling, he moved lower, his lips raining tiny kisses along the way.

"Oh, I like that," she said.

"More?"

Desire surged through her, making her voice raspy. "More."

His tongue explored lower, down her neck toward the opening of the shirt she'd borrowed from him. "You wear my clothes well."

"I'm glad you approve."

"Now, I think we need to get you out of them." His gaze meandered across her face, down to her chest. "The sooner the better."

"Oh, well, if you insist."

"I insist."

He groaned, his breathing becoming shallow as he

started undoing the shirt. One by one he released the buttons, spreading the material apart with his lips. When he'd undone four of the buttons, he lifted up and leered down at her. Grabbing the sides, he ripped the shirt apart.

A laugh bubbled from her lips. "Brute."

He grinned as his gaze returned to her chest. He clicked his tongue and studied her bare breasts. "Magnificent." He gulped, then tripped his gaze lower, his breath catching in his throat. "My dear, you're not wearing any pantaloons."

"Are you scandalized?"

He shook his head and sealed his lips to her. "Too much talk."

He shifted his weight to one side and dragged his hand along her bare belly, up to cup her breast again. She hadn't been prepared for the jolt of feeling his touch created. "Oh."

He stopped, and lifted his head with a questioning expression.

"Well, don't stop now."

He laughed. "I think we're taking this way too slowly."

"We finally agree on something."

"Then hold on tight, honey."

She grasped his shoulders just before he clamped his mouth over hers and thrust his tongue inside. At the same time he wedged his knee in between her legs. As her tongue dueled with his, she arched her back, pressing her naked, throbbing core against his thigh. He slid his hand to the small of her back and thrust his hips firmly into hers.

She knew what to expect, knew what would happen once he undressed. But she hadn't known she'd want it so badly. Had she once thought intimacy between a man and woman dirty and ugly? How naïve she'd been. A moan of desire yanked free from her, forcing her to pull away from his kiss. She threw her head against the pillow and cried out from the longing to mate with this man.

He took the opportunity to move off the bed and start yanking at his clothes. She hadn't thought a man could get out of clothes so quickly. Of course, he did have an incentive. A jolt of power surged through her, humbling her, arousing her.

Once naked, André stood beside the bed. He thought to give Faith one last chance to change her mind. She just looked her fill, her eyes widening as they connected with his need. "Oh, my."

"You don't have to do this."

She looked him straight in the eye and smiled. The siren's call in her gaze beckoned to him. Before he lost the rest of his shattered willpower, André took a moment to admire her. Her hair, freed from the confines of its knot, cascaded in a midnight waterfall against the white pillow. He tortured himself further and moved his gaze lower. Two tight nipples strained toward him, moving in tandem from the quick hard breaths sailing out of her lungs.

As he lowered his gaze further still, it occurred to him that he would be the first to explore the dark, thick curls surrounding her feminine secrets.

A snarl lifted his gaze back to hers. Eyes drenched with passion stared into his. "You going to stand there eyeing my charms all night?"

"I might."

Impatience written all over her face, she snarled again. "I'd highly advise against it."

"Demanding, aren't we?"

"Du Bois . . ."

He pounced. She giggled. And as hard as he was, as serious as what they were doing was for them both, he couldn't help but bask in the glow of her laughter, her happiness.

He hadn't felt this alive, this young, in over eight years.

He wanted to savor every moment with this woman, but he was too far over the edge to take things slowly.

"You know what's going to happen?"

"Yes."

"I'll try not to hurt you."

Her eyes gentle, she let a smile waltz across her mouth. "I know." Her trust, her ultimate confidence in him, pushed him to his limit. He had to join with her. *Now.* Watching her face, he reached his hand between her legs.

Her delighted gasp increased his need to explore. He smoothed his fingers along her curls, seeking the hot moisture of her need for him. He rotated his finger in circles around her nub, then probed deep inside her. Her round eyes softened as he slowed his exploration, intentionally tantalizing her.

Her lids slowly shuttered closed as she wrapped her hand around his wrist and lifted her hips off the bed. He leaned down into her, breathing in her sighs of pleasure.

"More," she demanded. "I want more."

He spoke against her lips. "Yes, dear God, yes."

Giving her one, hard kiss, he moved over her. "Grab hold of my shoulders."

She did as he asked, and he pulled his hand out of her moisture and placed it on the bed by her hips. She moaned in protest, but he captured her lips again before she could voice her complaint aloud.

Without breaking the kiss, he repositioned his weight and moved in between her legs. "Look at me, Faith," he whispered against her mouth.

She opened her eyes and he entered her. He tried to push inside slowly, but she would have none of it. She grasped his hips and with one solid motion, she thrust forward, sheathing him fully.

He covered her shocked cry of pain with a kiss. She writhed below him, but he held steady. The more she moved, the harder it was for him to hold back his release.

But the fact that she wasn't squirming with pleasure kept him restrained. "Don't move, honey. The pain will go away in a minute. Then we'll start again."

She stilled. At the sign of her instant trust in him, his heart soared. "I didn't realize it would hurt," she moaned.

"I should have warned you."

"I . . . I think you did."

He kissed her on the forehead, the eyelids, the cheek. "Better yet?"

"I think so."

Trying to get her mind, and his, off her discomfort, he moved a hand to her breast and softly stroked her nipple.

"I like that."

"How about this?" With a gentle touch, he pinched.

"Try it a little harder."

He did. And she gasped. "Oh, my, I really like that."

"How about this?" He shifted, closed his lips around the hard orb, and sucked.

"Harder," she demanded.

He pulled more of her in his mouth and increased the pressure. Her fingers clenched into his shoulders and she arched. She squirmed a little more as he continued to toy with her nipple. Within seconds, she was whimpering in pleasure.

"Pain's gone," she whispered.

He lifted his head from her breast and grinned at her. "I noticed."

Thrusting, he found her rhythm and took charge. The throbbing warmth of her responding little pushes sent him hurtling toward ecstasy. He'd wanted her to peak before he did, but he knew he couldn't hold out much longer. Her sudden short gasps told him she'd almost made it. He wrapped his hands around the curves of her buttocks and thrust harder, deeper.

An instant later she cried out his name, her spasms

rippling around him just as he burst inside her, spilling his need inside her.

Gasping, he rolled onto his back, tugging her along with him. She collapsed on top of him, dragging in hard gulps of air.

Eventually, she found her voice. "Oh, André, I never knew."

He kissed the top of her head. "Me neither, Faith. Me neither."

"Is it"—she broke off, taking a deep breath—"is it always like this?"

How could she talk? "No," he rasped.

"Was it"—she hesitated—"special?"

He tightened his arms around her. "God, yes."

"I knew it."

Chapter Twenty-one

As night surrendered to the dawn and dawn lurched into day, Faith struggled to keep her emotions even, keep her irrational fears from overwhelming her. But try as she might, she couldn't stop her raging thoughts from overcoming her logic.

In a flurry of activity, she completed her share of the household chores earlier than usual, and found herself with too much free time to think. Needing something to do with her hands, she went to the kitchen and busied herself making biscuits.

Preparations complete, she grabbed a fistful of flour and dusted the dough waiting to be kneaded. The air clouded with white powder, making her eyes water and setting her to coughing. Swearing, she punched the dough into compliance. "Not only did I act rashly last night, now I'm going to choke myself."

Following her heart had seemed such a good idea the

night before. But now, back at the orphanage and alone with her thoughts, she wasn't so sure.

The soreness between her legs reminded her of the previous evening's events. Her innocence was gone, laid to rest in the hands of the man she loved. Sighing, she touched her pounding heart.

André Du Bois had been a perfect lover. Patient and yet passionate. Bold and altogether sweet. Though there had been no declarations of love, no promises, she knew he cared for her deeply. Perhaps even loved her. Her heart told her to trust him. Could she? Could she wait for . . .

What? What did she want from him?

She slammed her fist into the dough, biting her lip to keep from crying out. Panic wanted to flood inside her. She swallowed hard, holding it back.

Her feelings for André were too strong, too powerful. She was more in love than she'd ever thought possible. She wanted to weep, to cry out in misery, but she was too afraid to look that deep inside herself.

More flour and a hard slap to the dough still didn't make the images of her naked body twined in sensual intimacy with Du Bois disappear.

As beautiful as it had been, an ugly thought nagged at her, unrelenting.

Was she like her mother and Sally and the rest? Was there no turning back? And worse, did Du Bois think she was the same as a whore? Or had his eyes told the truth?

Did he love her?

No. Kneading with stiff fingers, she felt a thread of urgency weave through her worries. She should go to him, demand to hear the truth from his lips.

So intent was she on her thoughts, she didn't hear Katherine approach. "Are you going to beat that dough to death?" Katherine asked.

Jumping, Faith sighed and wiped her forehead on her

sleeve, then continued to pound. "The idea has merit."

Katherine poured a glass of water and offered it to her. Faith shook her head. "No, thanks."

"You want to talk about it?"

Faith's hands stilled. "Who says there's anything to talk about?"

Katherine eyed the mutilated dough. "Just a hunch. Here." Katherine handed her a towel. "Wipe your hands and come sit with me on the porch."

"I have biscuits to make."

Fingers wrapped around her wrist and squeezed gently. "Leave it."

Biting back a spurt of unnecessary oaths, Faith snatched the towel with exasperation. "Oh, all right."

She followed Katherine to the front of the house and out onto the porch. Settling herself in one of the rockers, she sighed. "I don't know what's wrong with me," she began.

Katherine perched on the edge of the railing and smiled down at her. "You don't?"

"Well, yes, I do. I just don't want it to be like this." She rubbed her hands up and down her thighs. "It's not supposed to be so complicated."

"It?"

Faith dashed a glance behind her, ensuring they were alone. "Falling in love."

"Ah. Does Mr. Du Bois know how you feel?"

"Who says it's Du Bois?"

Katherine waved her hand in the air. "You've been in love with him since that first night. So, have you told him?"

"No." She buried her face in her hands, and a whimper of shame slid through her teeth. "Oh, God, what if he thinks I'm a whore now?" It sounded so ugly once it was spoken aloud, but there it was. Her greatest fear. Not that he didn't love her, but that he'd assume she was a whore simply because she'd made love to him.

Katherine knelt in front of Faith. "Did you—"

Humiliation shot through her, and her hands dropped back into her lap in resignation. "Oh, Katherine, yes. I did."

A gasp flew from the other girl's lips. "Was it awful?"

Faith's head spun with memories. How could she explain the beauty, the intimacy, the intensity of their union? "It was *wonderful*. And he made it really special for me. He treated me with enormous tenderness." How could she have forgotten that part? How could a man make love with so much care and not respect her?

Relief slumped Katherine's shoulders forward. "Then what are you worried about?" A little line of fury dug between her brows. "Did he call you a whore?"

It was Faith's turn to gasp. "No, of course not. He'd never say such a thing."

Katherine reached out and placed a hand over Faith's. "Then what makes you so sure he would think it?"

"I . . ." Her breathing quickened as dread snaked its way through her. She had given her body in love, without the promise of marriage. And now there was a high probability that no offer would be forthcoming.

It was too late. She couldn't use the sheer force of her will to erase the last twenty-four hours. For the first time in her life, she couldn't handle a situation alone. And the only person who could help her, give her the answers she needed, was the very person who could destroy her.

Closing her eyes, she fought off a wave of emotion. "Oh, Katherine. What have I done?"

The sound of the front gate swinging open had Katherine turning to look over her shoulder. "Looks like you get to find out." And with those words the younger girl moved toward the porch door. "I'll be inside if you need me."

The very object of all Faith's worrying called out a greeting as he released the latch and entered the yard. Looking carefree and happy, Du Bois lifted the cage dangling from his left hand. "Anybody want a bird?"

At the sight of the man who held her fragile heart in his hands, a feeling of exquisite joy marched across Faith's soul. Her eyes connected with his and in that single look, all the feelings of the night before came back. She gave up the battle she'd waged against her emotions, and a choked sob escaped.

Eyes narrowed, Du Bois angled his head. "You all right, O'Malley."

Pushing her worries to the back of her mind, she climbed hastily to her feet. Forcing a delighted smile on her face, she said, "I forgot about Larkin."

Man and bird started forward, a jaunty gleam in both of their eyes. "Guess you had too much on your mind last night to remember," said André. "Seems I have that way about me."

She took to the game as though the banter could make her forget all the dangerous emotions brewing just below the surface. Smirking, she said, "At least as far as you know."

He drew up next to her and trailed a knuckle along her cheek. "Hoyden."

"Beast."

As his finger traced down her neck, his eyes swam with all the words she needed to hear but he had yet to say. In that moment, Faith knew all he had to do was ask and she'd do anything for him. Anything.

Holding her gaze, he swallowed. "Ah, O'Malley, I lo—"

"Awwwk. Pretty bird."

They jumped apart as though caught in a naughty game. Du Bois was the first to recover. Amusement dancing in his eyes, he lifted the cage again. "Seems my bird is the jealous sort. You've got quite a fan in him."

She lightly punched André's shoulder. "You mean, *my* bird."

"Right. This lovesick creature is all yours. Do with him what you will."

She sensed he spoke of more than the bird. Peering at her new pet, Faith grinned. "Katherine," she yelled. "Come look what André Du Bois has done now."

Faith left the children in Katherine's care with strict orders to keep the bird in his cage. Joining André on the porch, she clasped her hand over his and looked into his eyes. "Thank you. The children already love him."

Holding her gaze, he nodded. "You're welcome."

As one minute turned into two and then three, they continued to stare at one another. So much had been left unsaid between them and yet, now that the time had come, she couldn't find the words to start the conversation that would be the beginning of their future.

She wanted to be a part of his life, but she didn't know what that meant. She'd always been on her own. Alone, she'd carved out a place for her and the children in a world that didn't want to make room for them. All she knew was how to rely on herself and her resources.

Could she change so drastically, and open her heart and her life to a man? To this man?

Did she dare?

His features turned compassionate and loving, mingling with the intensity of other unnamed emotions in his gaze. "There's so much to say," he began. "But I don't know how to begin."

He'd spoken her thoughts aloud. Were they that connected?

Kissing her forehead, he blew out a puff of air. "I'm not a man of pretty words."

She clasped his hand tighter. "I don't need pretty words."

"Yes, you do. And I need to say them to you." He pulled out of her grasp, then in a single sweep crushed her against his chest. "There are so many things I have to apologize for."

Wrapping her arms around his neck, she placed a gentle kiss on his lips. "You apologized last night. Remember?"

A quiet, grave look passed in his eyes. "It's not enough. It'll never be enough. I treated you horribly these past few weeks." His hands rubbed along her spine. "My precious O'Malley."

She kissed him again, longer and with more feeling. "You didn't act alone. We both have much to atone for and much to forgive. Last night was the start."

Little worried lines appeared between his sharply arched brows. "Will it be enough?"

"I don't know. But I'm willing to find out." She attempted to lighten the mood. "Think of the fun we'll have trying."

He nodded, though his mood was still serious. "Then come back with me to the saloon now. I want to be alone with you in the same room where we started this. I want to say the words you deserve to hear this time, show you with my body the feelings that take my breath away."

She longed to be with him, to chase away the worries that had haunted her morning. "All right. Just let me make sure Katherine will be fine on her own for the day, and get my dress for later."

"Take your time. I'll wait right here."

Chapter Twenty-two

Faith followed behind André as he led the way into his room. White-hot emotion clogged her ability to speak as he nudged her forward, then struck the lock in place. Memories of the night before hammered desire through her belly, creating a throbbing ache between her legs.

She turned to face him, and a slow, sensual smile eased onto his lips. "You look a little shaky."

"I am."

His eyes proclaimed his love as he opened his arms to her. "Come here."

Without hesitation, she wrapped herself in his embrace. As she looked into his eyes, her lips, damp with the moisture her tongue had just trailed across them, trembled. "Kiss me, André."

His smile lowered to her mouth, joining their lips in a sensual mating. Heat curled in her stomach as his tongue met hers. The exquisite torment of his gentle ministering ripped a sigh from her core.

She broke free, her lips seeking the salty taste of his neck. Showering the hard, musk-scented muscles with tiny nips, she gasped out his name again.

He moaned. "What you do to me, O'Malley."

She smiled against his throat before she pulled back to look into his dazed expression. "I think it's what we do to each other that could prove quite a problem."

Cupping her breast, he drew circles around her nipple. "Are you sore from last night?"

She gave him an inviting smile. "Not anymore. Now I just ache." His thumb stroked harder. "Especially when you do that."

He ripped his hand away and knifed shaking fingers through his hair. "And I can't think straight when *you* react like that."

She pulled his hand out of his hair, then one at a time sucked each fingertip into her mouth. "Then don't think."

"I want you to know I—" He broke off the moment she started swirling her tongue along his palm. "Ah, God, that feels good."

She lifted her eyes to his, saw the struggle in his gaze, and stopped her teasing. "Oh, André, you look so serious. Do you really want to talk first?" She reached a finger up to his mouth and beat a sensual rhythm against his lips. "Or can it wait?"

He grasped her shoulders and placed her at arm's length. Her hand fell to her side. "I'm trying to tell you how I feel."

She smiled. "Yes?"

"Dammit. O'Malley, stop looking at me like that."

She stuck her hands on her hips and sighed. "Well, that's a nice snarling declaration. Got any more pretty words, Du Bois?"

He growled.

"You were doing better when you weren't talking," she said.

His smile turned deliciously roguish. "Well, then, to hell with words."

She edged just out of his reach. "Careful, you silver-tongued brute, my heart can't take all this tender affection."

He laughed, reached for her again, but she skipped out of range.

Chasing after her, he missed grasping her three more times. "For God's sake, would you let me catch you?"

She eased close to him, then dodged to her left, sending him tumbling onto the bed. "What would be the fun in that?" she asked, a flirtatious smile toying along her lips.

"O'Malley—"

"You want me, you gotta catch me."

He didn't move. Instead, he sprawled out on the bed and stared up at the ceiling. "God, I love you."

The air hissed out of her lungs in a single whoosh. "What did you just say?"

"I. Love. You." He lifted his head and crooked his finger. "Now come here and I'll say it over and over again."

She edged closer. Leaning toward him, she placed a restraining hand on his chest and smiled. "I love you too. You big brute."

The affectionate, lopsided grin on his face said more than words. He was right, she thought. To hell with words.

"Climb on top and let me show you with my body just how much my heart yearns for you."

Giggling, she vaulted forward. " 'Bout time you asked."

Faith had never felt this free, this full of love before. Knocking once on André's office door, she poked her head through the opening and said, "You wouldn't happen to be looking for me, would you?"

André swiveled in his chair and smiled. "Thought I told you to stay in bed as long as you'd like."

She aimed a sleepy grin at him, one that she made sure promised as much as it held back. "I still have a debt to pay."

"The independent hoyden to the end."

"Always the brute."

His answering smile was just as coy as hers. "That I am."

She floated over to him, wagging her finger as she approached. "You are the most conceited, arrogant man I know."

André rose and pulled her into his arms. Kissing her on the forehead, he said, "Just part of my charm."

"I wish I could think of something insulting to say to you, but I feel too good to work up enough lather at the moment."

"And here I was looking forward to that sharp tongue of yours." He kissed her on the nose. "I'd say let's go back upstairs, but you're too sore and I have a saloon to run."

She scrunched her features into a hopeful expression. "I'm not *that* sore."

He chuckled. "What have I created?"

Her breath hitched as the first stab of doubt splintered her good mood. "Complaining?"

"Not at all. I think you're handling me just fine." His eyes glazed over before he buried his face into her neck and took a deep breath. "Did I ever tell you I love the smell of you?"

"No."

He nibbled her neck. "How about the taste of you?"

She couldn't tell if her voice shook from desire or self-loathing. "Not that either."

He missed the worry in her tone, and kissed her jaw.

"Or that I have a hard time keeping my hands off you?"

"Oh?"

"We do well together, O'Malley." He closed his lips over her gasp. For a long time neither spoke.

Faith pulled away first. "André?"

He rolled his tongue along her neck. "Hmm?"

Just say it, Faith, just say it. "I have to ask you something."

He tugged her ear between his teeth. "Go ahead."

A shiver of desire passed through her, and she almost forgot what she wanted to say. But the feel of his need pressed against her sparked a memory of the exquisite satisfaction his love provided her. Spasms of regret trickled through the pleasure of his kisses. "I . . . André, this is kind of important." He was too busy kissing her neck to respond. She pushed her palms against his chest and pulled her head away from his seeking lips. "Are you listening to me?"

He grinned, and had the brass to look both handsome and boyish doing it. Damn the man. He covered the distance between them, joining his lips with the flesh just above the neckline of her black dress. "Absolutely."

Of its own accord, her breathing quickened. "It doesn't feel like you're listening."

He reached into her dress, clutched her breast, and teased the nipple to a stone-hard peak. "Oh, I'm listening."

No, he wasn't. And she was fast losing her own train of thought. "Do you think I'm like my mother?" she blurted out.

André stilled. Something in her tone alerted him that she was upset, worried. He shook his head, trying to remember what they'd been talking about, but he couldn't. Giving up, he asked, "What did you just say?"

Sniffing, she repeated her question. "Do you think I'm

like my mother?" With each clipped word, her jaw clenched tighter.

Confusion knit his eyebrows together. "I never knew your mother."

"That's not what I meant."

André thread his fingers through his hair. Slowly, understanding dawned. The fear laced behind her question came straight from her childhood as the timekeeper and money collector for her whoring mother.

How could he have been so stupid? Damn his randy soul to hell. He'd been so intent on his own pleasure, he'd completely forgotten about her fears and his pledge to ease her into the physical side of love. He ordered his passion to rest and concentrated on alleviating her worries.

Sensing she'd appreciate blunt candor more than fancy words, he said, "Faith, love, I don't think you're a whore. If that's what you're asking me."

She lowered her lashes, a tremble slicing through her calm. "But we made love. Twice."

He didn't want to lie to her now. "Yes, that's right. And there will be many more times to come."

Her gaze shot up, undisguised panic pouring into her eyes. "You, you don't think I plan to keep having, that is, I don't think I can keep—not that I wouldn't want to—but . . . Oh, Lord, I'm really spoiling this, aren't I?"

André smiled, his heart filling with affection. He took Faith's hands in his, determined to pledge his life to her. "Ah, honey, I know what you're trying to say."

Eyes scrunched closed, she howled, "I won't be your mistress."

"And I won't let you."

"I still plan to work off every dollar I owe you, at the faro tables."

"If that's what you want."

Her eyelids swept open. "You won't expect me to be

your mistress in return for . . . for the money I owe you?"

Such an insulting question, he thought. But he also understood it. "Hell, no, I don't want you to be my mistress. Faith, I want you in my life forever."

She took a shaky breath. "You mean my pedigree, or lack thereof, doesn't matter?"

"Of course not. Let me tell you a little story and then maybe you'll understand." He tucked her into a chair and told her about the Yankee Occupation of Louisiana after the war, the burning of his home because his family refused to pledge loyalty to the Union, the scrimping for food, the poverty.

Her eyes widened with each portion of his tale. When he was finished, she rushed to him, pulling him into her sheltering embrace. "I didn't know. You've always seemed to leak wealth straight out of your fancy, expensive clothes. You're so confident, so . . . *rich*." She shook her head, as though still unable to grasp the fullness of his story. "And all this time you were warring against those kind of memories."

For a moment he rested in the circle of her arms, stroking her hair as she leaned her head against his shoulder. "Make no mistake, Faith. I've worked hard to regain the life that was stolen from me." He let out a snort. "Funny, isn't it? You want nothing of the life you led as a child, and I want all of what I had."

"But money isn't everything, André."

"This? From you?"

She cupped her hands along his face. "Money is important, I won't pretend otherwise. But it's not guaranteed for life. It can be taken from you at any time."

He sniffed. "You sound like Trey."

Her lips spread into a self-deprecating grin. "I like the man better already."

"Understand, O'Malley. I'll never be poor again."

She shook her head. "But you pulled yourself out of

poverty once already. You could do it again." Brushing her fingers along his jaw, she smiled at him. "I'm sure of it."

Stunned speechless, André pulled out of her embrace and sat in his chair. He rubbed his palms against his thighs. Her simple belief in him splintered all his preconceived notions of who he was and what he wanted.

All this time, he'd thought he'd be less of a man if he didn't have wealth and success. But this woman, as she stood calmly staring at him with her unquestionable confidence, gave him a glimpse of something deeper than wealth.

Longer-lasting. Eternal.

A loud knock on the door jolted André out of his thoughts. Hank shoved unceremoniously inside, the sound of chaos and high-pitched shrieking trailing behind him. André rose out of the chair. "What is it, Hank?"

"Mr. Du Bois, you better come quick. We have a problem."

"I'll be right there."

Hank's frantic gaze darted to Faith. "Hurry, sir. This can't wait."

André tossed O'Malley an apologetic smile. "I'm sorry, honey."

She grasped his arm. "I understand. Go take care of your business." Her steady acceptance and the love shining in her eyes made him catch his breath.

"Wait for me?" he said.

"Of course."

Sensing an urgency to tell her one last time, he clutched her against his chest. "I love you, O'Malley."

Her heart pounded against his chest. "I love you too," she whispered.

Holding her tight against him, André couldn't shake a sudden sense of terrible loss, as though he'd never again enjoy this easy, open affection with her after tonight. He rested his lips against her head. "I'll be right back."

As he strode into the saloon, dread pushed against his throat and the heightened level of noise hit him like a physical blow. His saloon had never held such chaos. And all from the ranting of a small, emaciated blond woman throwing anything she could get her hands on.

With her back to him, André couldn't see her face, but her shrieking was impossible to ignore. A part of him recognized the voice; another part refused to accept that recognition.

He shot Hank a swift glance. Even as the man's pinched expression warned André of what he would see once the woman turned around, he denied it to himself.

The slurred words of the small hurricane spoke of too much drink or too much laudanum, or perhaps both. "Where's my husband?" she demanded, picking up a handful of cards and flinging them in her rage. "I know he's here."

Hank circled to the front of the woman. André moved in from behind.

André's gut churned again as she took another threatening step toward Hank. "Well? Where is he?"

Dear Lord, it couldn't be. God just couldn't be that cruel, but André knew only too well that He could.

"I know this is his saloon," she declared, and a little more of André's world came crashing down around him.

She kicked over an empty chair and picked up a full glass of whiskey. Aiming at Hank, she hurled it forward. Hank dodged the glass, but most of the amber liquid splashed him in the face.

Picking up another glass, she screeched louder. "I want to speak to André Du Bois right now."

André had a brief desire to turn tail and run, but he wasn't a man that ran from his mistakes. "I'm right behind you."

She swung around, the glass forgotten as it slipped

through her fingers. "André," she greeted him, the purr in her tone sounding more like a croak. "Always a pleasure."

"I'm sorry I can't say the same."

"Aren't you going to greet me properly?"

When he didn't move, she reached up, yanked his head to hers, and pressed mushy, bourbon-soaked lips to his.

André nearly flung her away from him. Dear God, the impossible had happened. Pearl LaRue had risen from the dead.

Chapter Twenty-three

As André stared at his wife, one thought swept though his mind. The years had been unkind to her. She looked harder, paler, more calculating and desperate. Though she'd changed much since he'd seen her last, one thing had remained the same. Pearl hadn't lost the use of her acid tongue.

"Bastard." She reached up to slap him, lost her footing, and tumbled to the floor. From a tangle of legs and skirts, she glared at him. "You could help me up."

He folded his arms against his chest. "I could, but I won't."

Spitting curses, she scrambled to her feet. "Bastard," she said again. After inspecting him from head to toe, she turned and surveyed the saloon. "Well, well. I see nothing can keep André Du Bois down."

"That's right, nothing." He lowered his tone. "Not even a lying, scheming, cheating whore who I had the bad judgment to marry."

"Still angry, huh?" She lifted a shoulder, as though she didn't really care what he thought, but the simpering that crept into her voice belied her calm. "I just knew you'd hold a grudge."

Angry, and finished with the small talk, he grabbed her by the arm. "Now that the subject's been broached, where's my money?"

She nudged his hand away, then took two steps back. Taking her time, she picked a piece of grime from under one of her fingernails. "Gone."

"Liar." He rushed forward, intent on shaking the truth out of her, but the collective gasps from behind him halted his attack. He gulped down his rage and circled his gaze around the saloon. All activity had stopped. The sudden silence—the stares, the questions—made him realize this was not a conversation for watchful eyes. "Go back to your tables. There's nothing to see here."

When no one budged, he wrapped his fingers around Pearl's arm and lowered his voice. "Come with me. We'll talk in my office."

This time she didn't push his hand away. Instead, she brushed up against him. "Why not in your room?"

He was sickened by her touch, and his stomach rolled. "My office. Now."

The smell of stale whiskey wafted out of her, and his stomach heaved again. He held his breath as she ran her finger along the top button of his vest. "We used to do our best talking in bed."

Revulsion moved through him. Though this woman was his wife, he didn't love her—had never loved her. Not like he loved Faith O'Malley. Dear God, he'd been so stunned and twisted up in his anger, he'd forgotten about O'Malley. He'd been on the verge of asking her to become his wife, to merge her life with his for all time.

But he was already married.

And now he'd turned the woman he loved into the whore she'd vowed never to become.

The depth of his unthinking betrayal weighed heavily on his soul. He looked up and saw O'Malley standing near the edge of the crowd, her eyes round and hurt, bottom lip quivering. In one word, she managed to cast her remaining hope at his feet. "André?"

He wanted to reassure her, tell her that everything would be all right. But he loved her too much to lie to her.

Dear God, how could Pearl LaRue still be alive? And how could he ever make it up to O'Malley? The most he could hope for now was that he didn't destroy her completely. "I'm sorry," he said, willing her to believe him, to see his love.

Her eyes clouded with warring emotions, then went blank. "Who is she?"

Before he could answer, Pearl pushed around him and wove through the crowd. Stopping inches away from Faith, she sneered, "I'm his wife."

Fast on Pearl's heels, André stepped between her and Faith. Too late. The damage had been done. As disbelief and disillusion shimmered in Faith's tears, the reality of what he'd done to her knifed through him.

She locked her gaze with his. "Wife?" The silent plea in her eyes begged him to deny the truth. "You're married?"

She swayed then, her trembling making her stumble into him. He reflexively reached out an arm to steady her.

Pushing away from him, she asked again, "Are you married?"

How could he kill the love in the only woman he'd ever wanted? Because she deserved the truth from him. "Yes. I thought she was dead."

Faith looked from him to Pearl and back again. "She

doesn't look very dead." Faith shuddered, shut her eyes for a long moment, then took a deep breath. When she raised her lids, all emotion had fled from her face. "I have to get to my table."

This was the O'Malley he'd met that first night. Desperate and closed off, hiding behind her bravado.

"Faith, wait."

She kept walking, head high, chin jutting forward. André stifled the urge to beg her to stop, to listen to him. After what he'd just done to her, he owed her this moment of dignity.

Pearl's snicker tore through him like a dirty, jagged blade. "Your little whore doesn't seem too happy to meet me. You forget to tell her about our marriage?"

Barely above a whisper, he snarled his warning down on her. "Don't you ever call Faith O'Malley a whore again."

He must have communicated his threat well, because Pearl closed her mouth and nodded.

"Let's go," he snarled.

Rage threatened to explode in his head as he steered Pearl toward his office. Too many questions filtered down into his confusion and anger to make coherent speech possible. But he would eventually find the words and get his answers.

He shouldered into his office, banging the door shut behind him. He didn't see the need to waste time with pleasantries. "I thought you were dead."

She spun around and glared at him. "As you can see. I'm not."

Her expression turned calculating. Reeking of smoke, unwashed skin, and stale liquor, she sidled up to him. "You've aged well, husband. I'd say you're more handsome than before." She touched his cheek. "It's your eyes. Sinful and devilish, makes a woman want to tame all that wildness in you."

He clutched her roving hand, adding enough pressure to get her attention before releasing it. She stepped away and rubbed her fingers in her palm. "I'd forgotten how big and strong you are." She gave him a look that had once turned his insides into jelly. But that was before he'd learned to recognize the hardness, the hint of cruelty behind the smile. Naïve and fascinated, he'd thought Pearl worldly. Now he saw the cunning.

Her voice lowered to a husky drawl. "I could show you some of the new tricks I've learned."

The whore in her shone like a tarnished nickel in a handful of gold. He saw it now, the cold passion, the way she used sex to get what she wanted.

Pearl moved forward. Reaching to his crotch, she molded her hands around him. "I used to make you ache for me."

He shoved her hand away. "Don't start. We may be married, but I'm not going to do this with you. Never again."

She looked at him for a long moment, her eyes turning dark with hatred. "Always a man of control, right, André?"

He didn't dignify the question with a response.

"Want to know how I did it?" she asked smugly.

He knew she was goading him now, would take her time telling him. But after five years of wondering, he had to know it all. "Yes."

Her eyes filled with artifice, her intent to hurt him obvious. Revealing nothing, he waited, watched.

She sat on his desk, scooted back, then dangled her feet back and forth. "Did you know the Pinkerton found me the very first month you hired him?"

"No."

She swung her feet. "He did."

"Go on. I know there's more."

"I had a lot of money then." She tapped her finger

against her chin and slid a glance at him from the corner of her eye. "It must have been several thousand dollars, if I recall."

"You had two hundred fifty-three thousand and ninety-nine dollars of mine."

She threw her head back and cackled with laughter, the sound a cruel imitation of joy. "I figured you'd know the exact amount. Money always did mean more to you than I did."

"Let's not rewrite history, Pearl. You knew who I was, and what I wanted out of life."

She laughed harder. "Better than you did."

André leaned forward. "What does that mean?"

"Oh, let's just say I knew losing all that lovely money wouldn't mean as much to you as you thought it would."

He'd only just discovered the truth of her words. How could she have seen it in him all the years ago? "You were telling me about the Pinkerton."

"Oh, yes." She surveyed the office. "Got anything to drink around here?"

She hitched her dress high up her thigh, opened the top desk drawer with her foot, and grinned. It was an ugly grin. "I see you still keep a bottle of your finest at the ready. You always were predictable. I think I hated that the most about you."

He could tell her a few things about hatred. "Just finish your story."

"Well, that Pinkerton . . . Oh, what was his name?" She shrugged. "I can't remember. Anyway, he was very official at first. He even went so far as to handcuff me." She grinned. "But he wasn't expecting my kind of persuasion. Or the fun we could have with handcuffs."

André could hardly believe his ears. It was too absurd to contemplate. "You seduced him."

"With my body. And *your* money. We had three lovely months together. When he was called back to Chicago,

I gave him twice the rate you were paying him to help fake my death."

"You bought off a Pinkerton?" It was impossible. Pinkertons were known for their honesty.

"Everybody has a price, darling."

"Not everyone."

"Oh, yes. I bet even that young woman you've dazzled has her price."

André moved fast. Before she could stop him, he wrapped his hands around Pearl's neck. "I told you to leave her out of this."

Pearl didn't even have the good sense to look scared. "Let me go."

"Why should I? You're dead. And not just to me, but to the world. That's the trouble with faking your own death." He tightened his grip. "I could kill you now and no one would know the difference."

She snorted at him. "You never could bluff me. You don't have it in you to hurt a woman."

Two warring desires battled one another in his head. He wanted to be free of Pearl, but not like this. With a snarl, he released her. "Where's the rest of my money?"

"Gone."

"Gone? No one could spend so much money that fast."

"It ran out a year ago."

"And you just came to me?"

She picked at her dirty, ragged fingernails, no longer able to meet his eyes. "I have several really rather enjoyable ways of earning money for myself, remember?"

"How could I forget?" The insult buried in his tone went unnoticed. "You are a woman of varied talents."

"Yes, I know."

André was through with the games. "How did you find me?"

She poured herself another drink. "I have my ways."

"Don't you think you've had enough?"

She glared at him. "I'm just getting started."

André took the glass from her. "You've had enough."

"You can't tell me what to do."

"You'll listen to me. This time, I'm in charge."

She ran her finger down his cheek. "You always liked me in charge. At least in bed."

André stepped out of her reach. "I'm not the young idealist I once was. You saw to that."

"We could always go upstairs and get reacquainted. I'll let you lead for a while."

"Never again."

Silence filled the moment as she measured him from below her lashes. "You mean it."

"Yes."

"Then just give me a little money and I'll be on my way." She hopped off the desk, stumbled, then a fit of coughing bent her over at the waist.

More out of habit than concern, André rushed to her side. "You sick?"

She coughed again, harder and longer. "I'm fine."

In that moment, André realized that old habits died hard. He no longer desired Pearl, but she was still his wife. He couldn't let her suffer alone. "Let's get you cleaned up. We'll talk about money after you've rested."

She smirked up at him. "I knew you'd see things my way."

Chapter Twenty-four

Cracking open the seal of a fresh deck of cards, Faith thanked God dealing faro required her complete concentration. Though she was outwardly calm, her heart ached. Numb with pain, she couldn't even collect enough anger to hate André Du Bois. But how could she deny the truth? He'd made love to her, given her a reason to hope for a future with him, and all along he'd been . . . *married.*

Agony swallowed her composure, making her hands shake, as she wondered if even now he would try to turn her into his whore. She realized he'd nearly done so already, when he'd offered to release her from her debt to him.

Completing her shuffle, she positioned the cards face-up in the dealing box. "Place your bets," she called.

She drew the first card from the box, the one that had no value, and discarded it to her far right to begin the soda pile. She nearly laughed at the irony of what she'd just done. Would Du Bois cast her into the soda pile of his life?

The hair on the back of her neck stood at attention. Turning her head, she caught sight of him escorting his wife out of his office, his hand in a solicitous hold on her elbow. With a gulp, Faith forced down the anguish choking her.

She played the next two cards, declared the winners and losers, then found herself unable to stop herself from wondering if André's reunion with his wife had been filled with vows of love.

The ache in her heart multiplied as she watched him steer his wife toward the stairs. She knew he was taking her to his room, to the very bed where he'd brought such joy and pleasure to Faith.

Oh, how she wished she could summon up at least some hatred, but her heart couldn't do it. The pain was real, and yet the love that Faith and André had created wouldn't let go of her soul.

She willed André to look at her. As though hearing her silent plea, he turned to her. She'd already discovered that she had few defenses against him, so she wasn't surprised when the expression on his face fractured the last of them.

The pure sorrow beating out of him joined with her answering despair. In that moment Faith knew that no matter what happened in the future, a part of her would always live inside André. She'd given him a piece of her soul. And he'd left a part of his with her.

His expression never altered, his silent pledge shouting over the divide between them. But he had a wife, and what Faith had shared with him for a brief two days could never be again. Determined to survive the loss with dignity, she hardened her heart to him.

Cold inside, she unlinked her gaze and dealt several

more rounds. But out of the corner of her eye she watched André lead his wife up the stairs.

For a heartbeat, she considered fighting for him. But she knew she wouldn't. All she had now was her pride. And somehow she would have to find the courage to live the rest of her life with only her self-respect for company.

As André and his wife disappeared into his room, Faith tried not to think about what was happening behind that closed door. When seconds turned into minutes and still the door didn't open, Faith forced her mind away from the couple and back onto her job.

She even managed to make it through several deals without thinking about anything other than faro. She was smack in the middle of concentrating on pulling another card when André drew up next to her table. "We have to talk."

Her body reacted, in spite of her determination to keep this man from affecting her. As his breath skimmed her neck, a delicious shiver ran down her spine.

She tried for calm, but her broken voice betrayed her pain. "I can't. I'm working."

"Rose will take over for you."

Without further argument, the other woman moved into place, scooting Faith out of the way with a none-too-subtle shove of her hip.

Faith glared at the woman, but Rose just smiled at her with sympathy. "Go on, everything will be all right. I know it."

Faith sighed, and faced the man who'd given her such lovely hope in one moment and had shattered her heart in the next.

André couldn't stop himself, he had to touch her, however briefly. He reached out to take Faith's elbow, but the look she shot him quelled his actions. Relenting, he allowed her to walk ahead of him. He wished he knew how to handle this situation, how to make things right between himself and Faith.

She moved inside his office, heading straight to the mantel. The moment he shut the door, she said, "You don't have a photograph of your wife."

He wanted only truth between them. "I thought she was dead."

He raised his hand to reassure her, but she jerked out of his reach as soon as he laid his fingers on her back. "Don't."

He knew she hurt. He could feel her pain as surely as his own. He tried again, resting his hand lightly on the top of her shoulder. "Look at me, Faith."

She shook her head, then dropped her chin to her chest. "I can't." Her words came out in halting syllables. "If I look at you, I'll forgive you."

"Would that be so terrible?"

"You know the answer to that."

"I don't want to keep talking to the back of your head. At least turn around."

She slowly did as he requested, but she kept her gaze firmly locked onto the floor.

André exhaled. "I love you."

Her gaze shot up. "Don't." The anger and the suffering mingling together in her eyes hurt him more than if she'd kicked him in his groin. "Don't lie to me anymore."

"I never lied to you."

"You're married."

"I thought she was dead." He repeated the words as if somehow, if he said them enough, they'd eventually make sense.

"You expect me to believe that?"

He rifled through the top drawer of his desk, searching for the document he'd nearly forgotten he had. Finding it at last, he urged her to take it. "Look at this and tell me what it is."

"I don't see the point—"

"Please, just do it."

Faith tugged her bottom lip between her teeth, then lowered her eyes to the piece of paper. With shaking fingers, she took it from him and read the inscription aloud. "It's a death certificate," she gasped. "For Pearl LaRue Du Bois."

"I was given this three years ago by a Pinkerton I had hired to find my wife."

She handed it back to him, setting her jaw in a stubborn line. "I don't understand."

André raked a hand through his hair. "I hardly understand it myself. Apparently, she paid the man to fake her death."

"That's absurd. Why would anyone do such a thing?"

The magnitude of Pearl's treachery was just starting to sink in. Pearl had stolen from him, lied, and staged her own death, all because she couldn't stand the life he'd offered her. He'd tried to get her straight, when all she'd ever wanted was his money. Trey had warned him that the business he'd chosen would lure the ugliest of hearts. How had he been so blind?

"André?"

"Oh, she had a reason. Actually, she had about two hundred thousand reasons."

"What do you mean?"

"Let me explain."

Faith gave him a forced smile. "Should I sit down for this?"

"I never told you I'd been married because, well, it never came up." She opened her mouth, but he stopped her with a wave of his hand. "I know that's not good enough. The other reason was that I didn't want you to know what a fool I'd been."

Faith angled her head. "You? I can't imagine you doing anything that wasn't well thought out." And as she said the words, she knew them to be true. She took a cleansing breath, realizing he would have never taken her into his heart if he hadn't believed he was free. And if he hadn't planned for their connection to be more than what it could never be now.

André blew out a slow breath. "Faith, you remember I told you I grew up on a plantation outside of New Orleans, a part of the wealthy elite of the South."

She nodded. "I remember. But what does that have to—"

He placed a fingertip to her lips. "Let me finish. We went from wealth to poverty in a matter of years. When my father died of malaria, and my mother shortly after him, I was through being poor."

"Oh, André. You don't have to tell me this."

He scrubbed a hand down his face. "Yes I do. Faith, understand me here, after those years I didn't just want money, I *needed* it. I was obsessed with it. Gambling was the quickest route to reaching my goal. I moved out West, traveling from card game to card game. By the time I was twenty-five, I'd earned enough wealth to never see poverty again."

"But then I went to Cripple Creek and met Pearl LaRue. She was ten years older than me and the most exotic woman I'd ever met." Faith flinched. He laid his hand on her sleeve. "I'm sorry this is hurting you."

"Go on. I want to hear the rest."

"Having grown up in New Orleans I thought I'd seen every kind of woman there was to see. But Pearl was different, exciting. I had to have her."

Faith's heart leaped to her eyes. "You loved her?" she asked.

André smoothed his finger down her cheek. "No, my relationship wasn't about love. At least, looking back now, I realize love had nothing to do with it. At the time I thought I'd die if I didn't win her."

"So you married her?"

"Not at first. She was a dance-hall girl and a prostitute, so I offered to put her up in her own home and take care of her. That way she wouldn't have to see all those other men. I wanted to save her from that life."

"Like the women you hire here?"

He looked embarrassed. It was enough to make Faith want to run to him and smooth away all his pains. But he was no little boy; he was a grown man who'd committed many sins. She had to keep that in mind, or else she'd start to do something foolish, like forget she could be nothing more than his mistress.

"What I didn't count on was that Pearl liked her life as a prostitute. She wouldn't quit, even after I set her up. She did, however, vow to change her mind if I made a more permanent commitment than just offering her a nice cottage."

"So you married her."

"I knew it was a mistake almost from the start. As soon as I was bound to her for life, the excitement disappeared."

A part of Faith died at the implication of his words. "You don't believe in marriage then?"

"Marriage is a holy sacrament. The two married couples I'd known intimately were my mother and father, and Trey and my sister. I wanted what they had, but what I got with Pearl didn't come close."

She suddenly saw André as that young, idealistic man, and her heart bled for all that had been lost because he'd wanted to do the right thing. "But you tried to make it work."

"It didn't take me long to realize that I couldn't change a woman who didn't want changing. But there wasn't much I could do. I was married. And marriage means forever."

"So what did you do?"

"I turned to my only solace. Gambling. I continued making money, working toward more and more wealth, and didn't dare allow myself to think about what Pearl was doing while I was playing cards. Every night I gambled, and won obscene amounts of money in the process."

"Oh, André."

"*No.* I can handle your scorn, your anger, but not your pity. I was young and stupid, but it was my mistake, so I lived with it as best I could."

"So what happened? You mentioned you hired a Pinkerton to find her. Did she run off?"

He sniffed. "Oh, she ran off, all right. With my entire fortune."

"She what? But how could she get away with that?"

"I kept most of my money in one of two places. The bank and my personal safe. Pearl learned the safe's combination by watching my fingers."

Guilt washed through her. "Just like me," she whispered. "You knew." That explained his presence in the alley that night.

"I was prepared for you to watch Hank work the safe."

"You set me up?"

"Yes, I did." Rubbing his stomach, he spread his lips into a pleasant smile. "I just didn't expect you to get loose quite in the way that you did."

Shame overtook her guilt. Groaning, she buried her head in her hands. What had she done? She'd stolen money from André, just like Pearl. She'd cheated him and run off, just like Pearl. And she knew he'd never be able to forgive her.

"Don't, O'Malley. I know what you're thinking. But you aren't like Pearl. You had a good reason to cheat for that money." His eyes softened. "I think deep down, I always knew you weren't the kind of woman who made a living stealing and conning your way through life. Perhaps that's why I let you get away so easily."

Disgrace over his effortless forgiveness clutched around her heart. "And that makes what I did all right?"

"No. But it makes it understandable."

This was the first time they'd ever really talked about that first night. It felt good to clear the air, to get it all out in the open. But nothing was solved.

"So, now you know," he said. "I was as shocked as you to see Pearl standing in my saloon."

"She wasn't exactly standing."

André's lips curled into a snarl. "No. She wasn't. She's a drunk, Faith. And although Pearl's timing wasn't perfect, perhaps it was for the best. You realize I was just about to ask you to marry me?"

She tried to stop it, but a lone tear escaped from her eye.

André drew her into his arms and caught the tear with a kiss. She was too weak with longing for what she couldn't have to push him away. "We might have married not knowing," he said. "Then what would we have done?"

Her heart skipped a beat, fresh agony making it hard to breathe. He leaned down to kiss her again, but she catapulted out of his embrace. "We can't." She didn't have to elaborate.

"Faith, Pearl has changed. She's out of money and she's ill."

Faith nodded. "I know. It's easy enough to tell she's lived a hard life. My mother looked like that just before she died of an overdose of laudanum."

"I have to take care of her. She's my wife. I can't divorce her and leave her to a life of poverty."

And that's why she loved him. "Yes, I know."

"I love *you*, Faith. But I'm married to another woman."

Instead of jealousy, or anger or bitterness, all Faith could feel at the moment was love for André. Perhaps that made her a real dolt, but she couldn't change the truth in her heart. "And because you're married, I can't be anything more than your employee."

"I know." He offered her his hand. When they reached the door, he planted a soft kiss on her forehead. "I'm going to miss you."

Tears welled against her lashes. "We'll see each other every day."

"It won't be the same," he said. For a moment, she thought he was going to ask her to run away with him. And for a moment she considered it. But instead of speaking, he placed his lips against her temple. "After this, I promise I'll never touch you again."

She smiled at him. "You said that once before. And we ended up together in your bed."

"This time is different." His eyes held a pledge in them. "I won't dishonor you. You are a part of my heart and I will never hurt you deliberately again."

And she knew he meant it. Which made it all the harder to live with the knowledge that the man she loved was married to another woman.

Chapter Twenty-five

Determined to survive each day as it came, Faith turned to routine for solace. Unfortunately, thoughts of André, and what they might have had together, never left her mind for long.

It helped to focus most of her energy on getting the older children ready to start the school year. And as the first day of school arrived, Faith spent the morning rushing around, surprised at the amount of effort it took to get fifteen girls and boys fed and out of the house in the morning.

At two minutes past eight, Faith collapsed in a chair and shut her eyes. Pleasantly exhausted, she took a minute to collect herself before facing the rest of the day's chores.

Breathing deeply, she let a smile curl on her lips. As of today, her children were no longer just the sons and daughters of whores, but normal schoolchildren.

She couldn't have hoped for more.

And she couldn't wait to hear about their day, but that would be hours from now. In the meantime, she would fill every moment with activity.

The hardest challenge would come later, when she went to work at the *Dancing Belles*. She would see André, and pretend the tentative friendship they'd forged was enough. But with that lie came more pain, more longing. There were moments when the urge to touch him, to feel his body pressed against hers, overwhelmed her. Too often in the last few weeks, she'd considered throwing away her pride and becoming his mistress.

Katherine's sympathetic voice lilted across her thoughts. "Do you want to talk about it?"

Faith slowly opened her eyes. "What more is there to say?"

"I don't know. But in my experience, talking seems to help. Remember when I came back from Miss Lindsay's Select School for Young Ladies?"

Faith swallowed her anguish in a sigh. "You were so confused. You couldn't get a job, and you didn't know what to do about your future."

"I mostly needed to talk it out. You listened." She wedged a chair close to Faith's. "Let me do the same for you."

Touched, Faith swiped at a tear escaping down her cheek. "Oh, Katherine, I'm trying not to wallow in self-pity. But it seems God is punishing me for all the mistakes I've made."

Katherine shook her head sadly. "Faith, God doesn't punish us for our mistakes. He just allows us to make them."

"And then leaves us to suffer the consequences? Like falling in love with a man I can never have?" She slammed her fists against the chair's arms. Angry as much at herself as God, she filled her words with disgust. "Why did I have to go to the Dancing Belles that night? There were so many other saloons I could have chosen. Then I would have never met André Du Bois."

She paused as what she'd just said sank in. Not meet him? *No.* She couldn't have gone through the rest of her life never knowing the beauty of loving the man, the pleasure of his touch, and his kiss. Sighing again, she continued. "Maybe if I hadn't taken out that last loan, I wouldn't have needed the money, and then I wouldn't have needed to cheat."

"I suppose you could look at it that way. But I like to think we find out who we are when we make our choices and then live with them."

Self-pity fought against the truth. "It just seems I've been given a much harder road than others."

Katherine's expression shifted into sympathy. "You're very strong, Faith. So I'll speak bluntly. You're where you are now because of choices you've made. Pure and simple."

Faith didn't deny it. "What other choices could I have made?"

Katherine stitched an age-old wisdom into her words. "Only you can answer that."

Faith thought hard about what else she could have done. She could have tried another bank. She could have bought a smaller house. In reality, she could have made hundreds of other decisions.

But she hadn't. And in the end, every choice she'd made had led her to André Du Bois and the anguish she suffered now. Even knowing this, she couldn't regret meeting him.

She was saved from further thought when Michael burst into the house, tears streaming down his face.

Her own worries forgotten, Faith jumped from her chair and fell to her knees in front of the boy. "Michael, what's the matter?"

"We—" He choked over a hiccup. "We were sent away."

"Sent away?"

Entering the house a few steps behind him, Johnny explained. "From school."

One by one, the rest of the children scurried through the front door.

Keeping a hand on Michael's shoulder, Faith drew to her full height. She surveyed the downtrodden faces, and her heart sank. Only a few had tears falling, while the others were red-cheeked with anger. But what concerned her most were the various hues of shame in each of their gazes.

Faith couldn't make words come out of her mouth. Thankfully, Katherine spoke for her. "Tell us what happened."

"They laughed at us, called us bastards, and said we were children of whores." Michael sniffed. "Faith, what's a whore?"

Faith instantly found her voice. "Oh, Michael." She ruffled his hair. "I'll explain later." She turned to Johnny. "The other kids laughed at you?"

"Yeah, and the teacher told us we had to go home."

Maggie added, "She said we could never come back again."

A sick feeling tumbled in Faith's chest. Her gaze linked with Katherine's.

Johnny continued. "She said the good folks of Denver wouldn't tolerate us mingling with their children."

Katherine sighed and shook her head. "No."

Faith raised her eyes to the ceiling, praying for a miracle, or at the very least, wisdom to know what to do.

Maggie pulled on Faith's sleeve, voicing the question that they all had. "What are we going to do now?"

Think, Faith ordered herself. Magically, an idea formed on its own. As seconds ticked through the silence, more of the details unfolded in her mind, and she felt a surge of excitement. If she and Katherine could pull it off . . .

"Hey, we made some cookies." She pointed to the kitchen. "Johnny, take everyone to the kitchen."

He stared at her as though she'd turned into a fish trying to swim up the middle of downtown Denver. "Cookies? Now? But what are we going to do about school?"

Faith gave him her most confident grin. "You leave that to me. I'll take care of everything." She ignored Katherine's frown, and beamed harder at the children. "I have an idea."

Katherine sighed. Faith spun on her heel. "Well, I do."

Katherine appeared resigned. "I know."

"It's a good one too."

Katherine shook her head. "It always is."

Faith started ushering the kids toward the kitchen. "Go on. I'll be there in just a minute to tell you what I have planned."

Michael pulled on Faith's skirt, worry wiping away his usual youthful enthusiasm. "We won't have to go back to that awful school again, will we?"

"Never again. I promise."

"Faith," Katherine warned, "let's not get hasty here. We were just talking about this very thing. You aren't thinking of making another decision that we'll regret later."

Faith nudged Michael out the door. "Of course not," she said, casting a smile over her shoulder. "I have a wonderful plan in mind. Really."

A shudder passed through Katherine. "I'm afraid to ask."

"Oh, pooh. You don't even know what I'm going to say." Faith poked a finger in the air. "So calm your worries right now."

Once the last of the children had filed into the kitchen, Katherine asked, "Well?"

"You'll teach them."

Gasping, Katherine covered her heart with a shaky hand. "Me? Have you gone mad?"

"Of course not. It's the perfect solution. The *right* solution."

"I don't . . . I never . . . No." She shook her head violently. "I can't."

"Oh, Katherine. You taught me. You can teach them."

Scowling, Katherine glared at her. "You're not thinking clearly, that's it."

"Of course I'm thinking clearly."

"Oh, really? What about desks? And blackboards? And books?"

"Those are small problems. But we'll work them out. We always do." Anticipation swelled, making Faith dizzy with all the possibilities. "We'd eventually need to purchase a building, though. That's a definite concern. The sooner the better."

"Faith, you're getting drunk on your own excitement." Katherine grasped her by the shoulders and shook. "Sober up. There are more than minor problems involved with starting a school."

Faith glared at Katherine's hands gripping her. The younger woman immediately released her hold.

"You still owe Mr. Du Bois over a thousand," Katherine said. "Where are you going to get the extra money to buy the supplies, the books, much less a building?"

Faith waved off her argument. "Details."

"Might I remind you this is the kind of thinking that got you into trouble *all* the other times."

Faith shut her mind to the argument. "This time is different."

"It's never different."

Eyes narrowed, Faith tilted her head to look Katherine

straight in the face. "Don't you want to teach the children?"

Katherine took a contemplative pause. "Well, yes. Yes, I do."

"Then leave the details to me."

One of the smaller children started crying. Katherine looked toward the second floor. "Sounds like Anne."

"You go take care of her. I'll let the children know what we're planning."

Katherine hesitated, her eyes concerned. "Don't you think it's a bit too soon to tell them? After all, nothing's really settled."

The answer was simple enough to Faith. "Didn't you see how upset they were?"

"I'm afraid you haven't learned one thing." Katherine started out of the room, then turned back around. "Perhaps you should discuss this with someone else. Why don't you go talk to Mr. Du Bois."

For a moment, Faith considered it. He'd told her once that she wasn't alone anymore and that he wanted to help her and the children. But that was before his wife had returned. "He has too much to worry about on his own."

"Yes, but he loves you and the kids. He's been here several afternoons. And he's really wonderful with them. He'll want to help. You should give him the chance."

"No. I have to do this alone." Like always. "And the first thing I'm going to do is go down to the school and tell that teacher just what I think of her. How dare she say such things to my children? Doesn't she know the damage she's done?"

Katherine raised her eyes to the heavens. "Faith, I can't help but think it would be a mistake to go over there right now. You should calm down first."

Faith slapped her palms against her thighs. "I can't calm down."

"You'll only make matters worse."

"Nothing could be worse."

Chapter Twenty-six

Faith marched along Market Street, even more angry now that she knew the full truth. The schoolteacher hadn't wanted to send the children away; she'd only been carrying out Prescott's orders. And since the shifty banker owned the school's building and paid the bulk of the teacher's salary, the woman hadn't had much choice in the matter.

Well, he wouldn't get away with it.

Before she lost hold of the anger propelling her forward, Faith smoothed her palms down her skirt, then dashed inside the bank. No matter what happened, she wouldn't leave until Prescott had made restitution for this unforgivable offense.

Her steps slowed as it occurred to her that she was about to take another gamble, bigger and more significant than any before. She couldn't help but wonder how many times she could keep pulling these stunts and win.

As often as needed.

The children, she reminded herself. *Think of the orphans*. In the past that refrain had been enough to bolster her courage. But not today. Perhaps because today she knew what she was going to do was wrong, and no amount of rationalization would spin it differently.

But what choice did she have really? The children needed a school, and she needed money for that school.

She gave the clerk her name and waited. Like all the other times she'd come to this bank, Prescott didn't keep her waiting long. She might have thought that odd, if she didn't have so much else on her mind.

"Miss O'Malley, what a surprise." The lie slid smoothly from smirking lips.

Trying to hide her dislike, she pasted on a smile and allowed him to lead the way to his office. As she watched him walk with his chest jutting, Faith was reminded of that crazy rooster in the Montana mining camp that used to swagger around the streets, crowing all day long. A train had hit the stupid bird. She wondered if there would be a train passing through the bank anytime soon.

Once inside the office, Prescott wasted no time getting to the point. Without offering her a seat, he asked, "What can I do for you?"

Squaring her shoulders, she held his gaze. "You know what."

His expression drew into a blank. "I'm sorry, but I don't."

"Let's not continue the pretense, Prescott. You had my children banished from the local school."

"Come to beg for their readmittance?"

"No."

"Ah." He scratched his beard. "Then you must be here to talk about money."

She stared at him, her hand itching to slap that smug grin off his face. She wished she could just walk away, but she needed his cooperation. "I want to start a school for the orphanage."

His smile warned her to be careful. In all their other dealings, Prescott had proven himself much more wily and devious than her. "You want a school of your own? Now isn't that interesting."

She bit hard on her lower lip. "You've given me no other choice."

"And now you want another loan."

She swallowed the last of her pride. "Yes."

Circling around his desk, he plopped into his chair. "I still haven't found out where all that money came from for the last loan."

"I told you, I had a benefactor."

Prescott's chair creaked as he leaned back. "A certain saloon owner perhaps?"

"Who told you that?"

He lifted a shoulder. "People talk."

"People gossip."

"Call it what you will. But from what I hear, you're his mistress."

Outrage had her gasping. "That's a lie."

Flattening his hands on the desk, he leaned forward. "Tell that to his wife."

In one sentence, he'd made her relationship with André sound ugly. And perhaps it was. Hadn't she made love to a married man? Sins didn't get any blacker than that. Shame braided through her memories, darkening what once had been a beautiful act of intimacy into a hideous deed of adultery. "I refuse to discuss André Du Bois with you."

"I have to wonder why you don't ask him for more money."

Because of people like Prescott and their dirty accusations. How could she accept money from André knowing what it would mean? "I want to leave him out of this."

"So how much money would you need for this school?"

Here was her one chance to get what she wanted. "I understand that Mr. and Mrs. Anderson are considering selling their home. I want to purchase the house."

"Thinking big again?"

"It's next door to the orphanage."

"You know, Miss O'Malley, you can't keep calling that place you run an orphanage. Very few of those bastards are truly orphans."

Faith bristled. She could accept the slurs about herself, but she would not listen to any more about the children. "We were discussing a loan."

His eyes gleamed. "You're asking for a substantial amount of money. The Anderson home is a mansion."

"I know how big it is."

"What terms of repayment would you consider."

"Ten years."

He leapt out of his chair and came around the desk. "Good-bye, Miss O'Malley."

"Wait, you have to—"

He took her elbow and turned her toward the door. "I said good-bye."

She wrenched her arm free. Desperate, she blurted out another set of terms. "Five years."

He peered into her gaze. "You think you could pay back nearly six thousand dollars in just five years?"

"I've repaid all my other loans." Taking the offensive, she edged toward him and smiled sweetly. "That makes me a good risk."

"Suppose I consider this business venture. What's in it for me?"

"Well, for one, the bastards stay out of your neighborhood and your school. And . . ."

"And?"

Time to play her trump card. "Your wife never hears about Michael."

His eyes hardened. Then he threw his head back and laughed. "You're getting smarter, Miss O'Malley. Even devious. Have to say I'm a bit impressed."

She lifted a single eyebrow. "I've learned from the lowest."

He had the brass to chuckle again. "All right. I'll take those terms." Holding up his hand, he waggled his fingers. "Five years. I'll write up the papers this afternoon. You can come tomorrow for the money."

That was it? He'd given up too easily, making her suspect she'd just walked into a trap. "So that we're clear on this, I want a clause stating you can't call in the loan early, except for lack of timely payment."

A hint of genuine respect flashed in his eyes. "You really are learning, Miss O'Malley." He reached to touch her cheek, but she jerked back a step and his hand dropped to his side. "Although, if you'd truly learned your lesson, you wouldn't be here now."

She refused to consider the truth in what he said. Of all things, she couldn't bear that Prescott might be right. Without another word, she spun toward the door. "Until tomorrow then."

Chapter Twenty-seven

Later that evening, André worked on his accounts as he waited for Faith to finish her last deal. Though they didn't last long, he always looked forward to their evening conversations. Sensing her presence from the fresh lilac fragrance filling his breath, he looked up from his paperwork. Standing in the doorway, she looked fragile and beautiful, and he suddenly wanted to beg her to run away with him and forget all that stood between them.

"Hello, O'Malley," he said, hating that he couldn't tell her how precious she was to him. But if he did such a foolish thing, he'd be professing his love to her in the next breath, and then he'd no longer be able to survive apart from her.

But survive he would. For the sake of a vow he'd made five years ago.

Her eyes softened with understanding. "Hello, Du Bois."

Her head turned. Her gaze connected with the cot

where he'd slept since Pearl had moved into his rooms. A silence forged between them.

"I find it to be a very livable arrangement," he said.

Her smile deepened. "Doesn't seem very comfortable."

"You worried about me, O'Malley?"

"Certainly not." But her eyes told him that she was very worried, and his heart soared.

"Here I was starting to get all warm and tingly inside, imagining you taking care of me."

Her smile dropped, and the look of longing in her eyes cut him at the core. He liked the idea that she wanted to take care of him, and he hated that she could never do it. He looked at her for a long while, wishing he could reach out and smooth his finger down her cheek, touch her hair. But that would lead to more touching and . . .

He broke off his own thoughts, knowing only his eyes could caress her now. Drinking in all of her lovely features, he noticed the lines of fatigue around her mouth.

"I'm through for the evening," she said.

"Sit down and talk to me while I finish adding this last column, then I'll walk you home." He studied her. She seemed preoccupied, as though mulling something over. "You look tired."

She sank back into the chair and sighed. "Long day."

There it was again, that flicker of . . . something. "Can I get you anything to drink?"

"No, I'm fine." Her bright smile was more forced than usual. "So how was your day?"

"The same as always."

She nodded, and he suddenly wanted to lash out at the unfairness of the situation. These simple little pleasantries between them were killing him. Why couldn't he just ask her what was wrong? And why couldn't she just tell him without his asking? They'd taken politeness beyond the absurd, never trespassing into areas that might push them toward deeper intimacy.

They were living a lie. And his patience was running out. As he waited for Faith to open up to him, he thought of the woman who stood between them.

Pearl. Her addictions were worse than he'd first thought. In the last month, he couldn't remember a moment when Pearl had been sober. He clenched his hands into tight, white-knuckled fists.

He was damn tired of the pretense. All he wanted was to be with Faith.

Exhaling, he linked his hands behind his back, willing them to behave before he pulled her into his arms and buried his problems inside her love. But he could see she had her own worries. And since she wasn't going to speak about them, he would. "You look upset. Something happen?"

Her expression shut him out. "No." Now he knew she was holding something back. Was it Pearl? Had his wife stuck to their agreement? He'd promised her full use of his funds, as long as she stayed away from Faith.

He broke his first and only rule—never touch Faith—and bent down to take her hands in his. "Tell me what's happened."

She stared at him, her eyes haunted.

"Is it Pearl?" he asked.

The sadness in her gaze deepened as she shook her head. "No. It's . . . Oh, André." The dam broke and she tossed herself into his arms. "I don't know what to do."

He couldn't help but revel in the feel of her warmth pressed against his chest. Her scent pushed dizzying waves of desire crashing through his restraint. She felt so damn good that he lost the threads of what they'd been talking about.

Promising himself this one small indiscretion, he kissed the top of her head. His whole body shook from the self-control it took to keep from ravaging her right here on the spot.

"What's happened?" he asked again.

He gently wiped the tears from her cheeks, wishing he could wipe away her problem as easily.

"It's the children," she said. "They were banned from the school today." She clutched his waist. "I went straight down to that school to tell that teacher just what I thought of her banning innocent children."

"You think that was a good idea?"

"Maybe not. But I was too angry at the time to think straight." She shoved out of his embrace and started pacing off her anger. "How dare she, I thought." She threw up her hands in the air, spun in a circle, and took big, angry strides. "What gave her the right to judge my kids?"

André reached out and grasped her arm. "Slow down, honey. You're making me dizzy."

She pushed away from him and started pacing again. "I can't believe it. I then found out it wasn't even her fault, and I'm still getting mad."

"I see that."

"Did I tell you Prescott was behind it?"

"You saw him at the school?"

She didn't answer him directly. "Turns out he was behind the whole thing. And he said . . . he said . . ." As her words trailed off, she came to a halt, then threw herself back into his arms. "It was awful."

As he tried to soothe Faith's anger, André knew this was more than a fight about the school refusing the children. This was Faith's fight against all she'd ever endured as the daughter of a prostitute.

For the first time he glimpsed what Faith's life had been like, and what she must have braved as a child. Here he'd moaned and railed against his years of poverty, but his family had always been respected. Hell, they'd worn their poverty as a badge of honor against the Yankees.

He tightened his arms around her and stroked her hair, trying to work her pain out of her and into him. How had he not seen it? Faith had been an outcast, a person treated lower than an animal. And now the children of Heart House suffered the same stigma of an unfortunate birth.

"I can help you find another school."

She shook her head. "I can't ask the children to go through that again." And he knew *she* couldn't go through it again either.

"Tell me what can I do? Anything, and I'll do it."

Faith clenched her fingers into the fabric of his shirt. This was her one chance to ask for his help. She needed money, he had money. She opened her mouth to ask him for a loan, but couldn't find the words.

He stroked her hair, and she relaxed her head on his shoulder. How could she accept money from him, and turn their love into the ugly sin Prescott had intimated? Worse, she feared taking money from André would be the first step toward becoming his mistress.

"I don't know what I'm going to do yet." It was partially the truth. "I need to do some more thinking."

He pulled away and stared hard at her, scrutinizing every feature on her face. It took all her courage not to squirm under his searching gaze. "You aren't planning to do anything drastic, are you, Faith?"

She shifted what she hoped was a vacant stare to the top of his right eyebrow. "Of course not."

Undaunted, he continued his inspection. "Promise me something."

She slid her gaze to the top of his left eyebrow. "All right."

A knock came at his door, but he ignored it. "Promise you'll come to me before you make any firm decisions."

She looked at the door, then back to his forehead. "I—"

He grasped her shoulders. "Promise me."

"I . . ." The knock came again, shattering her concentration. "Don't you think you better answer that?"

"Not until I get your promise."

A slurred, high-pitched voice spoke over her whispered response. "André, are you in there?"

Pearl. Faith jumped out of André's embrace, shame and guilt grinding through every plane in her body.

"Don't, Faith. We haven't done anything wrong."

"Haven't we? We've thought it."

"We haven't acted on it."

The incessant banging got louder. "I need more money." Pearl's voice grew louder. "I know you're in there, so open the door."

Faith gasped. Pearl wanted his money, demanded he give it to her whenever she wanted it. Was she herself any different than his wife? How could she have been foolish enough to think she could take money from André now? He was a married man, with a commitment to his wife first. And always.

Unable to bear another moment, Faith shoved out of his embrace, wrenched open the door, and rushed out, nearly slamming into Pearl. Ignoring the look of outrage on the other woman's face, Faith rushed out of the saloon.

Several moments later, footsteps pounded after her. She should have known André wouldn't let her walk home alone. She just hoped, for both their sakes, he'd sent Hank.

Chapter Twenty-eight

The next evening brought its own form of tortures for André. Sitting in a chair facing the bed, he dragged a wet cloth across Pearl's feverish forehead, wondering why she did this to herself. This was the second time in so many days that she'd taken too much laudanum.

When he'd first realized she had a problem, he'd tried to talk to her about it. But he'd only received oaths and curses in response, so he'd begun throwing out the bottles as fast as she could buy them.

She always managed to find more.

Pearl awakened with a cough, her eyes peeling slowly open. In a shaky voice, she said, "Water."

André moved out of the chair, cradled her head, and eased a glass to her lips. He could no longer see the woman he'd married in the eyes of this pale, rail-thin stranger. She looked more ghost than person, her dull sallow skin carrying a permanent stench of grime and illness. Her once-vibrant eyes had sunken into their sockets, small and unremarkable now.

André swallowed hard. God, it hurt to look at her. As she coughed down the liquid, he calculated how much longer she could do this to herself. A day, a week, a year?

"I need more laudanum. There's some in my red dress."

He'd not thought to look there. Where else was she hiding the elixir? "Pearl, I beg you to stop this madness."

She collapsed against the pillow. Pain swam in her eyes as her unfocused gaze hastened around the room. "Not now, André."

Despite her hostility and the pounding headache behind his eyes, André refused to let the matter drop. "Yes, now. This is the perfect time. Look at what you're doing to yourself."

Her lip curled. "Such a saint you are."

He thought of Faith then, how much he loved her and how much he'd hurt her. "I'm no saint."

Pearl snorted. "Just give me the medicine. I'll feel better after a little taste."

"A temporary cure at best. Let me help you, Pearl." It seemed he'd used those same words a lot lately. Why did the two women he wanted to help most deny him?

"You just keep giving me money," Pearl said, her voice thick with the coarseness of dehydration.

His response was immediate. "Money can't solve everything." And suddenly he knew it to be his truth. Ever since he'd been a boy, he'd thought money was the cure for all ills. Now he knew, as he stared at his ailing wife, that money could only buy *things*.

Nothing more.

He couldn't pinpoint when it had happened, but in the last few weeks, André had grown to hate his wealth. He felt trapped in his chosen life, no longer free to experience pleasure from the luxury he once found comforting. He'd sell the damn saloon, but he had Rose and all the other girls to consider. If he gave up the Dancing Belles now, what would happen to them?

It was a thought he'd hold off until later, when he was alone and able to think more clearly.

Pearl curled her legs up against her chest and rolled onto her side. "Give me the medicine," she howled. The sound reminded him of a wounded animal caught in a trap.

He ignored her pain and made another attempt to convince her. "No. In good conscience—"

She found enough strength to pick up one of the glasses off the bedside table and throw it at him. "To hell with your conscience," she said.

"Pearl." He dodged another glass. "The *medicine* is what's hurting you."

"It helps ease my pain."

"It's killing you."

She bared her teeth. "So that's it. You want me dead so you can marry your little mistress. Well, I don't think I'll oblige you tonight." She sucked in her breath and tossed her head against the pillow. "No. I plan to live for a very long time."

André blew out a hiss, a very real sense of loss clutching against his heart. Such a waste. "I don't want you dead, Pearl." And he meant it. As much as he loved Faith and wanted her in his life, he could never wish his wife dead.

And although he harbored much anger toward Pearl, he still wanted to see her return to the vivacious woman that he'd met five years ago. "I want you to get healthy, get your life straight. It's not too late."

A haunted expression crossed her face. He'd never seen her look so vulnerable, so scared—like a lost, lonely child. "I want that too," she admitted in a small voice.

He nodded. "I'll get the doctor."

Terror stole into her gaze. "I don't want a doctor. He'll butcher me, sure as I lie here."

"Not this doctor."

"*No*. Please, no."

André didn't understand her fears, but he wasn't in the proper state of mind to draw the source of them out of her. "He's young and handsome."

She gave a snort of laughter. "Do you think I care about that right now?"

André didn't feel the need to answer that question, when they both knew the truth. "I'll be back shortly."

He opened the armoire and searched the pockets of Pearl's red dress. The new dress *his* money had purchased. Strange how his perspective had changed in a matter of weeks. Money was just money. Dear God, he'd nearly turned the damn stuff into his god. Shaking his head, he wrapped his fingers around cold glass. Clutching tightly, André tucked the bottle into his palm.

"That's mine," Pearl screeched.

He looked back at her. "It's mine now."

She tried to push to a sitting position, but the effort appeared to be too much for her and she fell back on the bed. "You can't do this," she whispered.

"I am doing it."

"Bastard. Don't you dare take that away from me."

André turned his back to her. "I'll return with the doctor shortly."

He clicked the door shut behind him, praying he hadn't left her alone with trouble. He'd found three other bottles earlier. He hoped there weren't any more. For Pearl's sake.

Chapter Twenty-nine

André paced outside his room as the doctor examined Pearl in privacy. Every so often, he glanced over the balcony to survey the activity of the saloon, already in full swing for the evening.

He tried his best not to watch the busy faro tables, but his gaze continually wandered to Faith. She'd refused to talk to him since Pearl had barged into his office demanding money the night before. He supposed she had the right, but there was so much that still needed to be said between them.

As he looked at her now, sorrow twisted in his gut. Although he had every possible material thing a man could want in the world, he didn't have the one thing he wanted most. For years he'd sought security. And he'd thought he could find it through the accumulation of wealth. He knew better now.

He'd been such a fool. The night Faith O'Malley had walked into his saloon, he'd thought God had been punishing him for his past mistakes. But God had given him a second chance.

A chance for redemption.

Too late, André knew exactly what he wanted. And who.

Without Faith, his soul was empty.

The door swung open, slamming André back to reality and Pearl's dire situation. Dr. Shane Bartlett stepped out, worn and haggard beyond his years. His dark, rumpled hair looked as though he'd run his fingers through it too many times to count. Whatever the doctor had to say, André knew it wouldn't be good.

"How is she?" he asked.

The previously alert eyes of just an hour before were now rimmed with fatigue. "Resting."

André exhaled. "Give it to me straight. Is she dying?"

"I can't give you a definitive answer." Bartlett shook his head, a line of confusion snapping in his gaze. "For all the scientific breakthroughs of this century, the workings of the human body are still a great mystery to us. Its self-healing is miraculous at times."

"Are you saying Pearl is going to be all right?" The relief was staggering.

"For now."

"But not for good?"

"She could live to grow a full head of gray hair. *If* you can convince her to sober up and . . ." He broke off, his eyes darting around. "I don't know quite how to say this, it's a delicate situation."

At this point, nothing Bartlett said would shock André. "You may be candid with me, Doctor."

"She must stay away from the liquor, the laudanum, and the . . . men."

André could see that the doctor was clearly embarrassed by the situation, but he'd long since stopped worrying about propriety. "I understand. And if she doesn't?"

A shaking hand threaded through the shaggy hair, the worry deepening in his eyes. "Hard to tell. She could continue this kind of life for an indefinite amount of time, though I doubt it very seriously."

"Indefinitely? How could anyone sustain that sort of life for any length of time?"

"Look, Mr. Du Bois. I honestly can't predict what will happen to your wife. I don't know her history, and she wasn't very forthright with it when I asked. The truth of the matter is, she could last a month, a year, maybe ten."

"Ten years? Even with the drinking?"

"Sadly, it's not unheard of."

André repeated the doctor's words aloud, more to anchor his spinning thoughts than for any other reason. "Ten years of drunkenness." He couldn't bear to watch Pearl destroy herself for that long.

Dr. Bartlett touched his shoulder, regaining his attention. "That is if she doesn't take an overdose. You must do everything you can to get her sober. Permanently."

André suddenly felt as though the world had just set itself atop his shoulders. "I've tried."

The other man's voice turned surprisingly forceful. "Then keep trying."

"What do you suggest I do, short of locking her in my room?"

"You could speak to the apothecary, make it clear he's not to sell her any more laudanum."

"I've done that, she just gets someone else to buy it for her."

"Don't give her any money."

André's gut coiled in helpless defeat. "She has ways to earn it herself."

The doctor shuddered. "Could you have someone follow her?"

"That didn't work either." André blew out a hiss of

frustration, so far he'd tried everything the doctor suggested. "Anything else?"

"There is one more thing you could try."

At this point André was willing to try anything. "What's that?"

"Pray."

Tonight, even the intricacies involved in dealing faro weren't enough to distract Faith. She mechanically pulled cards out of the dealing box. Unfortunately, her concentration kept wandering upward, her gaze moving to the balcony railing as André conversed with the doctor in the hallway.

She wished she knew what had happened. Her own worries had vanished the moment she'd seen André escorting Dr. Bartlett up the stairs an hour earlier. Retrieving the doctor could mean only one thing—Pearl was in real trouble this time.

Faith had watched Pearl slowly destroying herself over the past weeks. The thought of the woman's unhappiness sparked memories of the last days of Faith's own mother's life.

Before Pearl, Faith had thought her mother had been happy in her chosen profession, or at least resigned. Faith had just assumed the liquor and laudanum another part of the life required for lying with strange men.

But as Faith had witnessed Pearl's mindless self-destruction, she realized that perhaps her mother had been just enduring, drinking to quiet her shame.

As she watched André walk the doctor outside, Faith's heart constricted. Could she finally be on the road to forgiving her mother? Was it time?

André stopped for a brief moment at her table before heading to his office. Although he didn't owe her an explanation, he gave her a brief sketch of Pearl's condition, ending with a vow. "I have to try to get her sober."

"I know." Offering her support, she covered his hand with her own. It was only a brief contact, but the sparks that traveled out of him and into her shattered her composure. Tears edged to the tips of her lashes. Blinking, she looked into the haunted eyes of the man she loved, and her heart ached. "I wish there was something I could do to help."

"You can come see me before you go home tonight."

If he asked her to, Faith would have walked off the edge of the earth. "Not now?"

His expression closed. "No. I need to be alone a while to think."

Faith tried to understand, but the spasm of remorse that he didn't want her with him right now was hard to ignore. "Of course."

She worked the rest of the evening with half her mind linked to André's situation and Pearl, while the other half filled with worries over the loan agreement she'd signed in Prescott's office that morning.

She'd been so upset last night she'd made a hasty decision. And before she allowed second thoughts to water down her resolve, she'd rushed to the bank first thing this morning and signed the loan papers.

Now the second thoughts were coming, twice as severe. André had asked her to consult with him before she made any decisions. But with his problems with Pearl, she hadn't been able to find the courage to do it.

Oh, who was she kidding?

She hadn't gone to him because of her silly pride. She'd told herself she hadn't wanted to ask for money because it might sully the intimacy that they'd share. But if she were honest, she'd admit that she hadn't asked because she wanted to handle her problems on her own. Like always. And maybe protect herself from further hurt?

At the end of the night, she gathered the house's winnings at her table. She organized the money, then handed it to Hank on her way to André's office. Later, after she'd gone home, she knew, Hank and André would count the money. The next evening, André would show her the book with the tally of her daily take.

Her earnings were staggering at times. She supposed it was because she was personable and fair and always had a full table. At this rate, her debt would be paid before the first snowfall. And then she would never have to see André again.

The thought depressed her.

Squelching her worries, she knocked on the closed office door. Seconds ticked by before Faith heard a muffled "Enter."

Stepping only partly into the room, she asked, "You wanted to see me?"

He rose from his paperwork. "I did."

It surprised her that his smile was a little shaky, a little unsure of itself. "How's Larkin settling in with the children?" he asked.

She tilted her head, searching his face. "Getting a lot of attention. And loving every minute of it. He's become very talkative these days."

"I'm glad."

"You should come see him for yourself."

He nodded. A look of pleasure flitted in his gaze, but retreated just as quickly. "I think that could be arranged."

"Good."

Silence fell between them. Faith fiddled with the doorknob, then made a firm decision to say what was on her mind. She shut the door and gathering her courage, turned back to face him. "Thank you for what you did for Sally."

He waved his hand toward her. "It was nothing."

"Nothing? You set her up in that sanitarium in Arizona, away from temptation here. You probably saved her life."

He shrugged. "Anyone would have done the same."

Gratitude sent tears wiggling around in her eyes. "Claim what you will, but I know better. You saw a woman in trouble and you helped her."

"She was your friend. I know you worried about her."

His concern for her and her friends humbled her. She wanted to express her appreciation, explain her true feelings but the words clogged in her throat. She started pacing, using the activity to help her think more clearly.

"I know we see each other every day," she began. "But it's like we don't." She stomped her foot and scowled. "No, that's not what I mean." Twirling in a circle, she sighed.

"You're getting me dizzy again."

She ignored him, ran a finger along the mantel, then blurted out, "I miss you. No, that's not what I mean either."

"You seem to know a lot about what you don't mean."

"I'm trying to thank you, André, and to tell you I—" She spun to her left, then shimmied two steps to her right. "Oh, I can't explain it."

Out of the corner of her eye, she caught his lips twitching. "Just spit it out, O'Malley."

She stopped and stared at him. "That's it."

He folded his arms in front of him and shot her a sarcastic look. "Oh?"

She pointed to his chest. "That's it too. That's what I mean."

"Now that you got it all figured out, you want to enlighten me?"

She laughed. "Oh, André, don't you see? It's the way you scowl and throw out barbs and call me O'*Malley* with all that affection."

"Affection? I was mocking you."

He looked affronted, even a bit peevish. And, oh, it

was lovely. "Of course not. At least, not when your eyes twinkle at me like that."

He cocked his head. "You going mad? Is that it?"

"Since you're being intentionally obtuse, I see I'll have to explain."

"By all means."

She aimed a frown at him, but her heart danced with joy. "I can't stand all the refinement and courtesy we've had between us." She sighed. "I liked it better when we fought, before you decided you *liked* me. Strange as it sounds, I felt closer to you then. I actually liked it when you—"

Before she could finish, he caught her against his chest. Her heart pounded in tandem with his as he buried his face in her hair. Tears pricked against her eyelids as he kissed her ear, her eyelids, her neck, and finally her lips. When he broke away from her, he said, "I've miss you too . . . *O'Malley*."

André allowed his lips to curve into a smile, kissed her again, then reluctantly pushed her firmly out of his reach. If he touched his lips to hers one more time, he wouldn't be able to stop. *Ever*. "You realize we have to go back to the formality, Faith. It's the only way."

He shoulders slumped. "I know. I guess I should probably go." She gave him a sad look. "And you better send Hank to accompany me home tonight."

André pulled out a chair and tapped the seat cushion. "Tell me about your day first."

She shrugged, breaking eye contact in an uncharacteristic show of timidity. *Here we go again*, he thought. *Dammit*. She was hiding something and, by God, he wouldn't stand for it anymore. "Don't, Faith."

She still didn't look at him. "Don't what?"

"Don't keep holding secrets back from me. What's happened now? More problems with the kids?"

"Promise you'll listen before you judge?"

"Lord, what have you done?"

"I . . . Oh, what's the use." She smacked her palms against her thighs and made her confession. "I took out another loan."

"With Prescott?"

She rolled her shoulders forward. "Yes."

His gut lurched. After all they'd been through, she hadn't come to him, she'd turned to another man for help. "You'd rather go to him than ask me for money?"

"It's not like that," she whispered.

He tried to keep his anger contained. "Then tell me, what is it like?"

"With Prescott, it's business."

"Bad business."

"I know that. But what other alternative do I have? I have to start a school, and we can't run it out of the house indefinitely. It would never work, there isn't room."

"You're rationalizing, Faith. You could have made it work. And if not, I would have given you the money."

Her head snapped up, fire spitting out of her gaze. "And turn me into your whore?"

"How can I do that when we aren't intimate anymore?"

Her fiery eyes shot well-aimed flames of anger straight through him. "Just how long do you think you'll be able to say that? It gets harder and harder. And every day brings weakness, not strength."

She was right. Even now, angry and disappointed in her, he ached to take her in his arms and finish what they'd started. "Faith, I want to help you. Let me."

"I can't."

"Why not?"

"It might one day change how you see me. I couldn't bear that. And the truth is, I've never relied on anyone. I don't know if I can start now."

He heard the fear underneath her declaration, but he hardened his resolve to make her see the error of choosing

Prescott over him. "Just like the night you ended up here."

"That was one time." She puffed out her chest. "And it was for the kids."

"You can't keep justifying foolish behavior like this."

"I have no other choice." Her voice lowered to a whisper. "I'm alone."

He fought against the temptation to touch her, to soothe her. "No, you're not." And then a thought occurred to him. "Would it make a difference if I gave the money directly to Heart House, and not you personally?"

She didn't answer him right away. Her eyebrows knitted in the way they did when she was in deep thought. "How would that work?" she asked eventually.

"I'll repay the loan, in Heart House's name."

She gasped. "You'd do that?"

"It's just money."

"But I thought—" She shook her head, tossing a tendril of hair out of her face with trembling fingers. "What you said before. The years after the war. I don't understand this sudden change in you." But the spark of hope in her eyes told him she wanted to believe it was real.

"Let me do this for you, Faith. Consider it a gift, freely given."

She eyed him, working the idea around in her brain. "All right."

Blood hammered in his ears. She'd agreed. "You won't regret this."

Before he could tug her into his embrace, she jumped out of the chair and threw her arms around his neck. Laughing, she pressed very soft, very warm, very grateful lips against his. He forgot to breathe, forgot to think, as he settled into the feel of Faith O'Malley. He didn't hear the door swing open, until it banged against the wall.

"*Whore*. Get your hands off my husband."

Chapter Thirty

For a moment, Faith couldn't make her mind grasp what was happening. Hard as she tried, events would not unfold properly through the terrible haze of shame blanketing her.

André brushed his knuckles against her cheek. "Let me handle this," he said.

Still unable to comprehend why the pain in her heart suffocated her, she nodded. But then a slurred, overloud oath hissed in her ear and a jab on her shoulder spun her around. "I knew you wanted him for yourself. You're nothing but a whore."

Faith's head cleared, and she opened her mouth to deny the harsh accusation. "No. I . . ." Although the truth slowly unwrapped itself in her mind, she still fought against it. "I'm not."

André moved between her and his wife. "You're drunk, Pearl." He grasped her shoulder and turned her around toward the saloon. "You need to follow the doctor's orders and rest now."

Pearl shrugged off André's hand and spun on her heel. "You bastard." The venom in her expression ripped a gasp out of Faith. "You can't send me off like this. I won't let you."

"You can hardly stand."

She shifted her blurry eyes to Faith. "I finally see everything clearly now. You." She stabbed a finger in the air. "Keep your hands off André. He's mine."

Faith tried to maintain some semblance of composure, but with each word, each accusation, her world shattered around her. "You're right. He is your husband."

And for a moment, she'd foolishly forgotten. She'd been willing to throw every convention away, and in the process had nearly sold her soul. Agreeing to take money from André, even in the guise of support for Heart House, surely made her the whore Pearl claimed.

André's voice boomed through her chaotic thoughts. She shuddered at the anger in his tone, but then she realized he wasn't directing his words at her. "You're getting hysterical. Nothing's happened here, Pearl."

He nudged Pearl forward, but she thrust André's hand away from her. "I'm not stupid. I've got eyes. I saw you and that *whore* kissing."

André reached out to her, but she sidestepped him. Anger filled his gaze, his tone lowered to a hush. "Don't you ever call Faith a whore again."

Faith's voice trembled as she added her words to the fray. "But it's what I am, isn't it? I nearly took money from you. And for what?"

He spun to look at her, his eyes begging her to listen to him. "For help. I offered you that money from one friend to another."

"Would you have given the money to Katherine if she'd asked for it?"

"Dammit, Faith, I'm offering you the money because I don't want you dealing with Prescott."

Because he didn't answer her directly, he'd damned them both. "You said it was for Heart House."

"And *you*."

"Oh, God. You've turned me into a whore, and I let you."

"No. You owe me nothing for the money. Can't you see? A gift is a *gift*."

Torn, confused, and riddled with humiliation, Faith didn't know what to think anymore. But as her emotions struggled against each other, something about the sincerity in André's expression demanded honesty from her. "I don't know how to believe in you."

Her words came out barely above a whisper as the truth knocked the breath out of her. Right now, she wanted to trust in him, even more than she wanted his love. "How can I know for sure that you mean what you say?"

André gave her his full attention. "You can't. You have to trust me. What is it that makes it impossible for you to believe that turning to me for money is a good thing?"

"Because we . . . we . . ." She broke off, unable to admit out loud that she'd shared the most intimate of acts with him. And because of that, she could never truly be sure he cared about her as a person first and not as a woman he'd shared passion with in his bed.

"I knew it," Pearl declared. "You see, André, even she recognizes her fate." Pearl's smile turned sinister. "You see, I've done some checking, Faith, darling. I know all about your mother."

Faith shuddered at the memories haunting her now. The endless fear, waiting, and wondering when her mother would be through for the evening. The humiliation of keeping the time, thirty minutes a customer.

"You're just like her. You're just like me." Pearl dug deeper into the open wound. "Perhaps you don't sell your body nightly, but you're just like all of us in your own way."

As Pearl voiced Faith's greatest fear aloud, making it ugly but true, a part of her died. She'd nearly sold her love to a man for money. It didn't matter that the money would be used for a school.

André's distraught voice meshed into her thoughts. "Don't listen to her, Faith. She's drunk."

Faith's heart broke a little more. "She's right, though." She commanded his gaze. "I had sex with you, and now you're going to give me money. Like mother, like daughter."

André reached out to her, but she shoved past him, then walked through the doorway, never looking back.

André set out after her, but Hank stopped him. "Haven't you done enough? Leave her with some dignity."

The scorn in Hank's voice stopped him cold. Until that moment André hadn't realized what he was truly doing to the woman he loved. He turned to Hank. "Will you see she gets home safely?"

Hank's eyes showed accusation, sympathy, and pity. "I'll watch over her. I always do."

"St. André," Pearl snorted her disgust. "Always trying to protect his woman of the moment."

André gathered his temper with two hard swallows, then turned to face Pearl. For the first time since she'd plowed into his office, he looked directly at her. Her eyes swam in their sockets, her skin ashen and bloodless. Pearl had gotten ahold of another bottle of laudanum.

"Where'd you find it?"

She laughed at him. "It doesn't matter." She swayed, but caught hold of herself by leaning into the door. "Now, about you and that whore."

As if they had a life separate from him, his fingers gripped her arm. "Not another word out of you."

She glared at his hand. "Oh, I'm just getting started."

"I'm warning you, Pearl. I won't stand here and have you hurt her like this. Never again."

A bitter, sinister snarl flew out of Pearl's lips. The look on her face wasn't human. "Is that threat supposed to scare me? You may be a lot of things, but like I said once before, you don't have it in you to hurt a woman."

But he had hurt a woman. With his selfishness, he'd hurt the only woman he'd ever loved.

And now he wanted to hurt this woman too.

Never before had he been closer to losing his self-control. As he stared at Pearl's gloating expression, he understood how a man could commit murder. "Perhaps I've changed," he said, his voice low, menace riding under the surface.

"Not you, André." Though her words were bold, her eyes wavered. "You haven't changed since I first met you."

"Are you willing to gamble your life on that?"

She reached up to pat his cheek, her clammy fingers leaving traces of sweat along his skin. "Such a good man. You might have tried to save my wretched soul, but you failed." She laughed harshly. "I'm your greatest failure."

She buckled over, a violent cough racking her frail body. He reached out to help her stand. When she raised her face to his, the look of utter despair underneath her false bravado splintered his anger and gave him hope that he could perhaps rescue her yet.

"Time for you to get back in bed." He grasped Pearl by the shoulders and with very little effort, herded her to the stairs.

She wheezed through another cough. "You coming with me?"

"I'll get you settled."

They took the first step side by side. He supported her

full weight by the second. On the third, she collapsed. He reached down and scooped her into his arms. "Get Dr. Bartlett," he yelled to the last of the two bartenders still working.

Pearl's eyes fluttered open. "It's too late," she whispered.

He remembered his anger of only moments earlier, all the ugly thoughts he'd had about this woman, all the times he'd rejoiced over her death through the years. Dear God, he didn't want her to die like this. He wanted her to live, to fight. "Don't give up on me now."

A spasm contorted her face, and she gulped for air. "I'm sorry."

A lump formed in his throat. "I'm sorry too."

Tears welled in her eyes. "You were too good for the likes of me. Always too good." Just before her eyes fell shut, Pearl uttered two words that set him free. "Forgive me."

Chapter Thirty-one

The incessant knocking dragged Faith reluctantly awake. A memory tugged at her sleep-filled brain, but she brutally shoved it back into the corner of her thoughts. Her sanity demanded she stay inside her blissfully muddled state of mind.

The knocking continued, getting louder and more forceful with each bang. Groggy, Faith opened her eyes. She tried desperately to focus on anything solid in the shadow-darkened room. Images danced in front of her, but nothing concrete formed. After a moment, Faith realized the banging had stopped.

"Thank God."

Just as she buried her head back in the pillow's softness, a gentle tap on the door intruded once more on her sleep.

A key in the lock turned. Katherine peeked inside the room. "André Du Bois is here to speak with you," she said.

At the mention of his name, all the dreadful memories

of the night before came crashing in on her. *No.* She wouldn't let them. She squeezed her eyes shut.

"I think you should see him."

A moan escaped her lips. "Go away and let me go back to sleep."

Katherine approached the bedside table and lit the lantern resting there. "He looks devastated."

Faith yanked the covers over her head. "I can't face him. Not after what I've done."

Warm fingers pried the blanket from her grip. "You've done nothing except fall in love with a man who obviously loves you very deeply as well."

Faith covered her eyes behind the crook of her arm. "He's married."

Katherine tapped on her raised elbow. "You fell in love with him before you knew that, and before he knew it too."

Lowering her arm, Faith said, "Are you defending us?"

Without answering, Katherine straightened and folded her hands in front of her.

"Why did I have to fall in love with him at all?" Faith asked.

"He's your future husband."

"No." Another moan slipped from her lips. "Oh, Lord, I almost became his mistress."

Katherine gave her a steady smile. "But you didn't."

"Not yet." But the memories of the night before dashed any hopes Faith might harbor that she could remain pure for long. "I kissed him, knowing he was married. I allowed myself to forget." She searched her heart, the truth screaming out in her mind. "And God help me, wife or no wife, I still want him. On any terms."

She'd meant it as a confession of her sin. And now that she'd taken an honest look at who she was, and what she'd become, she couldn't face André again. After all the times she'd wondered if she was like her mother, now she knew. She buried her head behind her hands. "I'm detestable."

Katherine touched her shoulder. "No. I'd say you're human. Now stop this and go talk to him."

"I don't know if I can see him and not beg him—oh, my." This couldn't be happening to her, not now.

"Perhaps it's time you found out what you're made of?"

"What if I'm nothing but a . . . whore?"

Katherine regarded her with blank, patient eyes, giving Faith the uneasy feeling that she considered her a real dolt. "Loving a man doesn't make you a whore. Even loving the *wrong* man doesn't make you one."

"Perhaps not. But loving him again would turn what we had ugly and dirty."

Katherine tugged her to her feet. "Go talk to him. He's waiting."

Faith sighed. Was she a woman of courage and strength, able to play the hand that fate had dealt her? Or was she a woman willing to do anything, no matter how vile or sinful, for the love of her man? The only way to find out was to face André again. "Tell him I'll be down shortly."

After Katherine left the room, Faith didn't waste time waffling. Dressing quickly, she hurried into the hall, then down the stairs. At the bottom, she drew in a shaky breath. The moment she looked into his eyes, she would know who, or rather *what*, she was.

As she stepped into the parlor, her gaze sought and found the only man she would ever love. He stared back, and she took in his disheveled clothing, the fatigue and pain etching across his features. She'd never seen him so distraught.

When he didn't speak right away, her heart hurt from the ache of its rapid beating. Then he lifted his arms in invitation.

If he'd gloated, or said something sarcastic, or perhaps

arrogant, she could have found the courage to deny him. But his eyes held the yearning that lived in her own soul. She hurt, and only this man could make the pain go away.

She rushed into his embrace, throwing away all she'd considered noble for the feel of his healing warmth. As his lips crushed against hers, her mind tangled with regret and lost pride. It didn't take her long to realize she'd failed the test. With every sigh and breath they shared, she became irrevocably his mistress.

No. No, no, no. She didn't want him this way.

She shot from his embrace. "I can't become your mistress." She spun on her heel and dashed out of the room.

André's crashing steps followed after her. "Faith. Wait." He caught her by the arm. "Stop for a moment and listen to me. I need you now. And I need to tell you—"

Covering her ears with her hands, she shook her head. "No. Don't do this, André. I won't be your whore, sneaking around, rationalizing it's all right because I love you."

He tugged her hands down to her sides. His gaze gentled and his love shone in his eyes. "You will never be my whore. I love you, O'Malley."

Her stomach dipped. "You shouldn't call me that. You're not playing fair."

"No, I'm not." His fingers squeezed hers softly. "I learned how to cheat from the slickest."

Her shoulders slumped, and she lowered her head to her chest. "I suppose I deserved that."

He lifted her chin with gentle pressure. "Ah, honey, Pearl is—"

She finished his statement for him. "Your *wife.*" Before he could say another word to change her mind, she rushed out of the parlor, up the stairs, and slammed her bedroom door shut. She clicked the lock in place, then threw herself on the bed, finally allowing the tears that she'd fought against for three full weeks to flow unchecked down her cheeks.

When the banging on her door started, she yelled, "Go away."

"Let me in, O'Malley."

"Go away before you wake the children."

"They're already awake. You saw to that when you slammed your door."

"Go away."

"I'm not leaving until you hear what I've come to say."

She flung herself off the bed and walked to the door. Pressing her forehead against the cool wood, she whispered, "Please, leave me alone."

She almost felt his warmth through the door, as though he were pressing his forehead against the other side. "Faith, I appeal to our friendship. You're going to have to trust me enough to listen to what I've come to tell you."

"I can't keep doing this, André."

In a low but firm voice, he said, "I won't beg you again."

She didn't know what to say. After a long moment of silence, she whispered, "André?"

No answer.

Her heart stopped, then started again, its beating too fast, too erratic. "André? You still there?"

No answer.

She slowly opened the door and peered into the *empty*, darkened hallway. He was gone. For good.

Chapter Thirty-two

Three days passed and Faith didn't hear another word from André. On the afternoon of the fourth day, she lay alone on her bed staring at the ceiling, no longer able to deny the truth—his desertion hurt.

Of course, she hadn't sought him out either. Flipping onto her stomach, she cradled her chin on her hands. Had she stayed away from the Dancing Belles simply because she wasn't ready to face André?

Or was there another reason for her cowardice?

Several days of hard thinking had brought her to a few conclusions, none of them pleasant. André had once accused her of using deception to get what she wanted, rationalizing her bad behavior in the guise of helping her children.

He'd been right.

She'd always been willing to take chances for others. The Faith O'Malley who had walked into the Dancing

Belles saloon hadn't needed or wanted help from anyone. Now she had to ask herself. Why?

Had she craved the heady satisfaction of facing and beating the odds? Had her behavior been rooted in pride? And not, as she'd convinced herself, from the fear of turning into a woman like her mother?

There was one way to find out.

She had to return to work and face the man she loved. Her foray into the land of self-pity and misery was over.

Taking action was what Faith O'Malley did best. Now was the time to gather her courage and ask for his money, proving to him—and herself—that their friendship went beyond what had happened in his bed.

Entering the Dancing Belles, Faith wasn't prepared for the shock that stole the air right out of her lungs. Her first impression was that she'd somehow walked into the wrong saloon. But after checking the sign over the entryway two more times, she knew she had the right place.

Taking in the changes, she circled her gaze around the room. She was snarling by the time she finished her inspection. Confusion and astonishment made her faint with worry. And anger.

It wasn't just the rancid smoke filling the air, or the layer of grime that had already begun to form on the once-shiny fixtures. It was the *feel* of the place. No longer an elegant establishment, the Dancing Belles had turned into just another saloon.

The clientele had turned as grimy as the saloon itself, seedier, more dangerous. *Men* dealt at the faro tables, while unfamiliar women, smiling behind their painted faces and gaudy dresses, wove through the crowd, selling drinks and perhaps their personal wares as well.

Armed with her temper, Faith headed toward the back of the saloon, stopping short as she came eye to eye with Thurston P. Prescott III.

It took her a moment to get over her shock at the banker's presence. A sense of foreboding rooted deep inside her. "Prescott? What are you doing here?"

His gaze traveled down from her face, securing his eyes to the bare skin above her dress. Under different circumstances, she would have given into the urge to slap that leer off his face. But she needed answers, and from the self-satisfied look on the banker's face, she knew he was the man to ask.

"The question, my dear, is what are *you* doing here?"

She didn't like the hint of triumph in his tone. "I've come to deal faro."

"I have all the dealers I need, but if you would like another position . . ."

Her stomach rolled at the insinuation he put into his words. "No."

"Ah, more the pity." He drew out the words as his eyes roamed lasciviously down her body.

"I don't understand. Where's An—Mr. Du Bois?"

With an amused, predatory smile, he said, "Gone."

"What do you mean, gone?"

He blinked, and his smile never wavered. "I haven't seen him since he sold this saloon to me."

Sold the saloon? The sickening churn in her stomach kicked harder, making it difficult to speak clearly. "You're lying," she gasped. "He would never sell the Dancing Belles."

"I can assure you, I speak the truth. We made the transaction just two days ago."

"But it can't be true. He worked too hard to make this place special." She spun around, soaking in the changes, understanding them now. Two days and suddenly the Dancing Belles, as she'd known it, had died. Bile rose up from the knot in her belly. Placing her hand against her heart, she took a calming breath. "You've ruined this place. What have you done with all the fine crystal and the imported furniture?" She glanced at the ceiling, "And the chandelier?"

The longer Prescott leered at her, his smug expression almost unbearable, the sicker at heart she became. "Extravagant, all of it," he said. "Since I don't plan to waste money on drunks and gamblers, I sold the most expensive of the pieces. Back to Du Bois. At a hefty profit, of course."

Prescott placed a solicitous hand on her arm, but she shrugged it loose. "You really are a swindler."

"Miss O'Malley, I'm in the business of making money. Now, come with me."

She narrowed her eyes. "Where?"

He smiled again, then offered his hand with such charm she almost took it, before she noticed the malice behind the gesture. "We'll discuss the terms of my agreement with Mr. Du Bois in my office," he said.

His office? Oh, Lord, he really was the new owner. "What could your agreement with André possibly have to do with me?"

He spun around and headed to the back of the saloon. Faith dashed after him, the sinking feeling in the pit of stomach churning into waves of despair. "What have you done?" she demanded.

Prescott kept walking. Entering the office, he went directly to his desk and rummaged through the top drawer. While she waited, Faith surveyed the changes here too.

What had once been order was now chaos. Papers were strewn everywhere. The pictures on the mantel—gone. The armoire—gone. The grand pieces of furniture carefully selected and placed in perfect harmony with one another—replaced with a serviceable desk and three hard-back chairs.

Angry righteousness replaced her confusion. "How dare you do this to him."

"It would appear, Miss O'Malley, that you don't know your lover so well after all."

She cringed at both the accusation and the ugly summation of her relationship with André.

"Do you want to know why he sold me the saloon?" Prescott asked.

She eyed him warily. "I still don't understand what this has to do with the me."

Prescott shoved a handful of papers at her. "Here. You no longer have a loan with my bank."

She didn't look at the documents, choosing to keep her gaze planted on his. "What did you say?" She couldn't have possibly heard him right.

Impatience replaced his arrogance. "André Du Bois traded this saloon for your loan."

No. It couldn't be true. André had made it perfectly clear that he never wanted to experience poverty again. He'd offered her money, yes. But the saloon was his security, his future. He'd put his heart into the place. And yet he'd sacrificed it for her? "I can't believe it," she muttered.

"Nor could I, at first. Two days ago, he came to my office, offering his saloon in exchange for the loan you took out to purchase the Anderson home."

It just couldn't be true. She didn't *want* it to be true. Because that would mean . . . What?

What *did* it mean?

Either uncaring or unaware of her turmoil, Prescott continued. "He made it perfectly clear that he would not leave until we'd completed the transaction."

Faith could hardly grasp the meaning of Prescott's words. André had sacrificed his secure future for hers, and the children's. "What you tell me is the truth?"

"See for yourself. You're holding the transaction papers and deed to the house in your hands."

She looked down for the first time since he'd handed

her the papers. As she quickly skimmed the words on each document, her heart sank. "Why didn't you give these to him?"

"He asked that I give them to you personally. He must have known you would come here looking for him."

She didn't know what to think anymore. Suddenly, there was too much information for her brain to take in. "I . . . thank you."

"Don't thank me, thank him. I can't fathom it myself. After settling the funeral arrangements, he came directly to me."

Her thoughts snapped to attention. "What did you say?"

"Don't thank me, thank him." He wrapped his fingers around her arm and began ushering her out of his office. "Since you won't be working here, I've really had enough of you and this conversation."

Faith dug in her heels. "Wait. What did you say about a funeral? Whose funeral?"

"His wife's, of course. Tragic really. She died in the early morning, three days ago. An overdose of laudanum, I think."

"Pearl's dead?" Dear Lord, it couldn't be true. Faith didn't want Pearl dead. Not like this. She'd known the woman was on a path of self-destruction. But . . .

Oh, Lord.

It must have happened just before André had come to her, pleading with her to listen to him. She'd been so tangled inside her own despair, she hadn't realized he'd needed her. Thinking back, she recalled his glassy eyes. The sorrow lying just below the surface of his appeals.

He'd come for comfort, and she'd banished him with her silly fears.

Oh, André, what you must have gone through.

Prescott shoved her forward again, impatience meshed into his words. "Now, you really must be on your way."

Lost in her own confusing thoughts, Faith allowed him to escort her through the saloon. At the swinging doors, she wrenched her arm free and somehow scrambled out on her own.

Walking down the bustling sidewalk, she remembered the crumpled papers between her fingers. Looking down, she read them again. It was really true. André had sold his saloon for her school.

A gift, freely given.

Her mind tried to absorb all she'd just learned, but one thought kept rising above the others. She'd waited too long to accept his help. But he'd offered it to her anyway, with the sacrifice of his saloon.

Urgency had her increasing her pace. She had to find him, to tell him she understood. And beg him to forgive her. But where should she start?

Prescott might know. Yes, if anyone would know what had happened to André, the banker would. Spinning around, she retraced her steps. But she had only gone a short distance when she stopped, a sudden thought clogging her ability to move any further.

What if he'd left town?

The clip-clop of horses' hooves and the creaking of wagon wheels streamed together with the chaotic noises in her mind. Raucous laughter flowed around her, mocking her inability to capture her thoughts in some logical sequence.

She glanced around her, looking at everything and yet seeing nothing. The longer she stood glancing around her, the more she grieved for what might have been.

No. She wouldn't give up yet. She *couldn't.* Pushing forward, she stopped in mid-stride as a familiar voice cloaked its protective warmth around her. "Going somewhere, O'Malley?"

The beautiful sound of sarcasm dripping inside that arrogant tone washed over her. A gentle caress couldn't have felt as wonderful. In that moment, her options dwindled down to one.

If she was going to take the ultimate risk of the heart, now was the time.

But she had to do it right. No muddles, no shortcuts.

Turning around, she jutted out her chin, threw her shoulders back, and forced an equal amount of sarcasm into her words. "Well, as a matter of fact, I was just looking for a poker game."

His lazy scrutiny pulled a slow shiver from the bottom of her toes. She returned his open perusal, drinking in the sight of him. For once, she was glad for the hazy shades of dusk. Under the darkening sky, she looked her fill. As always, the simple fashion of his clothing added a measure of refined elegance.

In a gesture that had become as familiar as breathing to her, he raised a cigar to his mouth, tugged a slow drag, then blew the smoke downwind. "Poker's an honest trade, I suppose. Then again"—he let the meaning of his words trail through a long, silent pause—"there's no accounting for what might happen once a game is under way."

The temperature in her thighs burned hot and demanding. She ignored her body's reaction to this handsome man and forced her voice to be steady. "Oh, I'm not looking for just any poker game. What I have in mind is something . . . special."

He angled his head, dropping an expectant gaze on her. "Indeed? You want to be more specific for me?"

She jerked her chin at him. "I'm very particular, you know."

He lifted an eyebrow. "Sounds interesting."

"I'd like to find a game with an impossibly arrogant, rude, insufferable scoundrel. Know where I can get one of those?"

Moist lips curled into a devilish grin. "A game or a scoundrel?"

Oh, my. She bit her lip to keep from smiling, or acting on the sudden wave of lust crdling through her body. "Both, of course."

He inclined his head. "Naturally. And the stakes?"

She wished he wouldn't stare at her like that, all hot and eager. It made her want to forget all about poker and beg him to take her, here and now. The scandal would be worth every delicious moment. But then she wouldn't be able to prove to either of them that she'd changed for good.

No. Their future depended on her doing this right.

She cleared her throat. "Stakes are negotiable, to be determined for each hand."

His voice held a low, lusty promise. "Well, then, you're in luck. I've heard of just such a game."

She released a wide smile. "I knew I could count on you."

His eyes moved to her lips, and she found the tremor in his voice quite heartening. "Tonight. At the Palace Hotel, nine o'clock sharp."

She gave him one firm nod. "Right. I'll be there."

With a saucy flip of her hand, she tossed her hair behind her back, spun around, and sauntered away. Feeling his eyes bore into her, she stood a little taller, determined to play her role through to the end.

Before she moved out of earshot, she thought she heard him mutter, "Hoyden."

Renewed confidence pranced out of her soul. Yes. This time she would get it right.

Chapter Thirty-three

Thankful she'd accepted Sally's red dress as a gift before her friend had boarded the train for Arizona, Faith studied her figure in the full-length mirror with a critical eye. Tonight she would get it right. Every detail had to be checked—nothing could be left to chance.

Swiveling, she made a few necessary adjustments, then focused once more on her reflection. Perfect. She looked just as she had that first night at the Dancing Belles. The dress hugged her figure, setting off her coloring and adding an air of sophistication she hadn't seen the last time.

She took special care with the finishing touch. Twisting her hair on top of her head, she pulled a few tendrils loose and smiled.

"You'll do," she told her reflection.

"Awwk, you'll do. You'll do."

Grinning, Faith spun on her heel and glanced up at the bird shifting nervously on the perch inside his cage.

When she'd come into the room earlier, he'd had his head tucked under his wing.

"Well, Larkin. I see you're awake after all."

The bird blinked then shook his beak up and down. "You'll do. You'll do."

"And what makes you think I care about your opinion, you stupid bird."

"Pretty bird."

"Stupid"—she flicked her nose at him—*"bird."*

"Pretty bird."

Before falling into the pleasure of their daily game, Faith stopped herself from arguing a third time. "Right. I forgot."

Shifting from foot to foot, Larkin squawked. "You'll do. You'll do."

Grateful for his unwitting support, she reached up and stroked the cold metal of his cage. "Thank you, bird. I really needed to hear that just now."

"Awwk. It's not over."

At the sound of the familiar warning, she dropped her hand to her side. Dear Lord, the ramifications of what she was about to do tonight would decide the rest of her life.

Was she ready?

"You'll do. You'll do."

Confidence restored, Faith straightened to her full height and gave one swift nod. "You're right, Larkin. I am ready."

Head high, she waved to the chattering bird, sauntered out of her room, and marched briskly down the stairs to the parlor. Spinning around for the assembled group, she asked, "Well, how do I look?"

Katherine smiled, tears shining in her eyes. "Exactly like you did last time."

Faith plucked at a thread on her skirt, then smoothed

the material with surprisingly shaky fingers. "Do you think he'll understand?"

Leaning forward, Katherine kissed her cheek. "He'll know."

Johnny chimed in. "You're too fancy, Faith. I like you better when you're all normal-looking." He made a face. "You don't look like yourself."

Michael sidled over to her, grasping her hand. "Well, I think you look like a princess."

"Hey, does this mean André's going to come live with us after you two get married?" Johnny asked her.

Faith's heart tumbled to her stomach, then bounced back to her throat. She didn't want to get their hopes up. Heck, she didn't want to get *her* hopes up. "He hasn't asked me to marry him yet."

"Then ask him yourself," Katherine said.

Faith sighed. "If only it were that simple."

Always the voice of reason, Katherine stunned her with her quick retort. "Isn't it?"

Faith thought about it for a moment. Perhaps it was that simple. Perhaps it was all about taking matters into her own hands one last and final time. "You know, Katherine, that's not such a bad idea." She looked from Michael to Johnny and back again. "All right. It's settled. If he doesn't ask me to marry him, I'll just ask him." She raised a hand to keep them from hooting with joy. "But that doesn't mean he'll say yes."

With wisdom far exceeding his twelve years, Johnny said, "He'll say yes. So, it's settled. You ask him first. Heck, you've done crazier things than that."

"Oh, I have, have I?"

Johnny nodded vigorously. She ruffled his head in just the way he hated, pulling groans and grimaces from him. "Those days are over," she declared. She paused at the fib she'd just told. "*After* tonight."

She pulled one giant gulp of air in her lungs and placed

her outstretched hand between her and the children. "Cards, please."

With exaggerated show, Michael handed her a brand-new deck. "Cards."

She stretched out her other hand. "Gloves?"

Johnny slapped them into her palm. "Gloves."

"All set?" Katherine asked.

Faith took one last glance in the mirror over the fireplace and nodded. "Here I go."

"Good luck," the boys said at once.

"Yes, good luck," Katherine whispered. "And Faith?"

"Yes?"

A smile spread across the other girl's face. "I like who you've become since you met Mr. Du Bois."

Faith grinned. "Me too."

"Hurry, now." Katherine shooed her out the door. "You don't want to be late."

Outside Faith stopped short, laughing in delight when she spotted the man waiting for her at the bottom of the steps. "Hello, Hank."

Hank nodded. "Evening, Miss O'Malley."

She skipped down the last two steps. "This is certainly a surprise."

"Mr. Du Bois sent me. He wanted to ensure your safe delivery." His cheeks reddened. "And so did I."

"He has a good friend in you." She touched his sleeve. "And so do I."

Hank looked away from her, but she caught the shy smile hitching the tips of his lips. Struggling for composure, he wrapped her fingers into the crook of his arm. "Ready?"

"Ready."

The evening air was clear and crisp, perfect for a ride in an open buggy. On the way to the Palace Hotel, Faith discovered several details of the events of the last few days that Prescott hadn't deigned to tell her. In the short time,

André had been busy. He'd found honest employment for all the women who'd once worked for him.

And although he'd put most of his fortune into the Dancing Belles saloon, he wasn't completely broke. He'd already begun negotiating a purchase price with the owner of an empty building on Curtis Street.

"But he can't open a saloon there, can he?"

Hank shook his head. "He doesn't want to open a saloon. He plans to start a fancy restaurant, the likes of which Denver has never seen. He's modeling it after Antoine's in New Orleans," Hank explained.

Faith had never been to New Orleans, so she didn't know exactly what Antoine's was like. But she knew that André thought big. His restaurant would be refined and elegant, an establishment to make the good citizens of Denver proud.

As though finishing her thoughts for her, Hank added, "It'll be magnificent. The finest food in the West."

"A project like that will take time and money."

"He has time. And the money will come."

Hank pulled on the reins outside the Palace Hotel. The nine-story building was one of a kind, known as the fanciest in town because of both its elegance and superb service. Built exclusively from red granite and sandstone, the hotel towered over the other structures on the street. Its very existence had changed Denver from a prairie boomtown into a beautiful city.

Faith never tired of marveling over the structure.

"Well, this is where I leave you," said Hank.

Suddenly nervous, she fiddled with the cards in her hand. "Hank, am I doing the right thing?"

He didn't answer right away. Pushing the brake forward, he hopped down and came around to her side. Offering his hand, he said, "Go on. You know what to do." Then he gave her an encouraging smile similar to the one he'd given her the first night when she'd shown up for work at the Dancing Belles.

So much had changed since that night.

With Hank's support tucked in her heart, she made her way into the hotel lobby. Unsure what to do next, she walked to the registration desk and addressed the man behind the counter. "I'm here to see Mr. André Du Bois."

The gentleman gave her a warm smile. "You must be Miss O'Malley. He's expecting you in the restaurant."

She stood staring at him.

The clerk must have seen her dilemma. "Over there, to your right."

She granted him a shaky smile. "Thank you."

Upon entering the hotel, her feet must have accumulated ten pounds of lead each, making every step across the lobby agonizingly slow. Barely taking in the décor, Faith crossed toward the restaurant.

What had happened to all her spunk and fortitude? Where was the Faith O'Malley that only a month ago had defied an arrogant saloon owner, a shady banker, and a U.S. marshal? This reluctance was just plain absurd. Pulling herself together, she lifted her chin and walked the remaining distance with more confidence.

Her gaze instantly locked onto André, sitting at a small table in the farthest corner of the room. His back to the wall, he returned her stare with a fixed smile curving his lips. For a moment, she boldly drank in the sight of him.

Stalling for a moment, she whipped open her fan and peered at him through the slats. As though by some sort of silent understanding, he too wore the exact clothing he'd donned the first night they'd met.

Rather than taking away from his severe good looks, the crisp white shirt, red silk vest, and matching tie added to the refined dignity that defined him. A girl could go all wobbly inside if she liked the hard, brooding type.

And, oh, yes, the arrogant, brutish sort most definitely appealed to her.

She snapped her fan closed with a sigh. Her feet itched to run across the room to him, but she forced herself to take slow steps. This was her one chance to show him how much she'd changed since they'd first met. She hoped he recognized and understood what she planned to do here tonight.

As she approached the table, his hot gaze ran along her hair, her face, and lower, stopping at her chest. At the smoldering look burning in his eyes, warmth crept through her, reminding her of the intimacy they'd shared.

Twice, they'd consummated their love. The beauty he'd shown her with his body and his sacrifice had cured her once-skewed thinking. Loving André Du Bois with her heart and her body was good and right. Intimacy with him would always be safe, protected in the confines of their love and expressed in the lifelong vow of marriage.

Now was her chance. "I heard there was to be a poker game tonight."

He shot her an unreadable expression.

She took that as an invitation to sit. Placing the cards on the table, she shoved the deck toward him.

He shook his head. "It's the lady's deal."

Faith took a hidden, calming breath and continued to hold his stare. "Must I?" The trembling in her voice was real. Now that the time had come to prove her trust in him, she couldn't quite calm her tremors.

"Call your game and deal." He placed his palms flat against the table and leaned forward. "Now."

At the light of mischief dancing in his eyes, excitement tripped along her spine.

Taking a long-suffering sigh, she swallowed. "Five card draw?"

He nodded, keeping his twinkling gaze steady.

Faith batted her eyelashes, adding a careless toss of her head. "Well, here we go then."

Capturing a giggle inside another sigh, she made a marvelous show of shuffling the deck. This time she moved her fingers slowly, fairly, with no signs of flummery. She took her time, drawing out the suspense longer than necessary.

"Let us get down to business, shall we?" he said.

Unable to resist, she glanced one final time deep into his eyes. The love shining out of them awed her. A violent quiver captured her heart, drawing her into the secret world of feeling she shared with only André Du Bois.

Powerless to move her eyes from his, she squared the deck. As she went to deal the first card, his hand shot across the table and wrapped around her wrist. "You forgot a step."

Her pulse jerked, but she quickly schooled her features to hide her lusty reaction to the simple joining of their flesh. She slowly lowered her gaze to his hand and back again. "I did?"

He gradually released her wrist and leaned back into his chair. "The stakes, O'Malley. We haven't settled the terms of play."

Faith knew from her countless mistakes that desperation could make her commit irrevocable blunders. Now, more than ever, she had to act rationally. But weeks of restraint made it simply impossible. She wanted this man. In her life. Forever.

Under the circumstances, there was really only one thing left to do.

Take extreme measures.

Swallowing, she took her first real personal risk ever. "If I win, you must make an honest woman of me. That is, once your grieving is over, of course."

His eyes clouded over for a second, communicating the sadness and loss that she respected as his due. "Of course."

She cut the deck, but before she could deal the first card, he angled his head. "Wait a minute. Let's say you are able to restrain your natural inclinations and you resist cheating. . . ."

The insult crackled in the air between them. Undaunted, she fluttered a card in front of her while fanning herself with her fan. "You wound me, sir. I always play fairly."

He smirked at her. "Naturally. Now, if *I* win, what do I get in return for my efforts?"

She rolled her eyes to the heavens. "In the unlikely event you win—"

"I will."

She made a face. "*If* you win, I will trust you without question in the future."

"Well, then." He lifted a single brow, but a snort of laughter slipped out. "It would appear that if I accept these stakes, I win either way."

She fanned faster. "That is the general idea."

"With those odds, how could I not agree? Begin your deal."

Calling upon the recklessness that had brought her this far, she pulled the first card off the top of the deck and began dealing, her fingers working quickly. They each picked up their cards, the competitive streak in her suddenly wanting to win this hand. She eyed her hand and inwardly groaned. She didn't have a single good card and nothing matched. With a blank expression, she placed them face-down on the table and asked, "Cards, Du Bois?"

A smirk lifted one corner of his mouth. "Not yet. I want to raise you."

"But the stakes are already set. You agreed."

"Afraid?"

She lifted her chin. "Of course not."

He nodded. "No matter who wins, you must promise

to never again play poker with anyone other than me."

She contemplated the bet. Since she'd already decided to never play the miserable game again, she didn't think it would hurt to agree. "That seems fair."

"And you can *never* cheat."

She wiggled her eyebrows. "Simple stuff."

He placed several cards face-down on the table. "I'll take three."

She made a grand show of drawing off the top of the stack. "It's my turn to raise," she said.

One arrogant eyebrow journeyed upward.

"If I cheat, you walk away from me forever."

She'd never before seen the look of pure panic that flashed across his features. "No. Definitely not. I won't agree to such terms." He shook his head. "Lunacy," he muttered. "Sheer lunacy."

She threw her shoulders back. "You don't think I can play without cheating?" she said accusingly.

His eyes searched her face. "Can you?"

She shot him a coy I-dare-you smile. "Perhaps you should take the wager and see for yourself."

He eyed her for a long moment. "Pretty confident, aren't you, O'Malley?"

She leaned forward. "Take the bet, Du Bois."

A slow, steady grin slid across his lips. "All right. I accept the bet."

She placed two cards on the table and dealt herself two more. Again, taking great pains to pull them from the top of the deck. She looked at her cards, and her heart surged with joy. Nothing. She had absolutely nothing. Not so much as one pretty face card. Careful not to give herself away, she smoothed all signs of her excitement off her face. With all seriousness, she said, "I call."

His fingers shook as he laid his cards, one by one, face-up on the table. There before her was the sweetest sight she'd ever seen. A pair of twos, a three, a ten, and the jack of hearts winked at her. She held back a smile and fanned out her miserable hand for him to see.

With lightning speed, André rose and walked around the table, stopping directly behind her chair. "I would like a word with you in private."

Her gaze shot to his, measuring. "Excuse me? I don't think I quite heard what you said."

He bent over her, resting his lips against her earlobe. "I said, come with me." He nipped her tender flesh with his teeth. "Or would you prefer I made my proclamation in public?"

She forced an impeccable amount of outrage and shock into her voice. "Sir, who do you think you are?"

He straightened and offered her his hand. "André Du Bois." She opened her mouth to speak, but he beat her to it. "The man you promised the next fifty or so years of your life to."

She batted her eyelashes at him. "Oh, really?"

"I can assure you, it is the truth."

She placed her tiny hand in his. "Well, then, lead the way."

"You will cooperate without a fight?"

"Depends on where you're taking me."

He smiled down at her. "Do you really need to know?"

She accepted his hand and rose. "I trust you." Her breath caught as she drew up next to him. The familiar scent of limes, covered over with a hint of cigar smoke, filled her senses.

Determined to play this out, she turned and walked with dignity, chin held high as André escorted her out of the restaurant and up the stairs leading to the second floor of the hotel. He ushered her into a lovely sitting room that led to another, equally magnificent, bedroom.

With a bang and a resounding click, he shut them inside the room together. Spinning around, she widened her smile. He opened his arms to her, inviting her home.

Before she ran into his embrace, she needed to say one thing. "André, I'm sorry about your wife. It . . . I never wished her dead."

"Nor did I." He lowered his hands to his side and his eyes darkened to a turbulent green. Threading fingers through his hair, he groaned. "I thought I could change her, save her from the life she'd chosen. But she didn't want my help. In all truthfulness, her life was a tragedy begun long before I met her."

"When did she die?"

"After you left."

Her knees buckled. "Oh, God." She sank into a chair. "I killed her, sure as doing it with my own hands."

He shook his head. "Neither of us killed her. She made choices."

"I guess we all do." She sighed. "André, I'm sorry I didn't listen to you when you came to me the other day. I was so caught up with my problems, I didn't realize, I never stopped to think, Pearl might have been in trouble. I didn't think about what you were going through."

Inclining his head, he grimaced. "These last few weeks have been hard on us all."

"Forgive me," she said.

"It's I who needs forgiveness." He folded his arms across his chest, as though needing to keep his hands from calling her to him. "When I first met you, Faith, I had a hard heart. I was consumed with taking back what I thought others had stolen from me. But you changed me. After falling in love with you, I looked at everything I had worked so hard to accomplish and it all seemed meaningless. Like I was chasing the wind. With your commitment to the children and your willingness to fight the odds on their behalf, you showed me the meaning of love. When I lost you, there was nothing worthwhile anywhere in my life. Can you forgive me?"

At the look of genuine remorse on his face, Faith's

heart constricted. "Yes," she said simply, honestly. "But wait." She held her palm in the air to keep him from advancing. "I've learned something too."

He smiled. "Oh?"

She pushed out of the chair. "I should have accepted your offer of money to help me with the children's school."

His arms dropped to his sides and he took a step forward. "What are you saying?"

"I know now that your offer was a gift, given freely."

He blew a puff of air. "The school is yours now."

"I know. And by accepting this gift, I won't become your whore. By accepting it, I become free."

A muscle in his jaw worked, and he blinked rapidly as his eyes filled with tears of joy. "You accept my gift?"

"Yes." She sighed. "Can you ever forgive me for my foolish pride?"

"It's never been about me forgiving you. It's always been about you forgiving yourself."

"I know that now. Most of my mistakes were rooted in my pride. I pushed your help away because I wanted to cling to the very independence that in the end provided me with only loneliness and misery. And now I realize I don't want to live my life alone anymore. I need you, Du Bois."

André closed the distance between them and pulled her into his embrace. Burying his face in her hair, he said, "O'Malley, you're a changed woman."

She nestled into his arms. "So, how about it? You going to make me an honest woman?"

He laughed against her neck. "Are you asking me to marry you?"

"Are you saying yes?"

He crushed his mouth against hers for a long, slow, tantalizing kiss. "That's a yes, in case you're confused."

"Thanks for clearing that up for me." She sealed her

lips to his again, her tongue seeking the depths of his love. A long time later, she pulled away and leered at him. "So, can I convince you to jump straight to the consummation part?"

He pushed her out of his embrace, a look of horror in his gaze. "Before the vows? Absolutely not. From here on out, we do this right."

She reached to his vest. Tracing a finger along the top button, she purred out her question. "Why start now?"

He wrapped his fingers around her wrist. "Because I love you, O'Malley. After all I've put you through, I owe you a perfect wedding."

She wiggled free from his grasp and moved her hand to toy with the hair behind his neck. "Don't I have a say in this?"

A spasm racked through his body. "No."

She aimed a promise at him with her eyes. "Can I at least tempt you into a hand of poker? Winner gets *her* way?"

He scowled, clearly tempted. "You remember, of course, that I won that last hand. That means you can't cheat. Ever."

She moved her other hand to join the first, pulling tiny, little shivers out of him as she explored. "I'll win with my superior skill."

He leaned his head back and released a groan. "Life with you, O'Malley, will never be boring."

She placed a kiss and then another along his neck. "Is that a yes?"

Without a word, he released her and walked to the desk in the far corner of the room. Pulling a deck of cards out of the top drawer, he tilted his head in her direction and raised an eyebrow in challenge. "This time it's my deal."

With honest play on both their parts, Faith beat André's pair of fours with three tens. Casting him a smug smile, she said, "Looks like I win."

André rose from the table and helped her out of her chair. Nudging her toward the bedroom, he said, "O'Malley, my love, we're both winners tonight."

The assurance of her love added a tremor to her voice. "Indeed."